HATE LIST

HA
LI

JENNIFER BROWN

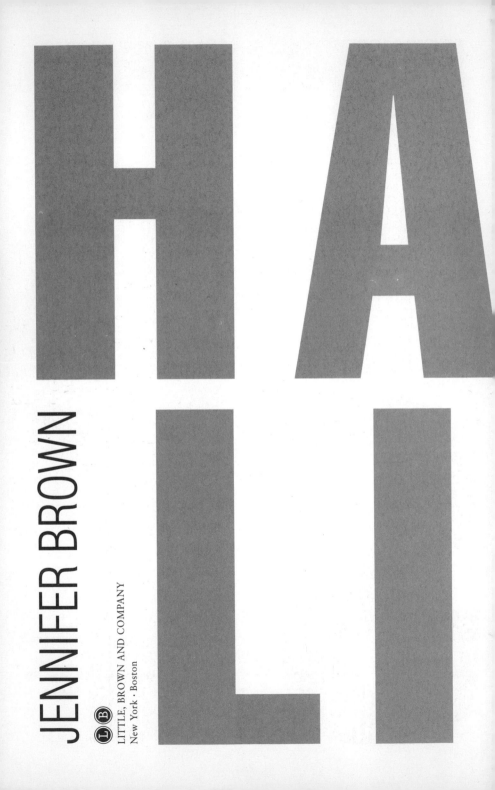

LITTLE, BROWN AND COMPANY
New York · Boston

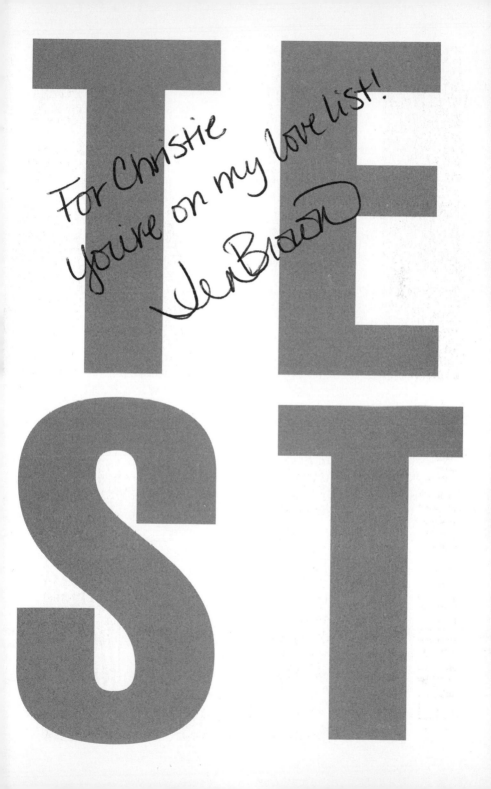

Little, Brown and Company
Hachette Book Group
237 Park Avenue, New York, NY 10017
Visit our Web site at www.lb-teens.com

Little, Brown and Company is a division of Hachette Book Group, Inc.
The Little, Brown name and logo are trademarks of Hachette Book Group, Inc.

First Edition: September 2009

The characters and events portrayed in this book are fictitious. Any similarity to real persons, living or dead, is coincidental and not intended by the author.

Library of Congress Cataloging-in-Publication Data

Brown, Jennifer, 1972–
Hate list / by Jennifer Brown.—1st ed. p. cm.
Summary: Sixteen-year-old Valerie, whose boyfriend Nick committed a school shooting at the end of their junior year, struggles to cope with integrating herself back into high school life, unsure herself whether she was a hero or a villain.
ISBN 978-0-316-04144-7
[1. School shootings—Fiction. 2. High schools—Fiction. 4. Emotional problems—Fiction. 5. Family problems—Fiction.
6. Forgiveness—Fiction.] I. Title.
PZ7.B1422Hat 2009   [Fic]—dc22   2008050223

10 9 8 7 6 5 4 3 2 1
RRD-H
Printed in the United States of America

For
Scott

We'll show the world they were wrong

And teach them all to sing along

— NICKELBACK

PART ONE

[FROM THE GARVIN COUNTY SUN-TRIBUNE,
MAY 3, 2008, REPORTER ANGELA DASH]

The scene in the Garvin High School cafeteria, known as the Commons, is being described as "grim" by investigators who are working to identify the victims of a shooting spree that erupted Friday morning.

"We have teams in there going over every detail," says Sgt. Pam Marone. "We're getting a pretty clear picture of what went on yesterday morning. It hasn't been easy. Even some of our veteran officers got pretty shaken up when they walked in there. It's such a tragedy."

The shooting, which began just as students were preparing for their first class, left at least six students dead and countless others wounded.

Valerie Leftman, 16, was the last victim shot before Nick Levil, the alleged shooter, reportedly turned the gun on himself.

Hit in the thigh at close range, Leftman required extensive surgery to repair her wounds. Representatives at Garvin County General list her in "critical condition."

"There was a lot of blood," an EMT told reporters on the scene. "He must have hit her artery just right."

"She's very lucky," the ER nurse on duty confirmed. "She's got a good chance of surviving, but we're being really careful. Especially since so many people want to talk to her."

Reports by witnesses at the scene of the shooting vary, some claiming Leftman was a victim, others saying she was a hero, still others alleging she was involved in a plan with Levil to shoot and kill students whom they disliked.

According to Jane Keller, a student who witnessed the shooting, the shot to Leftman appeared to be accidental. "It looked like she tripped and fell into him or something, but I couldn't tell for sure," Keller told reporters at the scene. "All I know is it was all over real quick after that. And when she fell on him it gave some people a chance to run away."

But police are questioning whether the shot that took down Leftman was an accident or a double suicide gone awry.

Early reports indicate that Leftman and Levil had discussed suicide in some detail, and some sources close to the couple suggest they talked about homicide as well, leaving police wondering if there is more to the Garvin High shooting than originally thought.

"They talked about death a lot," says Mason Markum, a close friend of both Leftman and Levil. "Nick talked about it more than Valerie, but, yeah, Valerie talked about it too. We all thought they were just playing some game, but I guess it was for real. I can't believe they were serious. I mean, I was just talking to Nick like three hours ago, and he never said anything. Not about this."

Whether Leftman's wounds were intentional or accidental, there is little doubt in the minds of the police that Nick Levil intended to commit suicide after massacring nearly half a dozen Garvin High students.

"Witnesses at the scene tell us that after he shot Leftman he pointed the gun to his own head and pulled the trigger," says Marone. Levil was pronounced dead at the scene.

"It was a relief," says Keller. "Some kids actually cheered, which I think is kind of wrong. But I guess I can understand why they did it. It was really scary."

Leftman's participation in the shooting is under investigation with Garvin County police. Leftman's family could not be reached for comment, and police will only divulge that they're "very interested" in speaking with her at this time.

* * *

After I ignored the third snooze alarm, my mom started pounding on my door, trying to get me out of bed. Just like any other morning. Only this morning wasn't just any other morning. This was the morning I was supposed to pick myself up and get on with my life. But I guess with moms, old habits die hard — if the snooze alarm doesn't do the trick, you start pounding and yelling, whatever kind of morning it is.

Instead of just yelling at me, though, she started getting that scared quavery sound in her voice that she'd had so often lately. The one that said she wasn't sure if I was just being difficult or if she should be ready to call 911. "Valerie!" she kept pleading, "You have to get up now! The school is being very lenient letting you back in. Don't blow it your first day back!"

Like I would be happy about going back to school. About stepping back into those haunted halls. Into the Commons, where the world as I knew it had crashed to an end last May. Like I hadn't been having nightmares about that place every single night and waking up sweaty, crying, totally relieved to be in my room again where things were safe.

The school couldn't decide if I was hero or villain, and I guess I couldn't blame them. I was having a hard time deciding that myself. Was I the bad guy who set into motion the plan to mow down half my school, or the hero who sacrificed herself to end the killing? Some days I felt like both. Some days I felt like neither. It was all so complicated.

The school board did try to hold some ceremony for me early in the summer. Which was crazy. I didn't mean to be a hero. I wasn't even thinking when I jumped in between Nick and Jessica. It's certainly not like I thought, "Here's my chance to save the girl who used to laugh at me and call me Sister Death, and get myself shot in the process." By all accounts it was a heroic thing to do, but in my case . . . well, nobody was really sure.

I refused to go to the ceremony. Told Mom my leg was hurting too much and I needed some sleep and besides, it was a stupid idea anyway. It was just like the school, I told her, to do something totally lame like that. I wouldn't go to something so dumb if you paid me, I said.

But the truth was I was scared of going to the ceremony. I was scared of facing all those people. Afraid they'd all believed everything they'd read about me in the newspaper and seen about me on TV, that I'd been a murderer. That I'd see it in their eyes — *You should've committed suicide just like him* — even if they didn't say it out loud. Or worse, that they'd make me out to be someone brave and selfless, which would only make me feel more awful than I already did, given that it was my boyfriend who killed all those kids and apparently I made him think I wanted them dead too. Not to mention I was the idiot who had no idea that the guy I loved was going to shoot up the school, even though he basically told me so, like, every day. But every time I opened my mouth to tell Mom those things, all that came out was *It's so lame. I wouldn't go to something so dumb if you paid me.* Guess old habits die hard for everyone.

Mr. Angerson, the principal, ended up coming to our house that night instead. He sat at my kitchen table and talked to my mom about . . . I don't know — God, destiny, trauma, whatever. Waiting around, I'm sure, for me to come out of my room and smile and tell him how proud I was of my school and how I was more than happy to serve as a human sacrifice for Miss Perfect Jessica Campbell. Maybe he was waiting for me to apologize, too. Which I would do if I could figure out how. But so far I hadn't come up with words big enough for something this hard.

When Mr. Angerson was in the kitchen waiting for me I turned up my music and crawled deeper in my sheets and let him sit there. I never came out, not even when my mom started pounding on the door, begging in "company-voice" for me to be polite and come downstairs.

"Valerie, please!" she hissed, opening the door a crack and poking her head into my room.

I didn't answer. I pulled the sheets over my head instead. It's not that I didn't want to do it; it's that I just couldn't. But Mom would never understand that. The way she saw it, the more people who "forgave" me, the less I had to feel guilty about. The way I saw it . . . it was just the opposite.

After a while I saw headlights reflecting off my bedroom window. I sat up and looked into the driveway. Mr. Angerson was pulling away. A few minutes later, Mom knocked on my door again.

"What?" I said.

She opened the door and came in, looking all tentative like a baby deer or something. Her face was all red and splotchy and her nose was seriously plugged up. She was holding this dorky medal in her hand, along with a letter of "thanks" from the school district.

"They don't blame you," she said. "They want you to know that. They want you to come back. They're very appreciative of what you did." She shoved the medal and letter into my hands. I glanced at the letter and noticed that only about ten teachers had signed it. Noticed that, of course, Mr. Kline wasn't one of them. For about the millionth time since the shooting, I felt an enormous pang of guilt: Kline was exactly the kind of teacher who would've signed that letter, but he couldn't because he was dead.

We stared at each other for a minute. I knew my mom was looking for some sort of gratitude from me. Some sense that if the school was moving on, maybe I could, too. Maybe we all could.

"Um, yeah, Mom," I said. I handed the medal and letter back to her. "That's, um . . . great." I tried to muster up a smile to reassure her, but found that I couldn't do it. What if I didn't want to move on just yet? What if that medal reminded me that the guy I'd trusted most in this world shot people, shot me, shot himself? Why couldn't she see that accepting the school's "thanks," in that light, was painful to me? Like gratitude would be the only possible emotion I could feel now. Gratitude that I'd lived. Gratitude that I'd been forgiven. Gratitude that they recognized that I'd saved the lives of other Garvin students.

The truth was most days I couldn't feel grateful no matter how hard I tried. Most days I couldn't even pinpoint how I felt. Sometimes sad, sometimes relieved, sometimes confused, sometimes misunderstood. And a lot of times angry. And, what's worse, I didn't know who I was angry at the most: myself, Nick, my parents, the school, the whole world. And then there was the anger that felt the worst of all: anger at the students who died.

"Val," she said, her eyes pleading.

"No, really," I said, "It's cool. I'm just really tired is all, Mom. Really. My leg . . ."

I pushed my head deeper into my pillow and folded myself into the blankets again.

Mom bowed her head and left the room, stooped. I knew she would try to get Dr. Hieler all worked up over "my reaction" at our next visit. I could imagine him sitting in his chair: *"So, Val, we probably should talk about that medal . . ."*

I know Mom later put the medal and letter away in a

keepsake box with all the other kid junk she'd collected over the years. Kindergarten artwork, seventh grade report cards, a letter from the school thanking me for stopping a school shooting. To Mom, somehow all those things would fit together.

That's Mom's way of showing her stubborn hope. Her hope that someday I'll be "fine" again, although she probably can't remember the last time I was "fine." Come to think of it, neither can I. Was it before the shooting? Before Jeremy walked into Nick's life? Before Dad and Mom started hating each other and I started searching for someone, something to take me away from the unhappiness? Way back when I had braces and wore pastel-colored sweaters and listened to Top 40 and thought life would be easy?

The snooze alarm sounded again and I pawed at it, accidentally knocking the clock to the floor.

"Valerie, come on!" she yelled. I imagined she had the cordless in her hand by now, her finger poised over the 9. "School starts in an hour. Wake up!"

I curled up around my pillow and stared at the horses printed on my wallpaper. Ever since I was a little kid, every time I got into trouble, I'd lie on my bed and stare at those horses and imagine myself hopping on one of them and riding away. Just riding, riding, riding, my hair swimming out behind me, my horse never getting tired or hungry, never finding another soul on earth. Just open possibility ahead of me into eternity.

Now the horses just looked like crappy kids' wallpaper art. They didn't take me anywhere. They couldn't. Now I knew they never could, which I thought was so sad. Like my whole life was all a big, dumb dream.

I heard clicking against the doorknob and groaned. Of course — the key. At some point, Dr. Hieler, usually totally on my side, gave my mom permission to use a key and come into my room whenever she pleased. *Just in case*, you know. *As a precaution*, you know. *There was that whole suicide issue*, you know. So now anytime I didn't answer her knock she'd just come right in anyway, the cordless in her hand, just in case she walked in and I was lying in a pool of razor blades and blood on my daisy-shaped throw rug.

I watched as the doorknob turned. Nothing I could do about it but watch from my pillow. She crept in. I was right. The cordless was in her hand.

"Good, you're awake," she said. She smiled and bustled over to the window. She reached up and pulled the Venetian blinds open. I squinted against the early morning sunlight.

"You're in a suit," I said, shading my eyes with my forearm.

She reached down with her free hand and smoothed the camel-colored skirt around her thighs. It was tentative, like it was the first time she'd ever dressed up before. For a minute she looked as insecure as I was, which made me feel sad for her.

"Yeah," she said, using the same hand to pat the back of

her hair. "I figured since you were going back to school, I should, you know, start trying to get back full time at the office."

I pulled myself to a sitting position. My head felt sort of flat in the back from lying down so long and my leg twinged a little. I absently rubbed the dent in my thigh under the sheets. "On my first day back?"

She stumbled over to me, high-stepping over a pile of dirty laundry in her camel-colored high heels. "Well . . . yeah. It's been a few months. Dr. Hieler thinks it's fine for me to go back. And I'll be there to pick you up after school." She sat on the side of my bed and stroked my hair. "You'll be fine."

"How can you be so sure?" I asked. "How do you know I'll be all right? You can't know. I wasn't okay last May and you didn't know that." I pulled myself out of bed. My chest felt tight and I wasn't sure I wasn't going to cry.

She sat, gripping the cordless in front of her. "I just know, Valerie. That day won't ever happen again, honey. Nick's . . . he's gone. Now try not to get all upset . . ."

Too late. I was already upset. The longer she sat on the side of my bed and stroked my hair the way she used to do when I was little and I smelled the perfume that I thought of as her "work perfume," the more real it was. I was going back to school.

"We all agreed that this was best, Valerie, remember?" she said. "Sitting in Dr. Hieler's office we decided that running away was not a good option for our family. You agreed.

You said that you didn't want Frankie to have to suffer because of what happened. And your dad has his firm . . . to leave that and start all over again would be so tough for us financially . . ." she shrugged, shaking her head.

"Mom," I said, but I couldn't think of a great argument. She was right. I'd been the one saying that Frankie shouldn't have to leave his friends. That just because he was my little brother didn't mean he should have to change towns, change schools. That Dad, whose jaw tightened angrily every time someone brought up the possibility of our family having to move to a new town, shouldn't have to build a new law firm after working so hard to build his. That I shouldn't have to be stuck in my house with a tutor or, worse, to switch to a new school my senior year. That I'd be damned if I'd slink away like a criminal when I'd done nothing wrong.

"It's not like everybody in the whole world doesn't know who I am anyway," I'd said, running my fingertips along the arm of Dr. Hieler's couch. "It's not like I could find a school where nobody has heard of me. Can you imagine how much of an outcast I'd be at a new school? At least at Garvin I know what to expect. Plus if I ran away from Garvin, everyone there would be even more sure I was guilty."

"It'll be tough," Dr. Hieler had warned. "You're going to have to face a lot of dragons."

I'd shrugged. "What else is new? I can handle them."

"Are you sure?" Dr. Hieler had asked, his eyes narrowed at me skeptically.

I'd nodded. "It's not fair that I should have to leave. I can do this. If it's terrible I can always transfer at the end of the semester. But I'll make it. I'm not afraid."

But that was back when summer stretched in front of us, impossibly long. Back when "going back" was just an idea, not a reality. As an idea, I still believed in it. I wasn't guilty of anything except loving Nick and hating the people who tormented us, and there was no way I'd slither away and hide from the people who believed I was guilty of something else. But now that it came down to putting my idea to practice, I wasn't just afraid; I was terrified.

"You had all summer to change your mind," Mom said, still sitting on my bed.

I snapped my mouth shut and turned toward my dresser. I grabbed a pair of clean underwear and a bra, then scavenged the floor for some jeans and a T-shirt. "Fine. I'll get ready," I said.

I can't say that she smiled just then. She did something that was kind of like a smile, only it looked a little painful. She took a couple false starts toward the door and then apparently decided it was a good decision and headed for it completely, gripping the phone in both hands. I wondered if she'd accidentally take the phone to work with her, thumb still poised over the 9.

"Good. I'll wait for you downstairs."

I dressed, pulling on the wrinkled jeans and T-shirt haphazardly, not even caring what they looked like. It's not like dressing well was going to make me feel any better or any less conspicuous. I hobbled into the bathroom and ran a brush through my hair, which hadn't been washed in about four days. I didn't bother with makeup, either. Didn't really even know where it was. It's not like I'd been to a lot of cotillions over the summer. For most of that time I couldn't even walk.

I slipped on a pair of canvas shoes and grabbed my backpack — a new one that Mom had bought a few days ago and that had sat empty in the very place she'd left it until she finally came in and stuffed it with supplies herself. The old backpack — the bloody one . . . well, that probably ended up in the garbage, along with Nick's Flogging Molly T-shirt, which she'd found in my closet and thrown away while I was stuck in the hospital. I'd cried and called her a bitch when I got home and saw that the shirt was missing. She totally didn't get it — that shirt didn't belong to Nick the Murderer. It belonged to Nick, the guy who surprised me with Flogging Molly tickets when they came to the Closet. Nick, the guy who let me climb up on his shoulders while they sang "Factory Girls." Nick, the guy who had the idea that we would pool our money to buy one T-shirt and share it. Nick, the guy who wore the shirt home and then took it off and gave it to me and then never asked for it back.

She claimed that throwing the shirt away was advice from Dr. Hieler, too, but I didn't believe it. Sometimes I had a feeling she just blamed all her ideas on him so I'd roll with it. Dr. Hieler would understand that Nick the Murderer didn't own that shirt. I didn't even know who Nick the Murderer was. Dr. Hieler understood that.

All dressed, I was struck with a sensation of being too nervous to go through with it. My legs felt almost too weak to take me out the door and a light coating of sweat covered the back of my neck. I couldn't go. I couldn't face those people, those places. I just wasn't strong enough.

With shaky hands, I fumbled my cell phone out of my pocket and dialed Dr. Hieler's cell phone number. He answered on the first ring.

"Sorry to bother you," I said, sinking down onto my bed.

"No, I told you to call. Remember? I was waiting for it."

"I don't think I can do this," I said. "I'm not ready. I don't think I'll ever be ready. I think it was a bad idea to —"

"Val, stop," he interrupted. "You can do this. You're ready. We've talked this through. It's going to be tough, but you can handle it. You've handled a lot worse over the past several months, right? You're very strong."

Tears sprang to my eyes and I wiped them off with my thumb.

"Just concentrate on being in the moment," he said. "Don't read into things. See what's really there, okay? When you get home this afternoon, call me. I'll have Stephanie patch you through even if I'm in session, okay?"

"Okay."

"And if you need to talk during the day . . ."

"I know, I can call."

"And remember what we said? Even if you make it through only half the day, it's already a victory, right?"

"Mom's going back to work. Full day."

"That's because she believes in you. But she'll come home if you need her. My prediction is you won't, though. And you know I'm always right." There was a smile in his voice.

I chuckled, sniffed. Wiped my eyes again. "Right. Whatever. I've gotta go."

"You're going to do great."

"I hope so."

"I know so. And remember what we said: you can always transfer after this semester if it doesn't work out. That's, what? Seventy-five days or so?"

"Eighty-three," I said.

"See? Piece of cake. You've got this. Call me later."

"I will."

I hung up and picked up my backpack. I started to walk out the door, but stopped. There was something missing. I reached under my top dresser drawer and fumbled around until I found it, tucked into the frame of the drawer, out of Mom's investigative reach. I pulled it out and looked at it for about the millionth time.

It was a photo of Nick and me at Blue Lake on the last day of school, sophomore year. He was holding a beer and I was laughing so hard I swear you could see my tonsils in the picture, and we were sitting on a giant rock right next to the lake. I think it was Mason who took the picture. I couldn't for the life of me remember what was so funny, no matter how many nights I stayed awake trying to drum it up.

We looked so happy. And we were. No matter what the e-mails and the suicide notes and the Hate List said. We were happy.

I touched the laughing still shot of Nick's face with my finger. I could still hear his voice loud and clear. Still hear him asking me out in his serious Nick way, at once bold and angry and romantic and shy.

"Val," he had said, pulling himself off the rock and bending to pick up his beer bottle. He picked up a flat rock with his free hand and took a few steps forward and skipped it across the lake. It skipped once, twice, three times before it dove into the water and stayed. Stacey laughed from somewhere nearby in the woods. Duce laughed just after her. It was getting on to nightfall and a frog started croaking somewhere to my left. "Do you ever think about just leaving it all behind?"

I pulled my heels up against the rock and grabbed my knees. I thought about Mom and Dad's fight the night before. About Mom's voice drifting up the stairs from the living room, the words unclear, but the tone venomous. About Dad leaving the house around midnight, the door shutting softly behind him. "You mean like run away? Definitely."

Nick was silent for a long time. He picked up another rock and slung it across the lake. It skipped twice and fell.

"Sure," he said. "Or, you know, like driving off a cliff and never looking back."

I stared at the setting sun and thought about it. "Yeah," I said. "Everybody does. Totally Thelma and Louise."

He turned and kind of laughed, then swigged the last of his beer and dropped the bottle to the ground. "Never saw it," he said. Then, "Remember when we read *Romeo and Juliet* in freshman English last year?"

"Yeah."

He leaned over me. "You think we could be like them?"

I crinkled my nose. "I don't know. I guess. Sure."

He turned again and stared out into the lake. "Yeah, we could. We really could. We think alike."

I stood up and brushed the backs of my thighs, which felt dimply from the texture of the rock we'd been sitting on. "Are you asking me out?"

He turned, lurched toward me, and grabbed me around the waist. He picked me up until my feet were dangling above the ground and I couldn't help it — I let out a squeal that turned into a giggle. He kissed me and my body felt so electric up against his even my toes tingled. It seemed like forever that I'd been waiting for him to do this. "Would you say no if I did?" he asked.

"Hell, no, Romeo," I said. I kissed him back.

"Then I guess I am, Juliet," he'd said, and I swear as I touched his face in the photo I could hear it again. Could feel him in the room with me. Even though in May he became a monster in the eyes of the world, in my eyes he was still that guy holding me above the ground, kissing me and calling me Juliet.

I stuffed the photo into my back pocket. "Eighty-three and counting," I said aloud, taking a deep breath and heading downstairs.

MAY 2, 2008

6:32 A.M.

"See you in the Commons?"

My cell phone chirped and I grabbed it before Mom or Frankie or, God forbid, Dad heard it. It was still early and dim outside. One of those tough mornings to wake up to. Summer break was right around the corner, which meant three months of sleeping in and not having to put up with Garvin High. Not that I hated school or anything, but Christy Bruter was, like always, giving me trouble on the bus and I had a D in Science because of a quiz I forgot to study for, and finals were going to be a killer this year.

Nick had been a little quiet lately. In fact, he hadn't shown up at school for two days, and had texted me all day long, asking about "the shits in homeroom" or "the fat bitches in P. E." or "that scab McNeal."

He'd been hanging around with this guy, Jeremy, for the

last month and every day he seemed to pull further and further away from me. I was afraid he was going to break up with me, so I just played along like it was no big deal that we hardly ever saw each other anymore. I didn't want to push him — he'd been so volatile lately and I didn't want to start a fight. I didn't ask him what he was doing on those days he didn't show up and instead just texted him back that "the shits in Bio need 2 B dunked in formaldehyde" and that "I h8 those bitches" and that "McNeal is lucky I don't have a gun." That last one would really come back to bite me later. Really, they all would. But that last one . . . that last one would make me vomit every time I thought about it for a long time. And it would inspire a three-hour conversation between me and Detective Panzella. And it would make my dad forever look at me differently, like I was some sort of monster deep down and he could see it.

Jeremy was this older guy — like twenty-one or some-thing — who'd graduated from Garvin a few years ago. He didn't go to college. He didn't have a job. From what I could tell, all Jeremy did was beat up his girlfriend and sit around smoking pot and watching cartoons all day. Until he met Nick and then he stopped watching the cartoons and started smoking his dope with Nick and only beat up his girlfriend on nights when he wasn't in Nick's garage, playing drums, too stoned to remember she existed. On the rare occasions that I'd been over there when Jeremy was there, Nick was a totally different guy. Someone I didn't even recognize, really.

For a long time I thought maybe I just never knew Nick at all. Maybe when Nick and I were watching TV in his basement or dunking each other at the pool and laughing, I was totally not seeing the real Nick. Like the real Nick was the one that showed up when Jeremy came over — that hard-eyed, selfish Nick.

I'd heard of women who were completely blind and ignored all these signs that their man was some sort of pervert or monster, but no way could you convince me I was one of them. When Jeremy wasn't around . . . when it was just me and Nick and I looked in Nick's eyes . . . I knew what I saw and it was good. He was good. He had a sick sense of humor sometimes — we all did — but no way did we mean it. So sometimes it makes sense to me that maybe it was Jeremy who put those ideas about shooting up the school in Nick's head. Not me. Jeremy. He's the bad guy. He's the one.

I picked up the cell and fumbled it down under the covers where I had been slowly waking up to the idea that I had to get through another school day.

"'Lo?"

"Baby." Nick's voice was thin, almost wired-sounding, although at the time I just figured that was because it was so early and Nick hardly ever got up early anymore.

"Hey," I whispered. "Going to school today for a change?"

He chuckled. Sounded really happy. "Yeah. Jeremy's gonna drive me."

I pulled myself to a sitting position. "Cool. Stacey was asking about you yesterday. Said she saw you and Jeremy driving out toward Blue Lake." I let the unspoken question hang in the air.

"Yeah." I heard the flick of his lighter and the crackle of a cigarette filter. He exhaled. "We had some stuff to do out there."

"Like . . . ?"

He didn't answer. Just the sound of the filter burning and his steady exhale.

Disappointment washed over me. He wasn't going to tell me. I hated the way he was acting. He'd never kept secrets from me before. We'd always talked about everything, even the hard stuff like our parents' marriages and the names kids called us at school and how sometimes we felt like nothing. Like less than nothing.

I almost pressed him, told him I wanted to know, I deserved to know, but decided to change the subject instead — if I was finally going to get to see him, I didn't want to waste that time fighting with him. "Hey, I've got some names for the list," I said.

"Who?"

I rubbed the corners of my eyes with my fingertips. "People who say 'sorry' after everything. Fast-food commercials. And Jessica Campbell." *Jeremy*, I almost added, but thought better of it.

"That skinny blond chick that goes out with Jake Diehl?"

"Uh-huh, but Jake's okay. I mean a little jockish, but he's

no way as annoying as her. Yesterday in health I was totally just spacing out and I guess I was looking in her direction. So all of a sudden she looks at me and goes, 'What're you looking at, Sister Death?' and she had this scowl on her face and she rolled her eyes and goes, 'Hell-o, mind your own business,' and I was all, 'Trust me, I don't give a shit about what you were saying anyway,' and she was like, 'Don't you have a funeral to go to?' and then her stupid friends started laughing like she was some sort of stand-up comedian or something. She's such a bitch."

"Yeah, you're right." He coughed. I heard a rattle of papers being turned and could imagine Nick sitting on his mattress writing in the red spiral notebook we shared. "All those blond chicks should just disappear."

At the time I'd laughed. It was funny. I agreed with him. At least I said I did. And, okay, I really thought I did. I didn't feel like a horrible person, but I laughed because to me, *they* were the horrible people. They deserved it.

"Yeah, they should be run over by their parents' Beemers," I said.

"I put that Chelle girl on the list, too."

"Good one. She won't shut up about making varsity. I don't know what her problem is."

"Yeah. Well."

We sat in silence for a minute. I don't know what Nick was thinking. At the time I took his silence to be some sort of unspoken agreement with me, like we were speaking at the same time in some wavelength that had no breath.

But now I know that's just one of those "inferences" Dr. Hieler was always telling me about. People do it all the time — assume that they "know" what's going on in someone else's head. That's impossible. And to think it's possible is a mistake. A really big mistake. A life-ruining one if you're not careful.

I heard some mumbling in the background. "Gotta go," Nick said. "We gotta take Jeremy's kid to day care. His girlfriend's being a pain in the ass about it. See you in the Commons?"

"Sure. I'll have Stacey save us a seat."

"Cool."

"Love you."

"You too, baby."

I hung up, smiling. Maybe whatever was bugging him was resolved. Maybe he was getting sick of Jeremy and Jeremy's kid and Jeremy's cartoons and Jeremy's pot. Maybe I could talk him into skipping lunch and walking with me across the highway to Casey's for a sandwich. Just the two of us. Like old times. Us sitting on the concrete median, picking onions off our sandwiches and asking each other music trivia questions, our shoulders butted up against one another, our feet swinging.

I jumped in the shower without bothering to turn on the light and stood enveloped by the steam in the dark, hoping maybe Nick would bring me something special today. He was pretty good at that — showing up to school with a rose he'd picked up at the gas station or sliding a candy bar into my locker between classes, slipping a note into my note-book when I wasn't looking. When he wanted to, Nick had a hell of a romantic side.

I got out of the shower and dried off. I took extra time on my hair and eyeliner and wore a torn black denim mini-skirt with my favorite pair of striped black and white tights with the hole in the knee. I stuffed my feet into socks and a pair of canvas shoes and grabbed my backpack.

My little brother, Frankie, was eating cereal at the kitchen table. His hair was spiked and he looked like one of those kids in PopTart commercials: perfectly coiffed skater types. Frankie was fourteen and totally full of himself. He thought he was some sort of fashion guru and was always dressed so stylishly he looked like he'd just stepped out of a cata-log. We were close, despite the fact that we tended to hang out with totally different crowds and we had completely different definitions of what was cool. He could be annoy-ing at times, but most of the time he was a pretty good little brother.

He had his American history textbook open on the table next to him and was frantically scribbling on a piece of notebook paper, stopping only to shovel a bite of cereal into his mouth every so often.

"Shooting a hair gel commercial today?" I asked, bump-ing into his chair with my hip on the way past.

"What?" he said, running the palm of his hand over the spikes of his hair. "The ladies love it."

I rolled my eyes, smiling. "I'll bet. Dad leave yet?"

He took another bite of cereal and went back to writing. "Yeah," he said around the food in his mouth. "He left a few minutes ago."

I grabbed a waffle out of the freezer and popped it into the toaster. "I see you were too busy with the ladies to do your homework last night," I teased, leaning over him to read what he was writing. "What did the women in the . . . Civil War era . . . think of excess hair gel, exactly?"

"Give me a break," he said, bumping me with his elbow. "I was talking to Tina until midnight. I gotta get this done. Mom'll freak if I get another C in history. She'll take my cell phone away again."

"Okay, okay," I said. "I'll leave you alone. Far be it from me to stand between you and Tina's riveting phone romance." The waffle popped up out of the toaster and I grabbed it. I took a bite of it, plain. "Speaking of Mom, is she driving you again today?"

He nodded. Mom drove Frankie to school every day, dropping him off on her way to work. It gave him a few extra minutes in the morning, which I guess would be nice. But since it would require me to sit within three feet of my mom and thus spend every morning hearing how my "hair looks atrocious" and my "skirt is too short" and "Why does a beautiful girl like you want to ruin her looks with all that makeup and hair dye?" I preferred to stand on the curb and wait for the bus full of jocks to come get me. And that's saying something.

I looked at the clock on the stove. The bus would be coming any minute. I shouldered my backpack and took another bite out of my waffle.

"I'm outta here," I said, heading for the door. "Good luck with your homework."

"See ya," he called to my back as I stepped out on the front porch, closing the door behind me.

The air felt crisper than usual — felt like winter was on the verge of rushing in on us rather than spring. Like right now the day was the warmest it was going to get.

2

[FROM THE GARVIN COUNTY SUN-TRIBUNE,
MAY 3, 2008, REPORTER ANGELA DASH.]

Christy Bruter, 16 — Bruter, Captain of the Garvin High
softball team, was the first victim and appeared to be
a direct target. "He bumped her in the shoulder," says
Amy Bruter, the victim's mother. "And some of the girls
who were there told us that when Christy turned around
he said, 'You've been on the list for a really long time.'
She said, 'What list?' and then he shot her." Bruter,
who was shot in the stomach, is described by doctors
as "damned lucky to be alive." Investigation confirmed
that, indeed, Bruter's name was the first of hundreds
on the now infamous "Hate List," a red spiral notebook

confiscated from Nick Levil's home just hours after the shooting.

* * *

"Are you nervous?"

I picked at the rubber that was peeling off the sole of my shoe and shrugged. There were so many emotions running through me I thought I might go screaming down the street. But for some reason all I could muster was a shrug. Which, now that I think about it, was a good thing. Mom was watching me extra close this morning. Any wrong move and she would run to Dr. Hieler and blow it all out of proportion as usual and then we'd have The Conversation again.

Dr. Hieler and I had had The Conversation at least once a week since May. It always went something like this:

He would ask, "Are you safe?"

"I'm not going to kill myself if you're asking that," I'd answer.

"I am," he'd say.

"Well, I'm not going to do it. She's just crazy," I'd answer.

"She's just worried about you," he'd say, and then we'd, thankfully, move on to something else.

But then I'd get home later and climb into bed and start thinking about it. About the suicide stuff. Was I safe? Was

35

there really a time I might have been suicidal and I didn't even know it? And then I'd spend about an hour, my room darkening around me, wondering what the hell happened to make me so unsure of who I even was. Because who you are is supposed to be the easiest question in the world to answer, right? Only for me it hadn't been easy for a very long time. Maybe it never was.

Sometimes, in my world where parents hated one another and school was a battleground, it sucked to be me. Nick had been my escape. The one person who understood. It'd felt good to be part of an "us," with the same thoughts, the same feelings, the same miseries. But now the other half of "us" was gone and, lying there in my shadowy room, I'd be struck with this realization that I had no clue how to be just me again.

I'd roll over on my side and stare at the dark shadowy horses dotting my wallpaper and wish they would giddy up and take me away the way I'd imagined them doing when I was a kid, so I wouldn't have to think about it anymore. Because not having a clue who you are hurts way too much. And one thing I did know for sure: I was tired of hurting.

Mom reached across the front seat and patted my knee. "Well, if you get halfway through the day and need me, I'm just a phone call away. Okay?"

I didn't answer. The lump in my throat was too big. It seemed surreal that I was about to be walking the same hallways with these kids who I knew so well, but who seemed like complete strangers. Kids like Allen Moon, who

I'd seen look directly into a camera and say, "I hope they put Valerie away for life for what she did," and Carmen Chiarro, who was quoted in a magazine as saying, "I don't know why my name was even on that list. I didn't even know who Nick and Valerie were before that day."

I could see her not knowing Nick. When he moved to Garvin freshman year, he was just a quiet, skinny kid with bad clothes and dirty hair. But Carmen and I had gone to elementary school together. She was totally lying when she said she didn't know me. And, given that she was good friends with Mr. Quarterback Chris Summers all of sophomore year, and given that Chris Summers hated Nick and would take every chance he could to make Nick miserable, and given that all of Chris's buddies thought it was hilarious whenever he tormented Nick, I found it highly suspect that she didn't know Nick, either. Would Allen and Carmen be there today? Would they be looking for me? Would they be hoping I wouldn't show?

"And you know Dr. Hieler's number," Mom said, patting my knee again.

I nodded. "I know it."

We turned down Oak Street. I could have driven this way in my sleep. Right on Oak Street. Left on Foundling Avenue. Left on Starling. Right into the parking lot. Garvin High straight ahead. Can't miss it.

Only this morning it looked different to me. Never again would Garvin High have that exciting and intimidating look it held for me as a freshman. Never again would I equate it with mind-bending romance, with euphoria, laughter, a job well done. None of the things most people think of when they imagine their high schools. It was just another thing that Nick had stolen from me, from all of us, that day. He didn't just steal our innocence and sense of well-being. He had somehow managed to rob us of our memories as well.

"You'll be fine," Mom said. I turned my head and looked out the window. Saw Delaney Peters walking down by the football field with her arm hooked through Sam Hall's. I had no idea they were together, and suddenly I felt as if I'd missed a lifetime rather than just a summer. Had things been normal, I'd have spent the summer at the lake or at the bowling alley or gas station or fast food places, picking up gossip, learning about new romances. Instead, I was holed up in my bedroom, afraid and sick to my stomach at the thought of so much as going to the grocery store with my mom. "Dr. Hieler feels strongly that you'll be able to handle today with flying colors."

"I know," I said. I leaned forward and my stomach started to tighten. Stacey and Duce were sitting on the bleachers like always, along with Mason, David, Liz, and Rebecca. Normally I would be sitting there with them. And with Nick. Comparing schedules, griping about who we got for homeroom, talking about being at some wild party together. My hands started to sweat. Stacey was laughing at something Duce had said, and I felt more like an outsider than ever.

We angled into the driveway and right away I noticed two police cruisers parked next to the school. I must have made a noise or had a look because Mom said, "It's just standard now. Security. Because . . . well, you know. They don't want any copycats. It makes you safer, Valerie."

Mom pulled up in the drop-off zone and stopped. Her hands fell away from the steering wheel and she looked at me. I tried not to notice that the corners of her mouth were twitching and she was absently picking at a hangnail on her thumb. I put on a wobbly smile for her.

"I'll see you right here at two-fifty," she said. "I'll be waiting for you."

"I'll be fine," I said in a tiny voice. I pulled on the door handle. My hands didn't seem to have enough strength to make it budge, but eventually it did, which disappointed me because it meant I was going to have to get out.

"Maybe tomorrow you'll wear a little lipstick or something," Mom said as I pulled myself out of the car. *What a strange thing to say*, I thought, but I tucked my lips in against each other anyway, out of habit. I shut the door and gave Mom a half-wave. She waved back, searching me with her eyes until the car behind her honked and she pulled away.

For a minute I was rooted to my spot on the sidewalk, unsure whether or not I could walk into the building. My thigh ached and my head was buzzing. But everyone around me seemed totally normal. A couple sophomores walked past me, talking excitedly about homecoming. One girl giggled as her boyfriend poked her in the side with his finger. Teachers stood around on the sidewalk, griping at kids to get to class. All things I remembered from the last time I was here. Strange.

I started walking but a voice behind me made me stop dead in my tracks.

"No way!" It seemed like someone hit the "mute" button on the world just then. I turned and looked. Stacey and Duce were standing there, holding hands, Stacey's mouth hanging open, Duce's screwed into a tidy little knot. "Val?" Stacey asked, not as if she didn't believe it was me, but as if she didn't believe it was me, *here*.

"Hey," I said.

David came around Stacey and hugged me. His hug was stiff and he let go right away, stepping back in line with the rest of the gang, dropping his eyes to the ground in front of him.

"I didn't know you were coming back today," Stacey said. Her eyes darted just briefly to the side, assessing Duce's face, and I could instantly see her begin to mold herself into a copy of him. Her grin took on a superior slant that was really awkward on her face.

I shrugged. Stacey and I had been friends since pretty much forever. We wore the same size, liked the same movies, dressed in the same clothes, told the same lies. There were stretches every summer when we were almost inseparable.

But there was one big difference between Stacey and me. Stacey had no enemies, probably because she was so eager to please all the time. She was completely moldable: you just told her who she was and she became it, just like that. She definitely wasn't one of the popular kids, but she wasn't one of the losers like me, either. She had always sort of walked this line in between, totally under the radar.

After "the incident" as my Dad likes to call it, Stacey came to visit me twice. Once, in the hospital, before I was speaking to anyone. Once at home after I was released, and I had Frankie tell her I was asleep. She never really tried to make contact again, and neither did I. I think maybe there was a part of me that felt like I didn't deserve friends anymore. Like she deserved a better friend than me.

In a way I felt sorry for her. I could almost see it in her face — her desire to go back to where we were before the shooting, the guilt she felt over holding me at arm's length — but I could also see how acutely aware she was of how being friends with me now made her look. If I was guilty by virtue of loving Nick, would she be guilty by virtue of loving me? Being my friend would be a tough risk to take — social suicide for anyone at Garvin. And Stacey would no way be strong enough to take that risk.

"Does your leg hurt?" she asked.

"Sometimes," I said, looking down at it. "At least I don't have to take P. E. But I'll probably never get to class on time with this thing."

"Been to Nick's grave?" Duce asked. I looked at him sharply. He was staring at me with hard contempt in his eyes. "Been to anyone's grave?"

41

Stacey elbowed him. "Leave her alone. It's her first day back," she said, but without much conviction.

"Yeah, c'mon," David mumbled. "Glad you're okay, Val. Who do you have for math?"

Duce interrupted. "What? She can walk. How come she never went to nobody's grave? I mean, if I was the one writing down all these names of people I wanted dead I'd at least go to their graves."

"I didn't want anyone to die," I practically whispered. Duce gave me one of those raised eyebrow looks. "He was your best friend, too, you know."

There was silence between us, and I began to notice that all around me were curious onlookers. Only they weren't curious about the confrontation. They were curious about me, as if they'd all of a sudden realized who I was. They walked past me slowly on all sides, whispering to one another, staring at me.

Stacey had begun to notice, too. She shifted a little and then looked past me.

"I gotta get to class," she said. "Glad you're back, Val." She was already walking past me, David and Mason and the others trailing behind her.

Duce moved last, shouldering past me, murmuring, "Yeah, it's real great."

I stood on the sidewalk, feeling marooned with this strange tide of kids moving around me, shoving me backward and forward with their motion, but never breaking me loose into the sea itself. I wondered if I could stand in this very spot until Mom came back at 2:50.

A hand fell on my shoulder.

"Why don't you come with me?" a voice said in my ear. I turned and found myself looking into the face of Mrs. Tate, the guidance counselor. She wrapped her arm around my shoulders and pulled me along, the two of us heading boldly through the waves of kids around us, leaving whispers in our wake.

"It's good to see you here today," Mrs. Tate said. "I'm sure you're a little apprehensive about it, no?"

"A little," I said, but I couldn't say more because she was pulling me along so fast it was all I could do to concentrate on walking. We broke into the vestibule before the panic in my torso could even well up, and somehow I felt cheated. Like I should at least have the right to panic about entering my school again, if that's what I wanted.

The hallway was a bustle of motion. A police officer stood at the door, waving a wand over students' backpacks and jackets. Mrs. Tate waved her hand at one of them and ushered me past him without stopping.

It seemed a little sparse in the hallways, like a lot of kids were missing. But otherwise it was like nothing had changed. Kids were talking, squealing, shoes were scuffling on shiny tile, the walls echoing with the *wham! wham! wham!* of lockers slamming in the hallways beyond my eyes' reach.

Mrs. Tate and I walked through the hall with purpose,

then rounded the corner to the Commons. This time the panic rose so quickly it made it to my throat before Tate could pull me into the large room. She must have sensed my fear because she squeezed my shoulders harder and pressed on more quickly.

The Commons — once the place to hang out in the mornings, ordinarily packed shoulder-to-shoulder — was empty, save for the clusters of empty tables and chairs. At the far end, the end where Christy Bruter had fallen, someone had installed a bulletin board. Across the top were construction paper cutout letters reading WE WILL REMEMBER, and the board was papered with notes, cards, ribbons, photos, banners, flowers. A couple girls — I couldn't tell who from this distance — were pinning a note and photograph to the bulletin board.

"We would have banned congregating in the Commons in the mornings if we'd had to," Mrs. Tate said, as if she could tell what I was thinking. "Just out of safety concerns. But it looks like nobody wants to hang out here anymore anyway. Now we only use the Commons for lunch shifts."

We walked straight through the Commons. I tried to ignore my imagination, which had my feet sliding in sticky blood across the floor. I tried to focus on the sound of Mrs. Tate's shoes clacking against the tile, trying to remind myself of all the things about breathing and focusing that Dr. Hieler had spent so much time coaching me on. At the moment I couldn't remember a single one.

We passed through the doorway at the other end of the Commons, where the administration offices were. Technically, this was the front of the building. More officers were searching backpacks and passing metal detector wands over kids' clothes.

"All this security is going to make our mornings get off to a slow start, I'm afraid." Mrs. Tate sighed. "But, of course, this way we'll all feel safer."

She whisked me past the officers and into the administrative offices. The secretaries looked on with polite smiles, but didn't say a word. I kept my face tilted to the floor and followed Mrs. Tate into her office. I hoped she'd let me stay there a long time.

Mrs. Tate's office was the opposite of Dr. Hieler's. Where Dr. Hieler's was tidy and lined with rows and rows of reference books, Mrs. Tate's was a haphazard conglomeration of paperwork and educational tools, like it was part guidance office, part supply closet. There were books stacked on just about every flat surface and photos of Mrs. Tate's kids and dogs everywhere.

Most kids came to Mrs. Tate to either complain about a teacher or look through a college catalogue, and that was pretty much it. If Mrs. Tate had gone to college hoping to counsel scads of troubled teenagers, she was probably pretty disappointed. If there can be such a thing as disappointment about not having enough troubled people in your life.

She motioned for me to sit in a chair with a torn vinyl seat and she edged herself around a small file cabinet and sat in the chair behind her desk, dwarfed by stacks of papers and Post-it notes in front of her. She leaned forward over the mess and folded her hands right in the middle of an old fast food wrapper.

"I was watching for you this morning," she said. "I'm glad you came back to school. Shows guts."

"I'm giving it a try," I mumbled, rubbing my thigh absently. "I can't make any promises I'll stay." *Eighty-three and counting*, I repeated in my head.

"Well, I hope you do. You're a good student," she said. "Ah!" she yelped, holding up one finger. She leaned to the side and pulled open a drawer of the file cabinet next to her desk. A framed photo of a black and white cat pawing at something wobbled as the drawer moved and I imagined her, several times a day, having to right the photo after it fell. She pulled a brown file folder out and opened it on the desk in front of her, leaving the file drawer hanging ajar. "That reminds me. College. Yes. You were considering . . ." she flipped through a few pages, ". . . Kansas State, if I remember correctly." She kept flipping, then ran her finger down a page and said, "Yep. Right here. Kansas State and Northwest Missouri State." She closed the folder and smiled. "I got the program requirements from each of them just last week. It's a little late to be just starting this process, but it shouldn't be a problem. Well, you'll probably have to account for some things on your permanent record, but . . .

really . . . you were never charged with . . . well, you know what I mean."

I nodded. I knew what she meant. Not that it needed to be on my permanent record, because I pretty much couldn't think of anyone in the country who hadn't heard of me by now. I was like best friends with the world. Or maybe worst enemies. "I changed my mind," I said.

"Oh. A different school? Shouldn't be a problem. With your grades . . ."

"No, I mean I'm not going. To college."

Mrs. Tate leaned forward, resting her hand on the wrapper again. She was frowning at me. "Not going?"

"Right. I don't want to anymore."

She spoke softly: "Listen, Valerie. I know you blame yourself for what happened. I know you think you're just like him. But you're not."

I sat up straighter and tried to smile confidently. This was not a conversation I wanted to get into today, of all days. "Really, Mrs. Tate, you don't have to say this," I said. I touched my back pocket with the picture of Nick and me at Blue Lake in it for reassurance. "I mean, I'm okay and everything."

Mrs. Tate held up a hand and looked me straight in the eye. "I spent more time with Nick than with my own son most days," she said. "He was such a searcher. Always so angry. He was one of those kids who was just going to struggle through life. He was so consumed with hate. Ruled by it, really."

No, I wanted to shout at her. *No he wasn't. Nick was good. I saw it.*

I was struck with a memory of the night Nick had shown up at my house unexpectedly just as Mom and Dad began to rev up for their usual after-dinner bitchfest. I could feel it coming: Mom slamming plates into the dishwasher, mumbling under her breath, and Dad pacing the floor between the living room and the kitchen, eyeing Mom and shaking his head. The tension was building and I'd begun to get that tired feeling I'd had so often lately, wishing I could just go to bed and wake up in a different house, a different life. Frankie had already disappeared into his room and I wondered if he got that tired feeling, too.

I was just climbing the stairs to my bedroom when the doorbell rang. I could see Nick through the window next to the door, shifting his weight from foot to foot.

"I'll get it!" I hollered to my parents as I ran back down the stairs, but the argument had already started and they didn't notice.

"Hey," I'd said, stepping out on the front porch. "What's up?"

"Hey," he said back. He'd held out a CD. "I brought this," he said. "I burned it for you this afternoon. It's all the songs that make me think about you."

"That's so sweet," I said, reading the back of the case, where he'd carefully typed all of the titles and artists of the songs. "I love it."

On the other side of the door, we could hear Dad's voice getting closer. "You know, maybe I *won't* come home, Jenny, that's a great idea," he was growling. Nick looked at the door, and I could swear I saw embarrassment creep through his face. And something else. Pity, maybe? Fear? Maybe that same weariness I felt?

"Want to get out of here?" he asked, shoving his hands in his pockets. "It doesn't sound too good in there. We can hang together for a while."

I nodded, opening the door a crack and dropping the CD on the table in the foyer. Nick reached out and grabbed my hand, leading me to the field behind my house. We found a clearing and sprawled on our backs in the grass, looking at the stars, talking about . . . anything, everything.

"You know why we get along so well, Val?" he asked after a while. "Because we think just alike. It's like we have the same brain. It's cool."

I stretched, wrapping my leg around his. "Totally," I said. "Screw our parents. Screw their stupid fights. Screw everybody. Who gives a shit about them?"

"Not me," he said. He scratched his shoulder. "For a long time I thought nobody would ever get me, but you really do."

"Of course I do." I turned my head and kissed his shoulder. "And you get me, too. It's kind of creepy the way we're so alike."

"Creepy in a good way."

"Yeah, in a good way."

He turned to face me, propping himself up on an elbow. "It's good that we have each other," he said. "It's like, you know, even if the whole world hates you, you still have someone to rely on. Just the two of you against the whole world. Just us."

At the time, my thoughts had been so consumed with Mom and Dad and their incessant arguing, I'd just assumed we were talking about them. Nick knew exactly what I was going through — he called his stepdad Charles his "Step du Jour" and talked about his mom's ever-changing love life as if it were some big joke. I'd had no idea he might have meant us against . . . everyone. "Yeah. Just us," I'd answered. "Just us."

I looked at the carpet of Mrs. Tate's office, once again struck with the feeling that I never knew Nick at all. That all of that soul-mate stuff we'd talked about was just bullshit. That when it comes to reading people, I'm an F student.

I felt a lump in my throat. How indulgent was that? The school outcast cries over the memory of her boyfriend, the murderer. Even I would hate me. I swallowed and forced the lump to go down.

Mrs. Tate had sat back in her chair, but was still talking. "Valerie, you had a future. You were choosing colleges. You were getting good grades. Nick never had a future. Nick's future was . . . this."

A tear spilled over. I swallowed and swallowed but it did

no good. How did she know about Nick's future? You can't predict the future. God, if I could have predicted what happened, I would've stopped it. I would've made it go away. But I didn't. I couldn't. And I should have. That's what gets me. I should have. And now my future doesn't have college in it. My future is about being known around the world as The Girl Who Hates Everyone. That's what the newspapers called me — The Girl Who Hates Everyone.

I wanted to tell Tate all of these things. But it was all so complicated, and thinking about it made my leg throb and my heart ache. I stood up and shrugged into my backpack. I wiped my cheeks with the backs of my hands. "I better get to class," I said. "I don't want to be late on the first day. I'll think about it. College, I mean. But like I said, I can't make any promises, okay?"

Mrs. Tate sighed and stood up. She pushed the file drawer in, but didn't move around the file cabinet.

"Valerie," she said, then stopped and seemed to reconsider. "Try to have a good day, okay? I am glad you're back. And I'll hang onto those program requirements for you."

I started toward the door. But just before I reached for the doorknob, I turned.

"Mrs. Tate? Have things changed much?" I asked. "I mean, are people different now?" I didn't know what I hoped her answer would be. Yes, everyone learned their lesson and now we're all one big, happy family, just like they say we are in the newspapers. Or no, there were no bullies — it was all in your head just like they say. Nick was crazy and you bought it and that's all there was to it. You were angry for no reason. So angry, but it was all in your imagination.

Mrs. Tate chewed on her bottom lip and seemed to really consider the question. "People are people," she finally said, turning up her palms in a helpless, sad shrug.

I think that was the last answer I wanted to hear.

MAY 2, 2008

7:10 A.M.

"She might cast a spell on you, Christy . . ."

Most days I found it totally ironic that Mom drove Frankie to school because he hated to ride the bus while I rode the bus because I hated the excruciating car ride with Mom. But some days I wished I'd gone ahead and braved Mom's morning critiques because the bus was just such crap.

Usually I could crawl into a seat somewhere in the middle, sink down into a C-shape, my knees propped against the seat in front of me, listen to my MP3 player, and completely disappear.

But lately Christy Bruter had been a real pain. It's not like that was news, since I couldn't stand Christy anyway. Never could.

Christy was one of those girls who was popular because most everyone was afraid not to be her friend. She was big and bulky and had a gut that stood out belligerently in front of her and thighs that were enormous and could crack a skull. Which was weird because she was the captain of the softball team. I never could figure that one out. I just couldn't imagine Christy Bruter outrunning anyone to first base. But she must have done it at least once or twice, I guess. Or maybe the coach was too afraid to cut her. Who knows?

I'd known Christy since at least kindergarten and never once had I thought I might like her. And vice versa. Every Back to School Night, my mom would pull the teacher aside and advise her that Christy and I should never sit at the same table group together. "We all have that one person . . ." Mom would say to the teacher with an apologetic smile. Christy Bruter was my one person.

In elementary school Christy called me Bucky Beaver. In sixth grade she started a rumor that I wore a thong, which, in middle school, was a huge deal. And in high school she decided she didn't like my makeup and clothes and so started the nickname Sister Death that everyone thought was hilarious.

She got on two stops after me, which could work in my favor on most days because I had time to get invisible before she got on the bus. Not that I was afraid of her or anything; I just got sick of dealing with her.

I sank into my seat, slid down where my head was barely peeking over the top of the backrest, and stuffed my earbuds into my ears, turning up the volume on my MP3 player with my thumb. I peered out the window, thinking that it would feel good to hold Nick's hand today. I could hardly wait to get to school and see him. I couldn't wait to smell the cinnamon gum on his breath and fold my head into the curl of his arm during lunch, sit shielded by him, all the rest of the world shut out. Christy Bruter. Jeremy. Mom and Dad and their "discussions" that always, always, always turned into screaming matches and ended with Dad slithering out of the house into a pocket of darkness, Mom sniffling pathetically in her room.

The bus slid to a stop, and then to another. I kept my eyes glued to the window, looking out at a terrier nosing through a trash bag in front of a house. The terrier's tail was beating the wind and his head was all but completely covered by trash bag. I wondered how he could breathe and tried to think of the things he might have found in there that would get him so excited.

The bus got going again and I turned up my MP3 player as the noise ratcheted up exponentially with the number of kids that got on. I leaned my head back against the seat and closed my eyes.

I felt a bump against my arm. I figured it was somebody walking past and ignored it. Then I felt a harder one and someone used the cord to snatch the earbud out of my right ear. It dangled in midair, tinny music spilling out of it.

"What the hell?" I said, pulling the bud out of my left ear and rewinding the cord around the MP3 player. I looked to my right and there was Christy Bruter's face grinning on the other side of the aisle. "Go away, Christy."

Her ugly friend Ellen (the equally Amazonian, red-haired, man-faced Garvin varsity softball team catcher) laughed, but Christy just stared at me with this fake innocent bat of her eyes.

"I don't know what you're talking about, Sister Death. Maybe you're having a hallucination. Maybe you got some bad X or something. Maybe the devil did it."

I rolled my eyes. "Whatever." I pushed the earbuds back into my ears and settled back to my C-shape, closing my eyes. I wasn't going to give her the satisfaction of fighting back.

Just as the bus turned into the Garvin driveway, I felt another shove against my shoulder, only this time there was a mighty yank on the cord of my earbuds and they were ripped out of my ears so hard the whole MP3 player flew out of my hand and skittered across the bus floor, settling under the seat ahead of mine. I picked it up. The green light on the side of it had blinked off and the screen was blank. I flipped the switch to turn it off and then on again, but . . . nothing. It was dead.

"God! What is your problem?" I asked, my voice getting loud.

Again, Ellen was snickering her man face off, and so were a couple other cronies sitting behind them. And again Christy was giving me this fake wide-eyed look.

The bus doors opened and we all stood up. That's some sort of kid instinct, I think. You could be in the middle of just about anything and if the bus doors opened, you stood up. It was one of the constants of life. You are born, you die, you stand up when the bus doors open.

Christy and I stood up within inches of each other. I could smell pancake syrup on her. She sneered at me, giving me a slow top-to-bottom look.

"In a hurry to get to a funeral? Maybe dump Nick for a nice cold corpse? Oh wait. Nick *is* a corpse."

I held eye contact with her, refusing to back down. After all these years she still hadn't tired of the same old stupid jokes. Still hadn't grown out of them. Mom had told me once that if I kept ignoring Christy, eventually it would get boring for her. But on days like today, ignoring her was easier said than done. I was so over this rivalry thing, but no way was I going to let her get away with breaking my stuff.

I pushed past her into the aisle, which had started moving. "Whatever your problem is . . ." I said. I held up my MP3 player. "You're going to pay for this."

"Oooh, I'm shaking in my boots," she said.

Someone else added, "She might cast a spell on you, Christy," and they all laughed.

I moved down the aisle and stepped down onto the sidewalk, cut behind the bus and jogged to the bleachers where Stacey, Duce, and David were hanging out as usual.

I climbed up to meet them, out of breath and furious.

"Hey," Stacey said. "What's up? You look pissed."

"Yeah," I said. "Look what that bitch Christy Bruter did to my MP3 player."

"Oh, man," David said, taking it out of my hands. He pushed a few buttons, tried to switch it on and off a few times. "You could get it fixed or something."

"I don't want to get it fixed," I said. "I want to kill her. God, I could just rip her stupid head off. She'll regret this. I'm totally going to get her back for this."

"Just blow her off," Stacey said. "She's such a cow. Nobody actually likes her."

A black Camaro roared into the parking lot and rolled up next to the football field. I recognized the car as Jeremy's and my heart sped up. For a second I forgot about the MP3 player.

The passenger side door opened and Nick stepped out. He had on the heavy black jacket he'd been wearing lately, and it was zipped up to his chin against the cool wind.

I skipped up to the top of the bleachers and yelled out to him.

"Nick!" I called, waving.

He caught my motion, tipped his chin upward slightly, and shifted his course in my direction. He moved slowly, methodically toward me. I bounded down the bleachers and across the lawn to him.

"Hey, baby!" I said, reaching him and wrapping myself around him. He sort of dodged me, but leaned down and kissed me, then turned me and slung his arm across my shoulders just like always. It felt so good to be under his arm again.

"Hey," he said. "What're you losers doing?" He used his free hand to do some sort of handshake thing with Duce and then socked David in the shoulder.

"Where you been?" David asked.

Nick smirked and I was struck by how odd he looked. Vibrant, almost buzzing or something.

"Been busy," was Nick's only reply. His eyes swept the front of the school. "Been busy," he repeated, but he said it so quietly I'm pretty sure I was the only one to hear him. Not that he was really talking to any of us. I could've sworn he was talking to the school itself. The building, the ant-like activity inside of it.

Mr. Angerson scuffed up behind us then and used his "principal voice," the one we liked to imitate at parties: *No, Garvin students, beer is bad for your growing brains. You must eat a healthy breakfast before coming to school, Garvin students. And remember, Garvin students, just say no to drugs.*

"All right, Garvin students," he said. Stacey and I elbowed each other and snickered. "Let's not linger this morning. Time to go to class."

Duce flicked Angerson a salute and started marching into the school. Stacey and David followed him, laughing. I started, too, but stopped under Nick's arm, which was still holding me in place on the sidewalk. I looked up at him. He was still staring at the school, a grin playing around the corners of his mouth.

"Better go before Angerson ruptures something," I said, tugging at Nick's arm. "Hey, I was thinking. Want to ditch lunch and get Casey's today?"

He didn't answer, but continued staring at the school silently.

"Nick? We better go," I said again. No response. Finally I kind of shoved him with my hip. "Nick?"

He blinked and looked down at me, the grin never changing, the bright look in his eyes never wavering. Maybe even growing more intense. I wondered what in the heck he and Jeremy had taken that morning. He was acting really weird.

"Yeah," he said. "Yeah. Got a lot to do today."

We started walking, our hips bumping one another with each step.

"I'd let you borrow my MP3 player for first period, but Christy Bruter busted it on the bus," I said, holding it up for him to see. He peered at it for a moment. His smile widened. He grabbed me tighter and walked toward the door more quickly.

"I've been wanting to do something about her for a long time," he said.

"I know. I totally hate her," I whined, squeezing all the attention I could out of the incident. "I don't know what her problem is."

"I'll take care of it."

I smiled, excited. The sleeve of Nick's jacket scratched along the back of my neck. It felt nice. Real somehow. Like as long as that sleeve was scratching along the skin of my neck everything would be normal, even if he was on something. For right now anyway, Nick was here with me, holding me, going to stand up for me. Not for Jeremy. For me.

We hit the doors and Nick finally let go of my shoulders. A breeze gusted right at that moment and swept down the collar of my shirt, billowing the front of it. I shuddered, my spine suddenly getting really cold.

Nick opened a door and waited for me to go in ahead of him.

"Let's go get this finished," he said. I nodded, heading toward the Commons, my eyes peeled for Christy Bruter, my teeth chattering.

3

[*FROM THE GARVIN COUNTY SUN-TRIBUNE,*

MAY 3, 2008, REPORTER ANGELA DASH]

Jeff Hicks, 15 — As a freshman, Hicks would have or-
dinarily not been walking through the Commons, ac-
cording to some students. "We don't go through there
if we can help it," freshman Marcie Stindler told report-
ers. "The seniors hassle us if we go down there. It's
sort of like an unwritten freshman rule to stay away
from the Commons except during lunch. Every incom-
ing freshman knows that."

But Hicks was running late on the morning of May
2nd and cut through the Commons in his hurry to get
to class, which some are calling a classic case of being
in the wrong place at the wrong time. He suffered a

*shot to the back of the head and died instantly at the
scene. A memorial has been set up in his name at Garvin
County State Bank. Police say it's unclear whether Levil
knew Hicks or if Hicks was accidentally hit by a bullet
intended for someone else.*

* * *

Because Mrs. Tate had kept me in her office for so long I
missed the first period bell and walked in right in the middle of Mrs. Tennille's First Day of School speech. I know
Tate had done it to keep me from having to brave the pre-
first period hallways, but I almost would have preferred
that to the eyes boring into me when I walked into class. At
least in the hallways I could sort of walk in the shadows.

I opened the door and I swear the entire class stopped
what they were doing and looked up at me. Billy Jenkins
dropped his pencil and just let it roll off his desk. Mandy
Horn's mouth flopped open so hard I thought I heard her
jaw crack. Even Mrs. Tennille stopped talking and stood motionless for a few seconds.

I stood in the doorway, wondering if it would really be
all that noticeable if I just turned around and walked out.
Out of the classroom. Out of the school. Back home to bed.
Tell Mom and Dr. Hieler that I was wrong, that I wanted to
finish high school with a tutor after all. That I wasn't as
strong as I originally thought.

Mrs. Tennille cleared her throat and put down the marker

she was using on the whiteboard. I took a deep breath and shuffled to her desk, holding out the hall pass Mrs. Tate's secretary had given me on my way out.

"We're just going over this year's syllabus," Mrs. Tennille said, taking the pass. Her face remained stonelike. "Go ahead and take your seat. If you have any questions on something we've already covered, you can ask me after the bell."

I stared at her for a beat longer. Mrs. Tennille had hardly been one of my fans to begin with. She always had a problem with the fact that I wouldn't participate in labs and with the fact that Nick sort of "accidentally" set fire to a test tube in third period once. I can't even count how many times she'd landed Nick's butt in detention, and she'd always glared at me when I loitered on the sidewalk in front of the school waiting for him to get out.

I couldn't imagine what she must feel for me now. Pity, maybe, for not seeing in Nick what she always saw? Did she want to shake me and shout, "I told you so, you stupid girl!"? Or maybe she felt loathing for what happened with Mr. Kline.

Maybe she, like me, replayed that scene over and over in her head a million times a day: Mr. Kline, the chemistry teacher, using his body to literally shield about a dozen students. He was crying. Snot running out of his nose, body shaking. He had his arms held out to each side, Christlike, and was shaking his head at Nick, defiant and scared.

I liked Kline. Everybody liked Kline. Kline was the kind of guy who'd come to your graduation party. The kind of guy who'd stop and talk to you in the mall — and none of that "Hello, youngster," Mr. Angerson the Principal kind of crap, either. Kline would say, "Hey, what's up? Keeping your nose clean?" Kline would turn a blind eye if he saw you sneak a beer at a restaurant and get away with it. Kline would give his life for you. We always kind of knew that about Kline. Now the whole world knew that about him.

Thanks to impressive TV coverage of the shooting, and that annoying Angela Dash writing for the *Sun-Tribune*, pretty much everyone in the world knew that Mr. Kline had died because he wouldn't tell Nick where Mrs. Tennille was. So I suppose it wasn't news to Mrs. Tennille. I also suppose that's why she looked at me like I was a plague set free in her classroom.

I turned and scuffed to an empty chair. I tried to keep my eyes rooted solely to the chair, but found it was impossible. I swallowed. My throat felt too thick. My hands were so sweaty my notebook was slipping out. My leg throbbed and I felt myself limping and silently cursed myself for doing it.

I curled into my desk and looked up at Mrs. Tennille. She stared at me until I was settled and then turned back to the whiteboard, clearing her throat again and finishing writing her e-mail address on the board.

Slowly the heads of my classmates turned back toward the front of the room and I felt myself begin to breathe once again. *Eighty-three*, I chanted in my head. *Eighty-two, if you don't count today.*

While Tennille talked about the best ways to contact her, I concentrated on my hands, trying to slow my breathing the way Dr. Hieler had taught me to do. I stared at my nails, which were chipped and ugly. I'd never found the energy to file them smooth and now I was oddly self-conscious about them. All the other girls would have prepared for the first day of school by doing things like painting their nails, picking out their best clothes. I'd barely even washed. It was just another way that I was different from all of them, and somehow, oddly, it was just another way that I was different from the way I used to be.

I tucked my nails into my palms. I didn't want them to show, afraid that someone would notice how ugly they were, but found myself strangely calmed by the feeling of them jabbing jaggedly into my palms. I lowered my hands to my lap and made hard fists, squeezing until the nails dug into my palms and I could take a breath without a wave of nausea rolling over me.

"E-mail me any time you have a question," Mrs. Tennille was saying, pointing to what she'd written on the board, and then she stopped short.

There was some commotion going on to my left. The kids were rustling around, one girl stuffing books and papers into her backpack quickly. Tears were streaking down her face and she was hiccupping, trying to keep it inside.

A few other girls were hovering over her, rubbing her back and talking to her.

"Is there a problem?" Mrs. Tennille asked. "Kelsey? Meghan? Is there a reason you're not in your chairs?"

"It's Ginny," Meghan said, pointing at the crying girl, who I now realized was Ginny Baker. I'd heard on the news about all the plastic surgery she'd had, but hadn't really realized how much it had changed her face until now.

Mrs. Tennille placed the dry erase marker into the tray at the bottom of the board, then quietly and steadily folded her hands in front of her. "Ginny?" she said in a voice so soft I wasn't sure at first it had come out of Tennille. "Is there something I can do to help? Do you need to go get a drink maybe?"

Ginny zipped her backpack and stood. Her whole body was shaking.

"It's her," she said, without moving. Everyone knew who she was talking about, though, and they all turned to look at me. Even Tennille glanced in my direction. I put my face back down toward my hands and squeezed my fingernails into my palms even harder. I sucked my lips inside my mouth and bit down on them hard from the inside, clamping them shut. "I can't sit here with her without thinking about . . . about . . ." she sucked in a breath and then let it out with a stream of anguish that made the hairs on the back of my neck stand up. "Why did they let her come back?"

She grabbed her backpack with both hands in front of her, hugged it to her belly, and rushed up the aisle, pushing both Meghan and Kelsey backward into desks.

Mrs. Tennille took a couple steps toward her and stopped. She nodded slightly and Ginny rushed out of the room, her contorted and ragged face pulled up into a grimace.

Everything was completely still for a minute and I squeezed my eyes shut and silently counted backward from fifty — another one of those coping methods I'd learned. From Mom or Dr. Hieler, I couldn't remember. I heard bells in my ears and I felt twitchy. Should I leave, too? Go after Ginny, tell her I'm sorry? Go home and never come back? Should I say something to the class? What do I do?

Finally, Mrs. Tennille cleared her throat again, turned back to the whiteboard, and picked up her marker. Her face looked unsettled, but her manner remained stoic. Good old steady Tennille. Couldn't charm her nor faze her.

"As I was saying," she began, and then she launched back into her lecture.

I blinked away the little white lights that were dancing in front of my eyes and tried to focus on what she was saying, which was hard because pretty much nobody stopped staring at me.

"The next unit will focus on . . ."

There was more restlessness and once again she turned and stopped. I glanced to my left and saw a couple kids talking heatedly among each other.

"Class," Mrs. Tennille said, her voice still stern but losing its grip on authoritative. "May I have your attention now, please?"

The kids stopped talking but remained restless.

"I would like to get on with this so we don't fall behind before the year even begins."

Sean McDannon raised his hand.

"Yes, Sean?" she said, a little exasperation creeping into her voice.

Sean coughed into his fist the way some men do when they want to change their voices from regular to super-powerful and manly. He looked at me, then looked away quickly. I tried a weak smile, but it was wasted because he'd already turned back.

Sean was an okay kid. Never a problem with anyone. Nobody really liked or hated him. He sort of flew under the radar most of the time, which can sometimes be the difference between getting along in high school and getting picked on in high school. He didn't get picked on that I ever knew about. He got good grades, joined academic clubs, kept his nose clean, had an unassuming girlfriend. And he lived about six houses down from me, which meant we'd played together as kids. We hadn't really talked much since about 5th grade, but there was no hostility between us. We said hi to each other if we passed in the hallway or at the bus stop. No big deal.

"Um, Mrs. Tennille, Mrs. Tate told us that we should talk about . . . um, about these things, and —"

"And it's not fair that Ginny should have to be the one to leave," said Meghan. While Sean had been pointedly not looking at me ever since that first glance, Meghan made an effort to swing her head around and glare at me. "It's not like Ginny did anything wrong."

Mrs. Tennille twisted the dry erase marker between her hands. "Nobody asked Ginny to leave, Meghan. And I'm sure Mrs. Tate meant that you could come up to her office to talk about these —"

"No," said a voice at the desk behind me. It sounded like Alex Gold, but my body felt frozen and I couldn't turn my head to be sure. My fingernails dug deeper into my palms, leaving painful purple crescents across them. "No, when the school had that trauma guy here he told us we should feel free to talk about stuff whenever we need to. Not that I need to or anything. I'm so over this."

Meghan rolled her eyes and shifted her hateful stare from me to a spot over my shoulder. "Well, good for you. But you didn't have your face blown off."

"Well, maybe that's because I never ticked off Nick Levil."

"Okay, that's really enough," said Mrs. Tennille, but by then the conversation had gotten well out of control. "Maybe we should get back to our discussion . . ."

"Neither did you, Meghan," Susan Crayson said, sitting just to Meghan's right. "Your face didn't get blown off either. You weren't even really friends with Ginny before the shooting. You just like the drama."

And that's basically when all hell broke loose. So many kids were talking on top of one another, it was almost impossible to tell who was saying what.

". . . all a bunch of drama? My friend died . . ."

". . . not like Valerie shot anybody anyway. She just had Nick do it. And Nick's dead, so who cares?"

"Mrs. Tate said arguing wouldn't solve . . ."

". . . bad enough that I have to have nightmares every night about it, but to come to class and . . ."

". . . you saying I liked that Ginny got shot because it was good drama? Are you seriously saying that?"

". . . had been nice to Nick, maybe this wouldn't have happened. Isn't that the whole point of . . ."

". . . ask me, he deserved to die. I'm glad he's gone . . ."

". . . what do you know about friends, anyway, you loser . . ."

It was kind of weird because eventually they were all so busy hating each other, they forgot about hating me. Nobody was looking at me. Mrs. Tennille had even sunk into the chair behind her desk and was just silently staring out the window, her fingers playing around her collar, her chin quivering just a little.

To hear the reporters on TV tell it, these guys were sitting around in the cafeteria holding hands and singing "Give Peace a Chance" every day. But it wasn't like that at all. They were at one another's throats. All the old rivalries, the old jokes, the old sour feelings were right there, festering under the plastic surgery and sympathetic head nods and crumpled Kleenex.

Finally my neck seemed to loosen and I felt able to look around — really look around — at the kids, who were yelling and waving their arms. A couple crying. A couple laughing.

I felt like I should say something, but I didn't know what to say. To remind them that I wasn't the shooter would make me sound defensive. To try to console somebody would be beyond weird. To do anything would feel like overload. I wasn't ready for this yet and couldn't believe that I'd ever thought I was. I didn't have answers to my own questions; how could I possibly answer any of theirs? My hand involuntarily drifted to the cell phone in my pocket. Maybe I should call Mom. Beg to go home. Beg to never come back. Maybe I should call Dr. Hieler; tell him that, for the first time, he was wrong. I couldn't make it eighty-three minutes, much less eighty-three days.

After a while, Mrs. Tennille was able to get the class back under control, and we sat there, tension riding above our heads like a cloud, while she finished going over the syllabus.

Slowly, people started to forget I was there. I began to feel like maybe this wasn't totally impossible, sitting in that desk, in that class. In that school. *You've got to find a way to see what's really there, Valerie,* Dr. Hieler had told me. *You've got to start trusting that what you see is what's really there.*

I opened up my notebook and picked up a pencil. Only, instead of taking notes on what Tennille was saying, I began sketching what I saw. The kids were in kid bodies, wearing kid clothes, their kid shoes untied and their kid jeans ripped. But their faces were different. Where I would normally see angry faces, scowls, jeers, instead I saw confusion. They were all just as confused as I was.

I drew their faces in as giant question marks, sprouting out of their Hollister jackets and Old Navy T-shirts. The question marks had wide, shouting mouths. Some were shedding tears. Some were tucked in on themselves, looking snaillike.

I don't know if it's what Dr. Hieler had meant when he told me to start seeing what's really there. But I know that drawing those question marks did far more for me than counting backward from fifty ever could have.

MAY 2, 2008

7:37 A.M.

"Oh my God! Somebody! Help!"

Nick and I plunged in through the school doors, the wind taking hold of mine and shutting it abruptly behind me. As always, the hall was packed with kids hustling to their lockers, griping about their parents or teachers or each other. Lots of laughter, lots of sarcastic grunts, lots of lockers slamming — early morning noises that are just naturally a part of the soundtrack behind high school life.

We rounded the corner into the Commons, where the orderly motion of the halls poured into a stagnant milling of kids getting in their before-school gossip. Some were at the Student Council table buying doughnuts, others sitting on the floors with their backs propped against the walls, eating doughnuts they'd already scored. Some cheerleaders were balanced on chairs hanging assembly posters. A few kids were tucked back against the stage area making out. The school losers — our friends — were waiting for us, draped over chairs turned backward at a round table near the closed kitchen entrance. A few teachers — the brave ones like Kline and Mrs. Flores, the art teacher — were wandering through the crowd, trying to keep some semblance of order among them. But everyone knew it was a losing battle. Order and the Commons rarely went together.

Nick and I stopped just after we entered the room. I stood on my tiptoes and craned my neck. Nick was surveying the entire room, a cold grin swiped across his face.

"Over there!" I said, pointing. "There she is!"

Nick scanned where I was pointing and found her.

"I'm so going to get a new MP3 player out of her," I said.

Nick unzipped his jacket slowly, but he didn't take it off. "Let's go get this finished," he said, and I smiled because I was so happy he was going to stick up for me. And I was happy that Christy Bruter was finally going to get what she had coming to her, too. This was the old Nick — the Nick I'd fallen in love with. The Nick who stood up to Christy Bruter and whoever else was making life miserable for me, who never backed down when one of the football players would come after him, trying to make him look small. The Nick who understood what it felt like to be me — crappy family, crappy school life, people like Christy Bruter constantly in my face reminding me that I wasn't like them, that I was somehow less than them.

His eyes took on a strange faraway look and he began

walking briskly through the crowd ahead of me. He wasn't paying attention to where he was going. He was just walking through people, his shoulders butting theirs and knocking them backward. He left me in a wake of angry faces and indignant shouts, but I ignored them and just followed him as closely as I could.

He reached Christy a few steps before I did. I had to crane my neck to see her over his shoulder. But I could still hear him. I was straining to hear him because I didn't want to miss a second of him scaring the heck out of Christy. So I'm sure of what I heard. I still hear it just about every day.

He must have bumped Christy on the shoulder or something, just like she'd done to me on the bus. I couldn't really see for sure because at that point his back was still to me. But I saw her pitch forward a little bit, almost knocking into her friend Willa. She turned around with a surprised look and said, "What's your problem?"

By then I had caught up with Nick and was standing just behind him. On the security video it looked like I was standing right next to him, all of us so close together it was impossible to tell whose body was whose. But I was just a step behind him, and all I could really see was the top half of Christy over Nick's shoulder.

"You've been on the list for a long time," he said, and I immediately went cold because I couldn't believe he'd just told her about the list. I was pissed, honestly. That list was our secret. Just between us. And he'd just blown it. And I knew that with Christy Bruter there would be hell to pay. She'd probably tell her friends and they would have something else to make fun of us about. She'd probably even tell her parents about it and they'd call mine and I'd get grounded. Maybe we'd even end up suspended and then I'd be screwed when it came to finals.

"What list?" she asked and then she looked down just slightly and her eyes grew big. She started to laugh, and so did Willa, and I started to pull up onto my tiptoes to see what they were laughing at.

And then there was the noise.

It wasn't so much a noise in my ears as it was in my brain. It sounded like the whole world was shutting down on me. I screamed. I know I did because I felt my mouth open and my vocal cords vibrate, but I heard nothing. I shut my eyes and let out a total scream and my arms instinctively flung themselves over my head and the only thought I had was *this is something bad, this is something bad, this is something bad*, which I'm pretty sure was my body going on autopilot. Lifesaving autopilot. It was more like a message from my brain to my body — danger: run away!

I opened my eyes and reached out to grab Nick, but he had moved to the side and instead I found myself looking at Christy, who had this totally shocked look on her face. Her mouth was open like she was going to say something, and her hands were both clutching her stomach. They were covered with blood.

She wavered and then began to fall forward. I jumped out of the way and she hit the floor between me and Nick. I looked down at her, feeling like I was in slow-motion, and saw that there was blood spreading across the back of her shirt as well and there was a hole in the fabric right in the middle of the blood.

"Got her," Nick said, looking down at her, too. He was holding a gun and his hand was shaking. "Got her," he repeated. He kind of laughed a little, this high-pitched laugh I still think was surprise more than anything. I have to believe it was a surprised laugh. I have to believe he was as surprised by what he did as I was. That somewhere underneath the drugs and the obsession with Jeremy was a Nick who, like me, thought it was all a joke, all a what-if.

And then everything snapped into real time. Kids were screaming and running, clogging the doorways and falling over one another. Some were standing around looking amused like someone had just pulled off a good prank and they were sorry they'd missed it. Mr. Kline was shoving kids out of the way, and Mrs. Flores was screaming commands at them.

Nick started to rush through the crowd, too, leaving me with Christy and all that blood. I turned my head and Willa and I locked eyes.

"Oh my God!" somebody screamed. "Somebody! Help!"

I think it was me screaming, but even today I can't be sure.

4

[FROM THE GARVIN COUNTY SUN-TRIBUNE,
MAY 3, 2008, REPORTER ANGELA DASH]

Ginny Baker, 16 — Baker, a straight-A honor roll stu-
dent, was reportedly saying goodbye to friends before
rushing to first period when the first gunshot rang out.
According to witnesses, Baker appeared to be a delib-
erate target, Levil bending to shoot her as she crouched
underneath a table.

"She was screaming 'Help me, Meg!' when he bent
down and pointed the gun at her," junior Meghan Nor-
ris said. "But I didn't really know what to do. I didn't
know what was happening. I didn't even hear the first
gunshot. And it all happened so fast. All I knew was
Mrs. Flores was yelling at us to get under the table and

cover our heads, so we did. And I just happened to dive under the same table as Ginny. And he got her. He didn't say anything to her at all. Just leaned down, pointed the gun in her face, shot her, and walked away. She was real quiet after he shot her. She wasn't asking me to help her anymore, and I thought she was dead. She looked dead."

Baker's mother could not be reached for comment. Her father, who lives in Florida, describes the incident as "the worst kind of tragedy a parent could imagine." He added that he will be moving back to the Midwest to help Baker through the extensive plastic surgery that doctors say will be required to reconstruct her face.

* * *

"So did your mom go back to work today?" Stacey asked. We were in the lunch line, getting our trays filled. We'd just come out of English together. Class had been tense but livable. A couple girls passed notes back and forth to one another and Ginny's seat was empty, but other than that things were quiet. Mrs. Long, my English teacher, was one of the few who'd signed that letter of thanks from the school board. Her eyes got kind of teary when I'd walked into the room, but she didn't say anything. Just smiled and nodded at me. Then she let me take my seat and she started class. Thank God.

85

"Yeah."

"My mom said your mom called her the other day just to talk."

I paused, tongs full of salad poised over my tray. "Really? How'd that go?"

Stacey didn't look back at me, but instead kept moving, eyes focused on her lunch tray. Nobody would have known for sure by looking at us if we were together or if she'd just been the unlucky one who had to stand next to me in the lunch line. She probably wanted it that way. It was so much safer for her to just be unlucky.

She picked up a bowl of rainbow colored Jell-O and put it on her tray. I did the same. "You know how my mom is," she said. "She told her that she doesn't want our family to be associated with yours anymore. She thinks your mom is a bad parent."

"Wow," I said. I felt a funny feeling in my stomach. Almost like I felt bad for Mom, which I hadn't allowed myself to do much. The guilt tore me up. It was much easier to think that she thought I was the worst daughter ever who'd ruined her life. "Ouch."

Stacey shrugged. "Your mom told my mom to blow it out her ass."

That definitely sounded like Mom. Still, I bet she went into her room and cried afterward. She and Mrs. Brinks had been friends for about fifteen years. We were both silent. I don't know about Stacey, but for me it was the stupid lump in my throat again that kept me from talking.

We picked up our trays and paid for our food, then headed out into the Commons to find a seat and eat our lunches.

Normally this would be a no-brainer. Before last year, Stacey and I would take our trays to the far side, third table from the back. I would kiss Nick and sit down between him and Mason and we'd all eat together, laughing, griping, destroying napkins, whatever.

Stacey walked in front of me, stopping at the condiment kiosk for some ketchup. I poured myself a tiny cup of ketchup, too, even though I had nothing to use ketchup on. I was just trying to avoid looking around and seeing how many faces were pointed in my direction. I had an idea it was more than a few. She picked up her tray again, as if she didn't know I was behind her, and I followed her. Maybe it was by habit, but probably it was more like I didn't know what else to do.

Sure enough, there was the gang sitting at the far left table near the back. David was there. So was Mason. Duce. Bridget. And Bridget's stepbrother, Joey. David looked up at us, waved at Stacey, and then sort of wilted as his eyes landed on me. He gave me a half-hearted wave that died midway through. He looked very uncomfortable.

Stacey set her tray down in the one empty spot left at the table, in between Duce and David. Immediately Duce started in on some conversation with her — something about YouTube — and she was laughing with him, squealing, "Oh, yeah! I saw that!" I stood a few feet away from the table, still holding my tray, unsure of what to do next.

"Oh, yeah," Stacey said, looking up at me. She had an almost surprised look, like she didn't realize I'd been following her. Like we hadn't just been walking together through the lunch line. Like she hadn't just been talking to me. She glanced at Duce and then up at me again. "Yeah. Um . . ." She pressed her lips together. "Val. We um . . . ran out of chairs, I guess." Duce hooked his arm around her and again that slithery little superior grin swept across her mouth.

David started to get up like he was either going to find me a chair or give me his. He wasn't eating. He almost never did.

Duce kicked the foot of David's chair, jolting him. He didn't look at David when he did it, but David stopped anyway and sat back down. He sort of shrugged shyly and turned his eyes to the table, as far away from me as possible. Duce started talking to Stacey again, very close to her ear. She giggled. Even David had gotten absorbed into something Bridget was saying. It was like, with Nick gone, the "family" had kicked me out. Or maybe I had kicked myself out; I don't know.

"No problem," I said, though nobody appeared to have heard me. "I can just sit somewhere else. No big deal."

What I really meant by that was that I would slink away and go sit outside somewhere alone where nobody would bother me and, more importantly, I wouldn't bother anyone else. It was for the best, really. What would I have talked to them about anyway? They had spent the summer

88

getting on with their lives. I had spent mine desperately scrambling to build a new one.

I turned around and looked across the cafeteria. It was weird — it all seemed the same as it had before. The same kids were sitting together. The same skinny girls were eating the same salads. The same jocks were loading up on proteins. The same nerds were acting invisible in the corner. The noise was deafening. Mr. Cavitt was wandering among the tables snapping, "Hands above board, kids. Hands above board!"

The only thing that had changed was me.

I took a deep breath and pressed forward, trying my best to ignore Stacey's laughs and squeals behind me. *This is what you wanted*, I told myself. *You wanted to push Stacey away. You wanted to come back to Garvin. You wanted to prove that you shouldn't have to hide. You wanted this, now you've got it. It's only lunch. Just suck it up and get through it.* I kept my eyes on my tray and on the floor in front of me as I walked out into the hallway.

I pressed my back into the wall just outside the Commons, leaned my head back, and closed my eyes. I let out a deep breath. I was sweating and my hands were starting to feel cold around the tray. I totally wasn't hungry and I wished this day would just go away. Slowly I sank down to the floor and set the tray on the floor in front of me. I rested my elbows on my knees and plopped my head into my hands.

In my head I went back to the only safe place I knew:

Nick. I remembered sitting on his bedroom floor, Playstation controller in hand, yelling at him, "You better not let me win. Damn it, Nick, you're letting me win. Cut it out!"

And him doing that thing he did with his mouth whenever he was being ornery — sticking his tongue out slightly to the side, mouth hanging open in a smile, snickering softly every few seconds.

"Nick, I said to cut it out. Seriously, don't let me win. I hate it when you do that. It's insulting."

More laughing every few seconds and then in one fiery swoop, purposely losing the game we were playing.

"Damn it, Nick!" I cried, smacking him in the arm with my controller, as my character flashed up on the TV screen in a victorious pose. "I told you not to let me win. God!" I crossed my arms over my chest and looked away from him.

He was laughing out loud now, bumping my shoulder with his. "What?" he said. "What? You won fair and square. Besides, you're just a girl. You needed help."

"Oh, you did not just say that. I'll show you help," I snarled, tossing my controller to the side and practically tackling him, making him laugh all the harder.

I pummeled him playfully on the shoulders and chest with my fists, his mischievousness ruining my pout. You didn't see it very often with Nick, but when he was in the mood to play around, it was contagious as hell. "Oh no! Oh don't, you big brute," he kept saying in this high, mocking voice between laughs. "Ouch, you're hurting me."

I lunged into him even harder, grunting and shoving

him. We rolled around and suddenly I found myself pinned under him. He was holding my wrists down against the floor, both of us breathing hard. He leaned over me, close to my face. "It's okay for someone to let you win sometimes, you know," he said, getting all serious. "We don't always have to be the losers, Valerie. They may want to make us feel that way, but we're not. Sometimes we get to win, too."

"I know," I said, but I wondered if he even realized how much I'd already felt like I'd won, just being in his arms.

"You can come sit with me," a voice said, ripping me out of my daydream. I opened my eyes, preparing myself for the rest of the joke. *You can come sit with me . . . when hell freezes over.* Or *You can come sit with me . . . not!* What I saw instead took my breath away.

Jessica Campbell was standing over me, her face showing no emotion whatsoever. She was dressed in her volley-ball uniform and her hair was pulled back into a ponytail.

Jessica practically ruled Garvin High. Easily the most popular, she could also be the cruelest, because everyone wanted to be her and would do just about anything to please her. Christy Bruter might have started the nickname Sister Death, but Jessica called me that name in a voice so cold and dismissive it made me feel small and stupid. She was the one who egged on Jacob Kinney to trip Nick in the hallways and the one who told Mr. Angerson that we smoked pot in my car in the parking lot in the mornings, which was a total lie, but earned us an in-school suspension just the same. She was the one who didn't even bother to make fun of us behind our backs. She did it in front of our faces. She was on the Hate List more than once. Her name underlined. With exclamation points behind it.

She was the one who should have the big dented scar in her thigh. She was the one who probably should have been dead. She was the one whose life I saved. Before May I'd hated Jessica. Now I had no idea how I was supposed to feel about her.

The last time I saw Jessica Campbell, she was cowering in front of Nick, her hands covering her face. She was screaming. Total throat-ripping screaming. She was almost delirious with fear. But then again, so was everyone else in the Commons at that point. I remember she had a streak of blood wiped across the leg of her jeans and some sort of food smashed in her hair. I have since thought how ironic it was that she was the most undignified I'd ever seen anyone in my life, but I couldn't revel in it because of what was happening. I should've really enjoyed seeing her like that, but I couldn't because it was all so horrible.

"What?" I croaked.

She pointed into the Commons. "You can eat lunch at my table if you want," she said. Still no smile, no frown, no emotion of any sort playing on her face. It felt like a trap. No way was Jessica Campbell seriously asking me to sit with her. She was setting me up to take me down, I just knew it.

I shook my head slowly. "That's okay. Thanks anyway."

She stared at me for a few minutes, cocking her head slightly to the side and chewing on the inside of her cheek. Odd, I don't remember ever seeing her chew on her cheek like that before. She looked . . . vulnerable somehow. Earnest. Maybe even a little bit scared. It was a look I wasn't used to seeing on her.

"You sure? 'Cause it's just Sarah and me over there and Sarah's working on some sort of research project for Psych anyway. She'll never even know you're there."

I looked past her to the table where she normally sat. Sure, Sarah was sitting there, her head bent over a notebook, but there were about ten other kids there, too. All of them Jessica's crowd. I seriously doubted they wouldn't know I was there. I wasn't stupid. And I wasn't desperate, either.

"No. Really. That's nice and all, but I don't think so."

She shrugged. "Suit yourself. But you can come over any time if you want."

I nodded. "I'll remember."

She started to walk away, but stopped. "Um, can I ask you a question?" she asked.

"I guess."

"A lot of people are wondering why you came back to Garvin."

Ah, so here it is. Here's where she calls me a name, tells me I'm not wanted, makes fun of me. I felt a familiar wall begin to build itself up inside me.

"Because this is my school," I said, probably a little too defensively. "I shouldn't have to leave it any more than anyone else here. The school said I could come back."

She chewed on the inside of her cheek again, then said, "You're right. You didn't shoot anyone."

She disappeared into the Commons again and I was struck with a thought that jolted me to the core: She wasn't making fun of me. She meant what she said. And I wasn't imagining things — Jessica Campbell didn't look like she normally did. She looked changed somehow.

I picked up my tray and threw the food in the trash. I wasn't hungry at all anymore.

I sat back down on the floor and angled myself to where I could see into the Commons. *See what's really there, Valerie*, Dr. Heiler's voice said in my head. I reached into my backpack and pulled out my notebook and pencil. I watched the kids inside. I watched them do what they normally do and I drew them doing it — a pack of wolves bent over their trays, their long snouts drawn up into snarls and sneers and smiles. Except Jessica. Her wolf-face stared delicately back at me. I was almost surprised to look down at what I'd drawn and see that her wolf-face looked a lot more like a puppy's.

MAY 2, 2008

7:41 A.M.

"Don't you remember our plan?"

When Christy Bruter hit the floor in front of me and the room erupted into this screaming rushing chaotic emergency, I had a bizarre moment where I felt sure that I was imagining all of it. Like I was still at home in bed, dreaming. Any minute my cell was going to ring for real and Nick would be calling me to tell me that he and Jeremy were going to Blue Lake for the day and he wouldn't be coming to school.

But then Nick rushed off and Willa fell to her knees next to Christy and rolled Christy over and there was all this blood. It was everywhere. Christy was still breathing, but it sounded really bad, like she was trying to breathe through a bowl full of pudding or something. Willa was pushing down on Christy's hands and telling Christy over and over that she would be all right.

I knelt next to Willa and started pressing down, too.

"Do you have a cell phone?" I yelled to Willa. She shook her head, no. Mine was in my backpack, but in all the chaos my backpack seemed to have completely disappeared. I saw in the security videos much later that it was actually lying on the floor behind me, soaking up blood. When I saw those videos I thought it was weird that I'd looked right at it but in my fear and confusion didn't recognize it. Like "blood" and "backpack" could in no way ever go together.

"I have my cell," Rachel Tarvin said. She was standing right behind Willa and was incredibly calm, like she dealt with shootings every day.

Rachel pulled the cell out of her jeans pocket and flipped it open. She started pressing numbers when there was another loud crack followed by more screaming. Followed by two more loud cracks. And then three more.

A crowd of kids surged in our direction and I jumped up, afraid that I would be crushed under them.

"Don't leave us," Willa cried. "She's going to die. You can't go. I need help. Help!"

But the crowd was surging me right along with them and before I knew it I was slipping across the floor on Christy's blood into a knot of kids that were trying to shove their way out of the Commons. Someone elbowed me in the lip. I tasted blood. Someone stepped on my foot, hard. But I was craning my neck too hard to notice. Christy now seemed an impossible distance away. Plus now I could see something worse.

Over by the Student Council doughnut table there was blood. And I saw two bodies underneath the table, not moving. Beyond that I saw Nick overturning chairs and dumping tables over. Occasionally he would crouch and look under a table, then drag someone out of it and talk to them, waving a gun in their face. Then there would be another one of those cracks and more screaming.

I started to put it together. Nick. The gun. The cracks. The screaming. My brain was moving slowly still, but was picking up speed. It didn't make sense to me. But then again, maybe it did. We had, in a way, talked about this.

"Did you hear about that school shooting in Wyoming or whatever?" Nick had said one night on the phone, just a few weeks before. I was sitting in my bed polishing my toenails with Nick on speakerphone on the night table next to me. One of a million talks we had, no more or less important than any other we'd had before.

"Yeah," I said, wiping the last of the wet fingernail polish off the side of my toe. "Wild, huh?"

"Did you hear the crap the media was giving about the guys who did it and how there were no warning signs?"

"Yeah. Sort of. I haven't watched much of it."

"They keep saying these guys were real popular and everyone loved them and they weren't loners at all and stuff. What a crock."

We were silent for a minute and I used the time to plug

my MP3 player into my computer. "Well. The media sucks. You know."

"Yeah."

More silence. I flipped through a magazine.

"So what do you think? Think you could do it?"

"Do what?"

"Shoot all those people. Like Christy and Jessica and Tennille and stuff."

I chewed on my finger and read a caption under a photo of Cameron Diaz in the magazine. Something about the purse she was carrying. "I guess," I mumbled, flipping pages again. "I mean, I'm not popular or anything, so it wouldn't really be the same."

He sighed — the noise came out of the speaker like thunder. "Yeah. You're right. But I could do it. I could totally blow those people up. It just wouldn't be a surprise to anyone."

We'd both laughed.

He was wrong. Everyone was totally surprised. Especially me. So surprised I was sure it was a mistake. A mistake I had to stop.

I shoved my way past a couple of girls who were hugging one another. I pushed through the cluster of kids by the door, going the opposite direction of where I wanted to go — where everyone else was trying to go. As I walked I got stronger, more forceful, shoving kids out of my way. Bumping into them and sending some of them sprawling on the floor, slipping in blood, landing with thwacks against the tile. I started running as I moved along. Shoving. Running. My throat making hoarse sounds.

"No," I was saying as I bumped kids out of my way. "No. Wait . . ."

Finally I found a small clearing and I rushed into it. I saw a kid I didn't recognize lying on the floor about two feet away from me. He was facedown and the back of his head was totally just blood.

Three or four more shots rang out, ripping my attention away from the dead boy.

"Nick!" I screamed.

Now that I was in the middle of the room I couldn't see him anymore. Too many kids were going in too many different directions. I stopped and looked around, whipping my head frantically from side to side.

Then I caught a familiar-looking blur to my left. Nick was approaching Mr. Kline, the chemistry teacher. Mr. Kline was standing his ground, his arms outstretched in front of a small group of kids. He was red-faced and appeared sweaty or maybe just covered with tears. I raced to catch up with them.

"Where is she?" Nick screamed. Several of the students behind Mr. Kline gave tearful squeals and pressed themselves tighter together.

"Put down the gun, buddy," Mr. Kline said. His voice was trembling, although I got the impression he was giving his best effort to keep it steady. "Just put it down and we'll talk."

Nick cussed and kicked a chair. It flew into Mr. Kline's legs, but he didn't budge. Didn't even flinch.

"Where is she?"

Mr. Kline shook his head slowly. "I don't know who you're talking about. Just put down the gun and we'll discuss this . . ."

"Shut up! Shut the fuck up! Tell me where that bitch Tennille is, goddamnit, or I'll blow your fucking head off!"

I tried to run faster, but my legs felt like rubber.

"I don't know where she is, man. Don't you hear the sirens? The police are here now. It's over. Just put the gun down and spare yourself . . ."

Another crack filled the air. My eyes closed instinctively. And when I opened them again I saw Mr. Kline falling to the floor, his arms still outstretched. He fell straight down like that, and then crumpled onto one side. I wasn't sure where he was hit exactly, but his eyes had a bad look in them, like he wasn't looking at the cafeteria anymore.

I stood immobile, my ears clogged up with the noise of the gun, my eyes burning, my throat raw. I said nothing. I did nothing. I just stood there looking at Mr. Kline lying on his side shuddering.

The kids who'd been hiding behind Mr. Kline were now trapped between Nick and the wall behind them. There were maybe six or seven of them, still huddled together and making puppy noises. In the back of the cluster was Jessica Campbell. She stood bent over at the waist, sort of in a crouch, her butt pressed against the wall. Her hair was tied in a ponytail, but had come out of the rubber band in clumps and was falling down around her face. She was shaking so hard her teeth were chattering.

I'd been too close to the last shot and my ears were muffled. I couldn't hear what Nick was saying, but part of it sounded like "get away" or "go away" and he was waving his gun around. The kids resisted at first, but he fired off a shot that hit Lin Yong in the arm and they all scattered, dragging Lin with them, leaving only Jessica crunched up against the wall all alone.

And I knew. Right then I knew what he was going to do. My hearing was still foggy, but not so foggy that I couldn't hear him screaming at her, and her screaming and crying at nobody in particular. Her mouth was stretched open and her eyes squeezed shut.

Oh my God, I thought. *The List. He's picking off people who're on the Hate List.* I started forward again, only this time it was like I was running through sand. My feet felt heavy and tired; my chest felt like someone had tied something around it, squeezing the breath out of me and dragging me backward at the same time.

Nick started to raise his gun again. Jessica pulled her hands up over her face and crouched lower against the wall. I wasn't going to make it in time.

"Nick!" I screamed.

He turned toward me, still holding the gun in front of him. He was smiling. No matter what else I remember about Nick Levil in my lifetime, probably the one thing I'll remember most was the smile he had on his face when he turned around. It was an inhuman sort of smile. But somewhere in it — somewhere in his eyes — I swear I saw true affection. Like the Nick I knew was in there somewhere, begging to be let out.

"Don't!" I screamed, closing in on him. "Stop it! Stop!"

He got this curious look on his face. The smile stayed put, but he looked like he didn't understand why I was running toward him. Like I was the one with a problem or something. He looked at me with that surprised smile and I couldn't hear him very well, but I was pretty sure he said something like, "Don't you remember our plan?" which kind of slowed me down a little because I couldn't remember anything about any plan. Plus, when he said it, he had this really creepy faraway look in his eyes, like he was totally absent from what was going on in the Commons. He didn't look anything like himself.

He shook his head a little, like I was so ditzy for forgetting the supposed "plan," and the smile grew wider. He turned back to Jessica and at the same time drew the gun upward again. I lunged for him this time, my only thought being *I can't watch Jessica Campbell die right in front of me.*

I think I tripped over Mr. Kline. Actually I know I did because the security camera shows me tripping over him. So I tripped over Mr. Kline and pitched sideways into Nick. We both stumbled several steps and there was another one of those cracks and I felt the Commons floor go out from underneath me.

All I knew then was that I was lying kind of halfway under a table about four feet away from Mr. Kline and Nick was looking at the gun in his hand with a much more serious surprised look and he was so far away from me I wasn't sure how I got that far away so quickly. And that Jessica Campbell wasn't standing in front of the wall anymore and I thought I could see the back of her running into the crush of kids at the Commons doors.

And then I think I felt more than saw, but definitely saw, too, a stream of blood pulsing out of my thigh, really thick and red. And I tried to say something to Nick — I don't remember what — and I think I raised my head like I was going to get up. Nick looked from the gun to me and his eyes were all glazed. And then all this gray fuzz appeared behind my eyes and I felt myself getting lighter and lighter or maybe it was more like heavier and heavier and then everything just went black.

5

[FROM THE GARVIN COUNTY SUN-TRIBUNE, MAY 3, 2008, REPORTER ANGELA DASH]

Morris Kline, 47 — As Garvin High's chemistry teacher and men's track coach, Kline was voted Teacher of the Year in both 2004 and 2005. "Mr. Kline would do anything for you," freshman Dakota Ellis told reporters. "Once he stopped on K Highway because he saw my mom and I had a flat tire. He helped us change the tire even though he was all dressed up like he was going somewhere really nice afterward. I don't know where he was going, but he didn't seem to mind getting dirty. That's just the way he was."

Although students are upset by the loss of Kline, few have expressed surprise at the way he died — like

a hero. Shot in the chest while protecting several stu-
dents and trying to talk Levil into putting down the gun,
Kline was "barely hanging on," according to EMTs who
arrived at the scene. He was later pronounced dead
at Garvin County General. Kline did not appear to be
a direct target of Levil, but rather shot in the heat of
the moment.

He is survived by his wife, Renee, and three chil-
dren. Mrs. Kline told reporters, "Nick Levil robbed my
children of a future with their father and personally I'm
glad he killed himself. He doesn't deserve a future af-
ter what he's done to all these families."

* * *

Mom was the first car in line and I couldn't have been more grateful to see that tan Buick. I practically sprinted for it when the bell rang, forgetting all about stopping by my locker for homework.

I slid into the car and took my first real breath of the day. Mom looked at me, frown lines stretching across her forehead. They looked pretty deep, like she'd been working on them for a long time.

"How'd it go?" she asked. I could tell she was trying to sound bright and cheery, but the worried edge was in there, too. I think she'd been working on that for a long time as well.

"Okay," I said. "Sucked, really. But okay."

She put the car into gear and pulled out of the lot. "Did you see Stacey?"

"Yeah."

"Good. That must have been nice to see your old friend."

"Mom," I said. "Just let it go."

Mom glanced away from traffic and looked at me, the frown lines deepening. Her lips were pressed together hard and I almost wished I had lied and told her everything went great today because I knew how important it was for her to hear that I got back with all my old friends and even made some new ones and everybody knew that I had nothing to do with the shooting and I was part of the big old happy crowd we kept hearing about on TV. But the glance really was for just a second and then she looked back into traffic.

"Mom, really, it's no big deal."

"I told her mother. I told her you weren't responsible for this. You would have thought she'd listen. She was your Brownie troop leader, for Christ's sake."

"Mom, c'mon. You know what Dr. Hieler said about how people were going to react to me."

"Yes, but the Brinkses should be different. They should know. We shouldn't have to convince them. You grew up together. We raised our girls together."

We were both silent for the rest of the ride home. Mom eased the car into the garage and shut it off. Then she leaned her forehead against the steering wheel and closed her eyes.

I wasn't sure what to do. I didn't think it was right to just get out of the car and bail on her. But I didn't think she necessarily wanted to chat, either. She looked like she'd had one heck of a bad day.

Finally I broke the silence. "Stacey told me that you talked to her mom." She didn't answer. "She said you told her mother to blow it out her ass."

Mom chuckled. "Well, you know how Lorraine can be. So uppity. I've wanted to tell her to blow it out her ass for a long time." She chuckled again, and then giggled, her eyes still closed, her head still against the steering wheel. "This was just my first good opportunity. It felt pretty nice."

She peeked at me with one eye and then started laughing harder. I couldn't help it — pretty soon I was giggling, too. Before I knew it we were both howling in the front seat of the car in the closed garage.

"What I really said is, 'blow it out your snotty fat ass, Lorraine.'" We both laughed harder. Between breaths, she said, "And I told her that Howard hit on me at last year's pool party."

I gasped. "Get out! Stacey's dad hit on you? Disgusting! He's like all hairy and nasty and old."

She shook her head, barely able to breathe long enough to talk. "I just . . . made . . . it up. God, I wish . . . I could have . . . been there when . . . she accused him . . . of it."

We sank backward into the seat then and howled for what seemed like forever. I couldn't remember smiling like that. Laughter felt weird in my mouth. It almost had a taste to it.

"You're evil," I said at last, once we started catching our breath again. "I love it, but you're evil."

She shook her head again, wiping her eyes with her pinkies. "No. The evil people are the ones who won't give you another chance."

I looked down at my backpack and shrugged. "I guess I can't blame them. I looked guilty. You don't have to stick up for me, Mom. I'll be okay."

Mom was wiping at her eyes with the cuffs of her jacket. "But they need to understand that Nick was the one who did this, honey. He's the bad one. I've been telling you that for years. You're so pretty — you really belong with a nice boy. Not a boy like Nick. You never belonged with a boy like Nick."

I rolled my eyes. Oh jeez, here we go again. Mom telling me that Nick was bad for me. Mom telling me that I shouldn't be hanging around with guys like him. Mom telling me that there was something wrong with Nick — she could see it in his eyes. Mom apparently forgetting that Nick is dead now and that she doesn't need to lecture me about how bad he was because it doesn't matter now anyway.

I reached for the door handle. "Not again. Seriously, Mom. He's dead. Can we move on?" I popped open the door and stepped out, schlepping my backpack behind me. I grimaced when I put weight on my leg.

Mom struggled out of her seat belt and got out of the car on the other side. "I'm not fighting with you, Valerie," she said. "It's just that I want to see you happy. You're never happy. Dr. Hieler suggested . . ."

My instinct was to glare at her. To tell her what I knew

about happiness, which was that you never know when it can change to terror. That it never stays around. That I haven't known happiness for a long time, before Nick was ever in my life in the first place, that she and Dad ought to know why. That, by the way, she was never happy, either, in case she hadn't noticed. But seeing her peer at me over the top of the car in her wrinkled suit, tears welling in her eyes, her face still flushed from laughing, saying all of those things would've just felt mean. Even if they were true.

"Mom. I'm okay. Really," I said. "I don't even think about Nick anymore." I turned and walked into the house.

Frankie was leaning against the kitchen counter, eating a sandwich. His hair was slightly wilted and his cell phone was in his hand, his thumb working the keypad, texting someone.

"What's up?" he asked when I came into the room.

"Mom," I answered. "Don't ask."

I opened the refrigerator and pulled out a Coke. I leaned against the counter next to him and opened it. "Why can't she just get it through her head that Nick's dead and she can quit bugging me about him now? Why does she have to lecture me all the time?"

Frankie turned in his chair and looked at me, chewing. "She's probably afraid you'll turn out like her and be married to someone you can't stand," he said.

I started to say something back, but heard the garage door rattle and knew Mom was coming in. I stole upstairs to my bedroom.

Frankie was probably right. Mom and Dad were anything but happy. Before last May they'd been all about getting a divorce, which would have totally been a blessing. Frankie and I were practically giddy at the thought of all the fighting coming to an end.

But the shooting, while it may have torn apart countless families, ironically brought mine back together. They said they were "afraid of fracturing the family further in an extreme time of stress like this," but I knew the truth.

1) Dad was a pretty successful attorney, and the last thing he needed was a bunch of news coverage insinuating to the world that his marriage problems were at the root of the Garvin High massacre.

2) Mom had a job, but nothing like Dad's job. Mom made money, but not that much money. And we all knew that some major psychiatric bills were coming down the pike.

Frankie and I were just along for the ride with their relationship, which was usually civil disregard, but sometimes bubbled into hostility that made us both want to toss their things in garbage bags and buy them plane tickets to anywhere else but here.

I walked into my bedroom, which looked a lot mustier and more cluttered than it had when I'd left it this morning. I stopped in the doorway and looked around, sort of surprised that I'd more or less lived in this room since May and had never noticed how disgusting it was. Depressing, really. Not that I was ever big on cleaning my room. But except for the Great Nick Extrication that Mom had done after the shooting, nothing had been picked up or cleaned in months.

I picked up a glass that had been on my nightstand for, like, forever and stacked it on top of a plate. I reached over and scrunched up a paper towel that was discarded nearby and stuffed it into the glass.

I had this fleeting feeling that maybe I should clean it all up. Make a clean start. Do a Great Valerie Extrication of my own. But I scanned the clothes crumpled on the floor, the books tossed to the side of the bed, the TV with its smudged and mucky screen, and I stopped in place. It seemed like way too much work, cleaning up my grief.

I could hear Mom and Frankie talking down in the kitchen. Her voice sounded agitated, sort of like it did when she and Dad were left in the kitchen together for too long. I felt a brief pang of guilt for leaving Frankie down there alone to bear the brunt of her frustrations since I was technically the one who had her frustrated. But Frankie never got it as bad as I did. In fact, ever since the shooting, Frankie really didn't exist much. No curfew, no chores, no limits. Mom and Dad were always too busy fighting with one another and worrying about me to remember they had another kid to worry about. I didn't know if I should feel really jealous of Frankie for that, or really sorry for him. Maybe both.

That weary feeling came back and I dropped the glass and plate into my trash can and flopped backward on my bed. I reached into my backpack. I pulled out my notebook and flipped it open. I chewed my lip, staring at the pictures I'd drawn throughout the day.

I rolled over and pushed the button to turn on my stereo and cranked it. Mom would be up in a few minutes hollering at me through the door to turn it down, but she'd already confiscated all my "concerning" music — you know, the music that she and Dad and probably Dr. Hieler and every other old fart in the world thought would incite me to slit my wrists in the bathtub — which still ticked me off since I bought most of that music with my own money. I turned up the volume loud enough that I wouldn't even hear her. She'd get tired of pounding long before I'd get tired of her pounding. So let her pound.

I reached into my backpack again and pulled out a pencil. I chewed on the eraser for a minute, looking at the picture I'd started of Mrs. Tennille. She looked so sad. Wasn't it funny that not all that long ago I would've said I'd wanted Tennille to feel sad? I'd hated her. But today, seeing how sad she was, I felt horrible. I felt responsible. I wanted her to smile, and I wondered if she smiled when she got home and held her kids or if she just came home and sat back in her recliner with a vodka and drank until she couldn't hear the gunshots anymore.

I bent my head and started drawing — drawing her doing both at the same time, curling around a little boy like a peanut inside a shell, her hand curling around a bottle of vodka like the shell clings to the vine.

PART TWO

MAY 2, 2008

6:36 P.M.

"What did you do?"

6

When I opened my eyes again, I was actually surprised to find that I wasn't still asleep in my own bed, waking to start a new school day. That's the way it was supposed to work, right? Nick was supposed to call and I was supposed to go on to school, hating every minute of it, worrying that he and Jeremy were at Blue Lake doing God-knows-what and agonizing that Nick was going to break up with me and getting pestered by Christy Bruter on the bus. I was supposed to wake up and the scraps that I could remember about Nick shooting up the Commons were supposed to be a dream, drifting away before I could even drum up the images fully in my awakened mind.

I woke up in the hospital. There were police in my room and the TV was turned on to a crime scene. Their backs were turned to me, their faces tilted up toward the TV screen. I squinted at the TV where images of a parking lot, a brick building, a football field, all vaguely familiar, blipped on and off of the screen. I shut my eyes again. I felt groggy. My eyes were very dry and my leg throbbed, and I started to remember not exactly what happened, but that something really bad had happened.

"She's waking up," I heard. I recognized the voice as Frankie's, but I hadn't seen him when I'd opened my eyes before and it seemed easier to just imagine him standing next to the bed saying that than to try to see him. So I let myself drift into this imaginary world where Frankie was standing nearby, saying *She's waking up* and it was true, but I wasn't in the hospital and my leg didn't hurt.

"I'll go find a nurse," another voice said. My dad's. That one was easy. The voice was tense, strained, terse. Just like Dad. He popped into my imaginary scene as well, in the background, floating out of view. He was tapping something into his PDA and he had a cell phone between his ear and his shoulder. He popped out just as quickly and it was just Frankie looking at me again.

"Val," Frankie said. "Hey, Val. You awake?"

The vision morphed into a morning in my bedroom. Frankie trying to wake me up to do something fun, like in the old days when Mom and Dad got along and we were just two little kids. Find our Easter baskets, maybe, or a Christmas present, or pancakes. I liked this place. I really did. So I have no idea why my eyes fluttered open again. They did it without my consent.

They opened onto Frankie, standing at the end of my bed, by my toes. Only it wasn't my bed, but a strange one with crisp, scratchy white sheets and a brown blanket that looked like oatmeal. His hair was completely limp and I had a minute of trying to clear my head because I honestly couldn't remember the last time I saw Frankie with limp hair. I had a hard time matching the fourteen-year-old Frankie face to the eleven-year-old Frankie hair. I had to blink several times before I could make sense of it.

"Frankie," I said, but before I could say anything else my attention was distracted to a wet sort of sniffling to my right. I turned my head slowly. My mom was there, sitting in a pink upholstered chair. Her legs were crossed at the knees and she had one elbow propped on top of them. In that hand she held a crumpled-up tissue she kept using to dab her nose.

I squinted at her. I somehow wasn't surprised that she was crying, because I knew that whatever the bad thing was that had happened, I was involved in it — even though I hadn't yet put together why I was waking up in what was beginning to look like a hospital bed rather than in my own bed waiting for Nick to call.

I reached out and placed my hand on Mom's wrist (the one holding the snotty tissue). "Mom," I whispered. My throat hurt. "Mom," I said again.

But she leaned away from me. Not jerked away — it was way too subtle of a movement to be considered a jerk. But more leaned away, out of my grasp. Leaned away, like she was physically separating herself from me. Leaned away, not like I was to be feared, but like she no longer wanted to be identified with me at all.

"You're awake," she said. "How do you feel?"

I looked down at myself and wondered why I wouldn't feel okay. I checked myself out and everything seemed to be there, including several wires that weren't normally a part of my body. I still wasn't sure why I was there, but I knew it had to be something I was going to live through. I'd somehow hurt my leg — that much I could glean from the dull throbbing under the sheet. Yet the leg still seemed to be there, so I knew there wasn't too much to be worried about.

"Mom," I said one more time, wishing I could think of something else to say. Something more important. My throat was achy and felt swollen. I tried clearing it, but found it was dry, too, and all I could do was make a squeaky little noise that did nothing to help it. "What happened?"

A nurse in pink scrubs fluttering around behind Mom moved to a little table and picked up a plastic cup with a straw hanging over the side of it. She handed it to Mom. Mom held it, looked at it like she'd never seen such a contraption before, and then looked over her shoulder at one of the police officers, who had turned away from the TV and was staring down at me, his fingers hooked into his belt.

"You were shot," the officer said plainly from over Mom's shoulder and I saw Mom kind of wince when he said it, although she was still facing him, not me, and I couldn't see her face exactly. "Nick Levil shot you."

I frowned. Nick Levil shot me. "But that's my boyfriend's name," I said. Later I would realize how stupid I sounded, and would even be a little bit embarrassed by it. But at the time it just didn't make sense, mostly because I hadn't put it all together yet and because I was just coming out of the anesthesia, and probably even a little bit because my brain didn't want me to remember everything right away. Once I saw a documentary about different things the brain will do to protect itself. Like when a kid who's abused ends up with multiple personalities and stuff. I think my brain was doing that to me — protecting me — but it didn't do it for very long. Not long enough, anyway.

The officer nodded at me, like he already knew this about Nick and I wasn't giving him any new information, and Mom turned around again and kind of looked down at the sheets. I scanned their faces, all of them — Mom's, the officer's, the nurse's, Frankie's, even Dad's (I hadn't seen him pop back into the room, but there he was, standing by the window, his arms folded across his chest) — but none of them were looking directly at me. Not a good sign.

"What's going on?" I asked. "Frankie?"

Frankie didn't say anything — just clenched his jaw in his pissed-off pose, and shook his head. His face was getting really red.

"Valerie, do you remember anything about school to-day?" Mom asked quietly. I won't say she asked it gently or tenderly or any of that motherly stuff. Because she didn't. She asked it to the sheets, in a low voice, a flat voice I barely recognized.

"School?"

And then things started flooding in on me. Funny, because when I first started waking up, what happened at school felt like a dream and I thought, *surely they aren't talking about that, because that was just some stupid, horrible dream.* But within a few seconds the realization that it wasn't a dream sunk in on me and I almost felt physically squashed beneath the images.

"Valerie, something terrible happened at school today. Do you remember it?" Mom asked.

I couldn't answer her. I couldn't answer anyone. I couldn't say anything. All I could do was stare at the TV screen, at the aerial view of Garvin High and all the ambulances and cop cars surrounding it. Stare at it until I swear I could see the individual little squares of color on the screen. Mom's voice was faraway, and I could hear her, but it wasn't like she was talking to me exactly. Not in my world. Not under this avalanche of horrible. I was alone here.

"Valerie, I'm talking to you. Nurse, is she okay? Valerie? Can you hear me? Jesus, Ted, do something!"

And then my dad's voice: "What do you want me to do, Jenny? What do I do?"

"More than just stand there! This is your family, Ted, for Christ's sake, your daughter! Valerie, answer me! Val!"

But I couldn't tear my eyes away from the TV screen, which I saw and didn't see at the same time.

Nick. He shot people. He shot Christy Bruter. Mr. Kline. Oh, God, he shot them. He really did it. I saw it and he shot them. He shot . . .

I reached down and felt the bandages wrapped around my thigh. And then I started to cry. Not loud crying or anything like that, but shoulder-twitching, lip-curling crying — the kind I once heard Oprah call the Ugly Cry.

Mom jumped up from her chair, leaning over me, but she wasn't talking to me.

"Nurse, I think she's in pain. I think you need to do something for her pain. Ted, make them do something for her pain." And I noticed, only barely and through a gauzy sort of wonderment, that she was crying, too. Crying so that her commands took on this frantic sort of gruffness, so that her words were hitched and desperate.

Out of the corner of my eye I saw Dad come up behind her and grab her by the shoulders and pull her away from the bed. She went reluctantly, but she did go, and she turned her face into Dad's chest, and they both walked out of the room. I could hear her harsh barks recede down the hall.

The nurse was pushing buttons on some monitor behind me and the cop had turned and was watching the TV again. Frankie stood staring at my blankets, motionless.

I cried until my stomach hurt and I was pretty sure I was going to throw up. My eyes felt sandy and my nose was completely plugged up. I cried a little bit after that even. I can't say what was going through my mind with all that crying — only that it was murky and dark and hateful and woeful and miserable all at once. Only that I wanted Nick and I wanted to never see him again. Only that I wanted my mom and that I wanted to never see her again, either. Only that I knew, somewhere back there in the recesses that my brain was keeping safe from itself, that in some way I was responsible for what had happened today, too. That I had a part in it, and that I never meant to. And that I couldn't say for sure I wouldn't have been part of it if I had to do it all over again. And I couldn't say for sure that I would.

Eventually the crying slowed enough so that I could breathe again, which wasn't altogether good.

"I'm going to throw up," I said.

The nurse produced a bedpan from out of nowhere and stuffed it under my chin. I heaved into it.

"If you'll step out for just a few minutes," she told the officers. They nodded and silently left the room. When they opened the door, I could hear muffled talking in voices that belonged to my parents out in the hallway. Frankie stayed put.

I heaved again, making ugly noises and letting my nose run in snotty ropes into the bedpan. I caught my breath and the nurse used a wet washcloth to wipe my face clean. It felt good — cold, soothing. I closed my eyes and rested my head back on the pillow.

"Nausea is normal after anesthesia," the nurse told me in a voice I can best describe as institutional. "It will subside with time. In the meantime, keep this close." She handed me a clean bedpan, folded the washcloth and laid it across my forehead then left the room on her silent shoes.

I tried to blank my mind. Tried to make myself turn those images in my mind black. But I couldn't do it. They shoved in on me, each one more horrible than the one before.

"Is he in jail?" I asked Frankie. Stupid question. Of course Nick would be in jail after something like this.

Frankie looked up at me, kind of startled, like he'd forgotten I was in the room with him.

"Valerie," he said, blinking, shaking his head, his voice husky. "What . . . what did you do?"

"Is Nick in jail?" I repeated.

He shook his head no.

"He got away?" I asked.

Again he shook his head.

I knew that left only one other option. "They shot him." I said this more as a statement than a question and was surprised when Frankie again shook his head no.

"He shot himself," he said. "He's dead."

MAY 2008

"I didn't do it."

7

It's funny that the name that would turn out to be the most recognizable of my class — Nick Levil — was a name nobody'd even heard of before our freshman year.

Nick was new to Garvin that year, and he didn't fit in. Garvin was one of those small suburban cities with a lot of big houses and rich kids. Nick lived on one of the few low-income streets that dotted the outsides of the city like boundary lines. His clothes were ratty, sometimes too big, and never stylish. He was skinny and looked like a brooder and had an I Don't Give a Shit air about him that people tended to take personally.

Right away I was drawn to him. He had these really sparkly dark eyes and a lopsided smile that was adorably apologetic and never showed his teeth. Like me, he wasn't part of the in crowd and, like me, he didn't want to be.

Not that I never belonged in the in crowd. When you're in elementary school, pretty much everybody is part of the in crowd and, sure, I was, too. I liked the things that were popular — the clothes, the toys, the boys, the songs that drove everyone wild at the school family fun nights.

But somewhere around 6th grade, all of that seemed to change. I began to look around me and think that maybe I didn't have all that much in common with those other kids. Their families didn't seem miserable like mine. I couldn't imagine them feeling the same frozen feeling at home like I did, as if they'd walked into a snowstorm when they opened their front doors. At school gatherings, their dads called them "Muffin" or "Baby Girl," while mine didn't even show up. As I began to doubt where I fit in, Christy Bruter, my "one person," gained momentum in popularity and suddenly it was no longer doubt, but truth: I wasn't like them.

So I liked Nick's attitude. I adopted a matching I Don't Give a Shit outlook and began cutting holes in my "cute" clothes to make them look ratty, to lose the pristine Valerie persona my parents totally bought into and had been trying extra hard to make me buy into lately, too. It also helped that my mom and dad would die if they saw me hanging out with Nick. They had this idea that I was Miss Popularity at school, which just showed how out of touch they were. Sixth grade was a long time ago.

Nick and I had Algebra together. That's how we met. He liked my shoes, which had been duct-taped around the toes, not to keep them together, but because I wanted them to look like they were falling apart. That's how we started, with him saying, "I like your shoes," and me answering, "Thanks. I hate Algebra," and him saying, "Me, too."

"Hey," he whispered later while Mrs. Parr was passing out ditto sheets, "don't you hang out with Stacey?"

I nodded, passing a stack of papers to the geeky kid behind me. "You know her?"

"She rides my bus, I think," he said. "Seems cool, I guess."

"Yeah, she is. We've been friends since kindergarten."

"That's cool."

Mrs. Parr told us to shut up and we went about our business, but every day before and after class we talked. I introduced him to Stacey and Duce and the gang and he fit in with us right away, especially with Duce. But it was obvious from the beginning that he and I fit better than everyone else.

Pretty soon we were walking to class together, meeting at his locker, and walking out of class together. And sometimes meeting on the bleachers in the mornings with Stacey and Duce and Mason.

And then one day I was having a really crappy day and all I wanted to do was get back at everyone who was making it that way. So I got this idea that I would write down all their names in a notebook, like the notebook was some kind of paper voodoo doll or something. I think I had this feeling that just writing down their names in the book would prove that they were assholes and that I was the victim.

So I opened my trusty red notebook and numbered every line down the column of the page and started writing names of people, of celebrities, of concepts, of everything I hated. By the end of third period I had half a page filled out, things like *Christy Bruter* and *Algebra — you can't add letters and numbers together!!!* and *Hairspray*. And I still didn't feel done, so I schlepped the notebook off to Algebra class with me and was hard at work on it when Nick walked in.

"Hey," he said, after he slumped into his chair. "I didn't see you at the lockers."

"I wasn't there," I said, not looking up. I was busy writing *Mom and Dad's marriage problems* in the notebook. That was an important one. I wrote it four more times.

"Oh," he said, and then he was silent for a minute, but I could feel him looking over my shoulder. "What's that?" he finally asked, kind of laughing.

"It's my Hate List," I answered, without even thinking.

After class, as we were walking out, Nick came up behind me and nonchalantly said, "I think you should add today's homework to that list. It sucks." I looked back and he was grinning at me.

I smiled. He got it, and somehow it totally made me feel better to know I wasn't alone. "You're right," I said. "I'll add it next period."

And that's how it started: the infamous Hate List. Started as a joke. A way to vent frustration. But it grew into something else I'd never have guessed.

Every day in Algebra class we'd get it out and write down the names of all the people in the school that we secretly hated, the two of us sitting in the back row, side by side, griping about Christy Bruter and Mrs. Harfelz. People who irritated us. People who got on our nerves. And especially people who bullied us, who bullied other people.

I think at one time we may have had this idea that the list would be published — that we could make the world see how horrible some people could be. That we would have the last laugh against those people, the cheerleaders who called me Sister Death and the jocks who punched Nick in the chest in the hallways when nobody was looking, those "perfect kids" who nobody would believe were just as bad as the "bad kids." We had talked about how the world would be a better place with lists like ours around, people being held accountable for their actions.

The list was my idea. My brainchild. I started it, I kept it going. It began our friendship and it kept us together. With that list, neither one of us was so alone anymore.

The first time I went over to Nick's house was the day I officially fell in love with him. We stepped into his kitchen, which was dirty and unkempt. I heard a TV off in the distance and a smoker's cough echoing over it. Nick opened a door just off the kitchen and motioned for me to follow him down a flight of wood steps into the basement.

The floor was cement, but there was a small orange rug tossed on it, right next to a mattress, which sat on the floor, unmade. Nick tossed his backpack on the mattress, and flopped back on it himself. He sighed deeply, running his hands over his eyes.

"Long day," he said. "I can't wait for summer."

I turned in a slow circle. A washer and dryer stood off against a wall, shirts draping off the corners of them. A mousetrap in another corner. Some moving boxes stacked by one wall. A squat dresser next to them, clothes spilling out of open drawers, an assortment of junk littering the top of it.

"This is your room?" I asked.

"Yep. Wanna watch TV? Or I've got Playstation."

He had flipped himself over onto his stomach and was fumbling with a small TV that sat propped on a box on the other side of the bed.

"Okay," I said. "Playstation."

As I settled on the bed next to him, I noticed a plastic crate between his bed and the wall, overflowing with books. I knee-walked across the mattress and picked one up.

"*Othello*," I said, reading the cover. "Shakespeare?"

He glanced at me, his face taking on a guarded look. He didn't say anything.

I picked up another. "*Macbeth*." And two more. "*The Shakespeare Sonnets. The Quest for Shakespeare.* What is this stuff?" I asked.

"It's nothing," he said. "Here." He thrust a Playstation controller at me.

I ignored it, kept digging in the crate. "*A Midsummer Night's Dream. Romeo and Juliet. Hamlet.* All of these are Shakespeare."

"That one's my favorite," he said softly, gesturing to a book in my hand. "*Hamlet.*"

I studied the cover, and then opened the book to a random page and read aloud:

"*O heavy deed!*
It had been so with us, had we been there:
His liberty is full of threats to all;
To you yourself, to us, to everyone."

"Alas, how shall this bloody deed be answer'd?" Nick said, quoting the next line before I had a chance to read it.

I sat back and looked at him over the top of the book. "You read this stuff?"

He shrugged. "It's nothing."

"Are you serious? It's cool. You totally have this memorized. I don't even understand what it's saying."

"Well, you kind of have to know what else is going on in the story to understand," he said.

"So tell me," I said.

He looked at me uncertainly, took a deep breath, and hesitantly started talking. His voice grew more and more animated as he told me about Hamlet and Claudius and Ophelia and murder and betrayal. About Hamlet's hesitation being his fatal flaw. About how he totally berated the woman he loved. And as he told me the story, quoted passages about divinity as if he'd written them himself, I knew. I knew I was falling in love with him, this boy with the ratty clothes and the bad attitude who smiled so shyly and quoted Shakespeare.

"How'd you get into this?" I asked. "I mean, you've got a lot of books here."

Nick ducked his head. He told me about how he discovered reading when his mom was divorcing dad number two, how he'd spent long nights at home alone, a kid with nothing to do while his mom trawled the bars for guys, sometimes not bothering to pay the electricity bill, forcing him to read for entertainment. How his grandma would bring him books and he'd devour them the same day. He'd read everything — *Star Wars*, *Lord of the Rings*, *Artemis Fowl*, *Ender's Game*.

"And then one day Louis — that's dad number three," he said, "He brought home this book he'd found at some garage sale. It was his big joke." Nick pulled *Hamlet* out of my hands and waved it in the air. "'Like to see you read this one, Smartypants,'" he mimicked in a gravelly voice. "He laughed when he said it. Thought he was being really funny. So did my mom."

"So you read it to prove them wrong," I said, flipping through the pages of *Othello*.

"At first," he said. "But then," he crawled up onto the bed next to me, leaning back against the wall just as I was, looking over my shoulder at the pages I was turning. I liked the heat of his shoulder against mine. "I started to like it, you know? Like putting together a puzzle or something. Plus I thought it was really funny because Louis was too stupid to know that he'd given me a book where the step-dad was the bad guy." He shook his head. "Moron."

"So your grandma bought you all these?"

He shrugged. "Some. I bought some myself. Most of them came from a librarian who helped me out a lot back then. She knew I liked Shakespeare. I think she felt sorry for me or something."

I dropped *Othello* back into the crate and then dug around and pulled out *Macbeth*. "So tell me about this one," I said, and he did, the Playstation controller forgotten on the floor next to the bed.

I spent my first days in the hospital remembering that day. Racking my brain until I recalled every little detail. The sheets on his bed were red. His pillow didn't have a pillowcase on it. There was a framed photo of a blond woman — his mom — perching on the edge of his dresser. The toilet upstairs flushed while we talked about *King Lear*. Footsteps creaked over our heads as his mom went from bedroom to bathroom to kitchen. Every detail. The more I remembered those details, the more unbelievable I found what they were saying about Nick on the news, which I'd turn on surreptitiously, almost guiltily, when everyone had gone home for the night and I was alone.

When I wasn't remembering that day in Nick's bedroom,

I was piecing together what had happened in the cafeteria, which wasn't easy for a lot of reasons.

First, I spent a lot of time during those two days in some sort of medicated alternate universe. Funny how you'd think the worst part of the pain when you get shot would be right when it happens, but that's not true. In fact, I really don't even remember feeling anything at the time that it happened. Fear, maybe. A strange heavy feeling, I guess. But not pain. The real pain didn't start until the next day, after the surgery, after my skin and nerves and muscles had a day to get used to the idea that something had forever changed.

I cried a lot during those first two days, and most of my crying was about wanting something to make the pain go away. This wasn't a bee sting. It hurt like hell.

So the nurse, who still didn't like me, I could tell, would come in every so often and give me a shot of this drug or a swallow of that one and next thing I knew everyone sounded weird and the room looked all grainy and stuff. I don't know how much of that time I was asleep, but I do know that after those first couple days when I stopped getting the mind-bending pain relievers and just started getting the regular ones, I wished I was asleep more often.

But the bigger reason it was tough to put the pieces back together was that it just didn't all seem to fit. Like my brain just couldn't make sense of it all. I felt like it had been snapped in two. Actually, I asked the nurse at one point if it was possible for the noise of the gun to make something in my brain get sort of jumbled up so I couldn't think straight. All I could really think was how much I wanted to sleep. How much I wanted to be in a different world other than the one I was in.

She said, "The body has many mechanisms to protect it from trauma," and I wished mine had more.

Every night when I would turn on the TV mounted to the wall across from my bed, I would watch pictures of my high school — aerial pictures that made it look about as faraway as I felt, and institutional and foreboding, not the place where I'd spent three years of my life — and I would have this weird sensation where I was sure I was watching some sort of fiction. But the nauseated feeling in my stomach reminded me that this was no fictional scenario. It was real and I was right in the middle of it.

Mom sat by my bed constantly for those first two days, the whole time dumping one emotion or another on me. One minute she'd be crying softly into a palmed tissue, shaking her head sadly and calling me her baby, the next she'd be an angry-faced, puckered-mouthed woman blaming me and saying she couldn't believe she gave birth to such a monster.

I really didn't have much to say to that. To her. To anyone. After Frankie told me Nick was dead, that he'd shot himself, I sort of just curled up like a salted slug. Turned to my side and curled up around my sheets and blankets, tucked my knees into my chest as best as I could with the bandaging and the throbbing in my thigh and the tubes and wires that kept me tethered to the bed. Just curled into a ball and after my body stopped curling my soul kept going. Curling, curling, curling into something tight, wound, tiny.

It wasn't some big decision that I would stop speaking or anything. It was just that I didn't know what to say. Mainly because every time I opened my mouth I wanted to scream in horror. All I could see in my head was Nick, lying dead somewhere. I wanted to go to his funeral. I wanted to go to his grave, at least. I wanted to kiss him mostly, to tell him I forgave him for shooting me.

But I also wanted to scream in horror for Mr. Kline. For Abby Dempsey and the others who'd been shot. Even for Christy Bruter. For my mom. For Frankie. And, yeah, for me, too. But none of those feelings seemed to really match up, like when you're putting together a puzzle and two pieces almost — maddeningly, just almost — fit. You could shove the pieces together and force them to fit, but even after they're successfully stuck together they still don't fit exactly, don't look quite right. That's how my brain felt. Like I was shoving odd puzzle pieces together.

And then on the third day my door swished open. I was staring at the ceiling, thinking about this time that Nick and I played laser tag at Nitez. I'd won the game and it had really ticked Nick off at first, but afterward we went to a party at Mason's house and he told everybody what a great shot I was. He seemed really, really proud of me and I felt so good about myself. We spent the rest of the evening holding hands and making googly eyes at each other and it was, like, the best night of my life.

When I heard the door open, I closed my eyes quickly, because I wanted whoever it was that came in to think I was asleep and go away so I could keep thinking about that night. I swear my hand was warm, like Nick's was in it right at that moment.

I heard footsteps scuff over to the side of the bed and stop. But the wires didn't move. I didn't hear any drawers or cabinets open like I normally would if a nurse was in the room. And I didn't hear Mom's telltale stuffed-up nose snorting. Didn't smell Frankie's cologne. Just a still presence beside me. I opened one eye.

A guy in a brown suit stood next to the bed. He was probably in his forties, I guessed, and he was completely bald. Not the kind of bald where all of his hair had fallen out, but the kind of bald where he'd lost enough of it to just give up and shave the rest off. He was chewing gum. He didn't smile.

I opened both eyes, but I didn't sit up. I also didn't say anything. Just looked at him, my heart pounding in my chest.

"How's your leg, Valerie?" he said. "I can call you Valerie, right?"

I narrowed my eyes at him, but didn't answer. My hand involuntarily moved to the bandage over my leg. I wondered if I should be prepared to scream. Was this some freaky horror-movie kind of guy who planned to rape and kill me in my hospital bed? I had half a thought that it would probably serve me right, that a lot of people out there would be happy to hear that something horrible happened to me, but it couldn't really form because he was moving and talking again.

"Better, I hope." He stepped back and pulled a chair forward. Sat in it. "You're young. You got that on your side at least. I got shot in the foot two years ago by some crackhead in Center. Took forever to heal up. But I'm an old man." He laughed at his own joke. I blinked. Still didn't move, my hand still on the bandages.

His laughter dried up, and he chewed his gum solemnly, staring at my face with his head cocked just slightly to one side. He stared at me for so long I finally spoke.

"My mom's coming right back," I said. I don't know why I said it because it was a total lie. I had no idea when Mom would be coming in. It just seemed like the right thing to say — that an adult would be coming along soon, so he probably should get rid of whatever rape plans he had.

"She's in the lobby. I've already talked to her," he said. "She'll be up later. Maybe after lunch or so. She's talking to my colleague right now. Might be a while. Your dad's down there, too. Seems like he's not overly happy with you right now."

I blinked.

"Well," I said. I thought that pretty much summed it up. Well. Well, when has he ever been? Well, who cares? Well, certainly not me. Well.

"I'm Detective Panzella," the guy in the brown suit said.

"Okay," I said.

"You can see my badge if you want to."

I shook my head, no, mostly because I still hadn't really put together why he might be there.

He eased into a chair and leaned forward, his face entirely too close to mine.

"We need to talk, Valerie."

I guess I should've known it was coming. It only made sense, right? Except at that point nothing made sense. The shooting didn't make sense, so how could a detective in a brown suit sitting across from my hospital bed make sense?

I was scared to death. No, I was more scared than that, even. I was so scared I felt cold all over and I wasn't sure I'd be able to talk to him at all about anything.

"Do you remember what happened at your school?" he asked.

I shook my head no. "Not really. Some."

"Lots of people died, Valerie. Your boyfriend Nick killed them. Do you have any idea why?"

I thought about this. In all the piecing together of what happened at the school, it had never occurred to me to even ask myself why. The answer seemed so obvious — Nick hated those kids. And they hated him back. That's why. Hate. Punches in the chest. Nicknames. Laughs. Snide comments. Being shoved into the lockers when some idiot with an attitude walked by. They hated him and he hated them and somehow it ended up this way, with everyone gone.

I remembered a night around Christmas. Nick's mom had loaned Nick her car, told him to take me out. It was rare that we had wheels and we were both really excited to go somewhere outside of walking distance. We decided on a movie.

Nick picked me up in the rusty, rattletrap car, the floorboard littered with lipstick-lined Styrofoam coffee cups and empty cigarette packs stuffed into the cracks of the seats. But we didn't care. We were too happy to be getting out. I scooted over to the middle of the front seat so I could sit close to him while he drove, hesitantly, as if it was his first time behind the wheel.

"So," Nick said. "Funny or scary?"

I thought it over. "Romantic," I answered, a mischievous smile on my face.

He made a face, glanced at me. "You serious? No way. I'm not sitting through a chick flick."

"You would if I asked you," I teased.

He nodded, grinning. "Yeah," he said. "I would."

"But I won't ask you to," I said. "Funny. I'm in the mood for a laugh."

"Me too," he said. His hand left the steering wheel and moved to my knee. He squeezed it softly, then left his hand resting there.

I leaned into him, closing my eyes and taking a deep breath. "I've been looking forward to this all day. My parents were so annoying last night, I swear I thought I was going to go crazy."

"Yeah, this is great," he answered, giving my knee another reassuring squeeze.

We pulled into the parking lot of the movie theater. The place was packed, people spilling out onto the sidewalk and lawn in front of it. Mostly teenagers, mostly people from our school. Nick's hand left my knee and reached back for the steering wheel as he drove slowly along, scanning for a parking space.

Chris Summers was walking past our car, a giant fountain drink in his hand. He was with his buddies, and they were goofing around like always. They cut across the parking lot right in front of us, causing Nick to step on the brakes hard.

Chris peered into the windshield and then started laughing.

"Nice car, freak!" he called and then cocked his arm and lobbed the giant drink onto the windshield. The cup split open and soda and ice splattered everywhere, leaving foamy streaks as it slid down onto the hood of the car.

I jumped, a little squeal escaping me. "Asshole!" I screamed, even though Chris and his buddies had already moved on and were pulling open the doors of the theater. Several of the kids on the lawn had looked up and were laughing, too. "You're such a jerk!" I screamed again. "You think you're so cool, but you're just a stupid ass!" I let a few more insults fly, directing my gaze at people who were laughing, including Jessica Campbell, who stood with her cluster of girlfriends, their hands over their open, laughing mouths. "God," I said, finally, sitting back against the seat again. "I wonder if he misses his brain, you know?"

But Nick didn't answer me. He was sitting absolutely still, his hands at ten and two on the steering wheel, the soda blurring the windshield. I leaned forward. His face, just a few minutes ago grinning, had totally fallen. Almost withered. His cheeks had bright red patches on them and his jaw was trembling. I could almost feel the embarrassment and disappointment radiating off of him, could almost see him crumple into defeat before my eyes. It scared me. Usually Nick got angry, fought back. But this time he just looked like he wanted to cry.

"Hey," I said, touching his elbow softly. "Forget about it. Summers is just a jerk."

But Nick still didn't say anything, didn't make a move, even though the cars behind us had begun honking.

I watched him a minute more, hearing his voice in my head: *Sometimes we get to win, too, Valerie*, he'd said. *Not tonight*, I thought. *Tonight we're still the losers*. "You know," I said, "I'm not really in the mood for a movie at all. Let's just go get something to eat. Take it back to your place. We can watch TV."

He looked over at me, his lips in a tight line, his eyes watery. He nodded slowly, then reached up and flicked on the windshield wipers, which whisked the cup away and made the soda disappear, as if it hadn't just completely ruined our night. "I'm sorry," he said in a ragged voice I could barely hear, then put the car into gear and slowly crept out of the parking lot like a whipped dog.

But sitting in my hospital bed, it didn't seem like this was what the detective really wanted to hear. He didn't want to know about Nick. He wanted to know about the perpetrator of a crime. "I don't know," I said.

"Wanna take a guess?"

I shrugged. "I wouldn't know. Nick would know. But you can't ask him because he's dead. Maybe Jeremy would know."

"Would that be Jeremy Watson? From, uh . . ." he checked some notes in a notebook that he'd produced from out of nowhere. "Lowcrest?" he said.

"I guess," I said. I realized I had no idea what Jeremy's last name was or where he lived. Only that he was Nick's friend and the last person to talk to Nick before this happened. "I don't really know Jeremy."

The detective's eyebrows raised just a little, like for some reason he expected me to be one of Jeremy's closest friends or something.

"I never really met him before," I said. "I just knew Nick was hanging out with him."

The detective pooched out his lips a little, a frown creasing his forehead. "Hm. That's funny, because Jeremy's parents sure know a lot about you. Knew your first and last names. Knew where you lived. Told me to look for you if I wanted answers."

"How would they know anything about me?" I pulled myself up onto my elbows. "I've never even met them."

The detective shrugged. "Maybe Nick talked about you a lot. Was this planned, Valerie? Did you and Nick plan the shooting together?"

"I didn't . . . No, I wasn't going to . . . No way!"

"We have about a dozen witnesses who all say Nick's words to you right before he shot you were, 'Don't you remember our plan?' You have no idea what plan he was talking about?"

"No."

"I don't think that's true."

"It's the truth," I said miserably. "I didn't plan any of this. I didn't even know he was planning this."

He stood and pulled his suit coat straight. He pulled a sheaf of papers out of a folder and handed them to me. I looked down at them and swear I stopped breathing.

To: NicksVal@aol.com
From: cadaver@gmail.com
Subject: Another way to do it
I think I would prefer gas over anything. You know, like go into the garage and turn on the car and just lay down on the seat and get high and get dead. That would be totally intense, man, if my parents walked in to the garage in the morning, ready to go to work and found me dead with a fatty in my hand.

Oh, and you know who I want to add to the list? Ginny Baker.

N

To: cadaver@gmail.com
From: NicksVal@aol.com
Subject: RE: Another way to do it
I don't know, I'm still liking the whole overdose thing.
Like o.d. on something sexy, like x or something. LOL
about your parents walking in on you in the car. That
would be too funny. Bet they'd finish smoking the weed
before they called the ambulance. Wouldn't you?

And why G.B.? I still have the list from when I was
looking through it in social studies. I can put it on for
you.
Val

To: NicksVal@aol.com
From: cadaver@gmail.com
Subject: RE:RE: Another way to do it
Why not? She's just another SBRB anyway. Write her
down. What number is she? I'm thinking somewhere
around 407. Too bad. She deserves to be way higher
on the list.
N

To: cadaver@gmail.com
From: NicksVal@aol.com
Subject: RE:RE:RE: Another way to do it
All of those SBRB's do. I wrote her down. 411, btw.
Wouldn't it be great if all of a sudden the mall blew up
and the SBRB Club was blown to smithereens?

Nothing but fake nails and blond hair all over the
place. LOL.

Val

The detective stared at me closely as I thumbed through
the rest of the papers — all files from my computer that
I later learned the police had confiscated hours after the
shooting.

"What are SBRBs?" he asked.

"Huh?" I mumbled.

"SBRBs. You guys both mention SBRBs. You say that
Ginny Baker was one of them."

"Oh," I said. "I need a drink of water." He reached forward and pushed the hospital tray closer to me. I grabbed the
water and drank. "SBRBs," I repeated. I shook my head.

"Don't remember?" The detective crouched down to eye
level. He glared into my eyes and I started to sweat. He
spoke in a low, growling voice and I could see that he could
turn into a real force to be reckoned with when he wanted
to. "Valerie," he said. "People want justice. They want answers. You can bet we're going to get to the bottom of this.
We will find out the truth. One way or another. You may
not remember what exactly happened in the cafeteria three
days ago, but I know you remember what SBRBs are."

I set the water glass back on the tray. My mouth felt frozen shut.

"I checked with the school. It's not some sort of school
organization. So I know it's something you and Nick made

up." He stood full height again and closed his folder. "Fine," he said, back in normal voice. "I'll figure it out. In the meantime, I'm just going to go ahead and assume that SBRB was your nickname for certain kids, at least one of whom died."

"Skinny . . ." I started and then I stopped and closed my eyes, tightened my jaw. I felt cold all over and thought I should maybe ring a nurse or something. But I had a feeling the nurse wouldn't do anything to help me. I took a breath. "Skinny Barbie Rich Bitches," I said. "SBRB. Skinny Barbie Rich Bitches. That's what it stood for. The SBRB Club. Okay?"

"And you wanted them to all be blown up."

"No. I never wanted anyone to be blown up."

"That's what you said. You are 'NicksVal,' aren't you?"

"We were joking. It was just a stupid joke."

"George and Helen Baker aren't laughing. Ginny's face is a mess. If she lives, she'll never look the same."

"Oh my God," I whispered, my mouth going dry. "I didn't know."

The detective stepped around the chair and shuffled toward the door. He pointed at the sheaf of papers that I was still holding. "I'm going to leave those with you for tonight. You can look them over and we'll talk about them again tomorrow."

I felt panicky. I didn't want to talk to him in the morning or any other time. "My dad's a lawyer. He won't let me talk without a lawyer. This has nothing to do with me."

I saw a flash of something cross the detective's face — anger, maybe, or maybe just impatience.

"This is no game, Valerie," he said. "I want to work with you, I really do. But you have to work with me. I've talked to your dad. He knows I'm talking to you. Your parents are cooperating, Valerie. So is your friend Stacey. We've spent the past two days going through Nick's things, and yours. We have the notebook. We're getting the e-mails right now. Whatever went on, we'll find out about it. This is your chance to clear things up. To clear Nick's name, if you think you can. But you have to talk. You have to cooperate. For your own sake."

He stood in the doorway for a few minutes just watching me. "We'll talk again tomorrow," he said.

I stared at my lap, trying to take in everything he'd said. The notebook? The e-mails? I wasn't sure exactly what he'd meant, but my guess was that it wasn't looking good for me. I was mentally scanning all the horrible things I'd said in that notebook or in late-night IMs with Nick. None of it was good. I was so cold now I could barely feel anything below my neck.

8

"So tell me about this nickname of yours — Sister Death,"
Detective Panzella said as soon as he walked in the door the
next morning. No *How's the leg? Better I hope* today, just
Tell me about this nickname of yours.

"What about it? It was a stupid nickname," I said, pushing the button to raise the head of my bed to a sitting position. I had been looking at the computer printouts he'd left
the day before — again — and was in a foul mood. All of
those things we talked about — why didn't I see it? Why
didn't I see that Nick was serious?

The detective flipped a few pages in his little notebook
and nodded. "Where did it come from?"

"What? You mean why did they call me that? Because
of my eyeliner. Because I wear black jeans and dye my hair

black. Because, I don't know. Why don't you ask them? It's not like I asked to be called names."

No, I hadn't asked for it. That I was sure of, even though some people on TV made it sound like I did. Christy Bruter was just *that one person*, as my mom had said all these years. That one person who saw someone looking weak and vulnerable and pounced on it. That one person who had enough people in her back pocket that any nickname she created was going to catch on. That one person who could make my life miserable if she wanted to. Christy liked to call me names. So did Jessica Campbell and Meghan Norris. Chris Summers liked to pick on Nick any chance he got. Why? How should I know?

"So it wasn't because you were planning to kill people with your boyfriend."

"No! I told you that already. I never planned anything with Nick. I never even knew Nick was planning anything. It was a stupid nickname. It's not like I created it. I hated it."

He flipped another page. "A stupid nickname started by Christy Bruter."

I nodded.

"The girl Nick supposedly shot first. The one we can't really see on the security video so well. All we see is you and Nick confronting her and then Christy hitting the floor and everyone scattering."

"I didn't shoot her if that's what you're thinking," I said. "I didn't."

He sank into a chair and leaned toward me. "Tell us what to think, Valerie. Tell us how it really went down. We only know what we see. And what we see is you pointing out Christy Bruter to your boyfriend. At least three other kids confirm that."

I nodded and rubbed my forehead with my fingers. I was getting sleepy, and I was pretty sure the wrapping on my leg needed changing.

"Want to tell me why you did that?"

"I wanted Nick to confront her," I nearly whispered. "She broke my MP3 player."

The detective stood and moved over to the window and slanted the blinds so that the sun was no longer driving into the room. I blinked. The room looked sullen now. Like Mom would never come back. Like I would forever be in this bed listening to this cop's questions, even if I were to be writhing in pain, the gunshot wound in my leg turning gangrenous and caving in on itself.

He pulled up another chair on the opposite side of the bed than he'd been sitting on. He sat and scratched his chin.

"So," he said. "You went into that cafeteria and pointed out Christy to your boyfriend. Next thing you know, she's got a big hole in her gut. What are we missing, Valerie?"

I felt a tear spill over. "I don't know. I don't know what happened, I swear. One minute we were walking into the Commons like every other day, and the next minute people were screaming and running."

The detective pooched his lips and closed his notebook, then leaned back against the chair, training his eyes to the ceiling like he was reading something off of it. "Eyewitness accounts say that you knelt by Christy right after she was shot and then got up and ran off. They say it was like you were making sure she was shot and then you moved on. Left her to die. Is that accurate?"

I squinched my eyes tight, trying not to see the image of Christy Bruter's bleeding gut, my hands pressed against it. Trying not to feel the panic that I'd felt that day welling up inside my throat. Trying not to smell gun powder in the air and hear screaming. More tears rolled down my cheeks. "No, it's not accurate."

"You didn't run off? Because we see you run off on the tapes."

"No. I mean, yes, I left her, but I didn't run off. Not because I was leaving her to die. I swear. I was leaving because I had to find Nick. I had to tell him to stop."

He nodded, flipped pages again. "And what was it again that you said to your friend Stacey Brinks when you got off the bus that day?"

My leg was throbbing, and so was my head. My throat was dry from talking for so long. And I was getting scared. Really scared. I couldn't remember what I'd said to Stacey. I was getting to the point where I couldn't remember much of anything, and those things I did remember I no longer trusted to be the truth.

"Hmm?" he said. "Did you say something to Stacey Brinks after you got off the bus?"

I shook my head.

"According to Stacey, your words were something along the lines of, 'I want to kill her. She's going to regret this.' Is that what you said?"

Just then a nurse popped into the room. "I'm sorry, Detective, but I've got to change her bandages before my shift is over," she said.

"Certainly," Detective Panzella answered. He stood and navigated through the various machines and wires. "We'll talk more later," he said to me.

I hoped by *later* he meant *never*. That somehow some miracle would occur between now and *later* and he'd decide I didn't have any answers.

9

I was sitting in a wheelchair next to my bed, wearing a pair of jeans and a T-shirt for the first time since the shooting. Mom had brought them to me from home. They were old, from maybe ninth grade or something, and way out of style. But it felt good to get into real clothes again, even if it meant I couldn't move much without the denim rubbing against the wound in my thigh and making me grunt and grind my teeth. It felt good to sit upright, too. Sort of. Not like there was much else I could do other than sit and watch TV.

During the day, when Mom and Detective Panzella and the nurses were around, I'd keep the TV tuned to Food Network or some other channel that wasn't showing coverage of the shooting. But at night, my intense curiosity won over and I would watch the news, my heart sometimes pounding in my chest as I tried to piece together who had lived, who had died, and how the school was going on about its business.

During the commercials my mind would sort of wander. I'd wonder about my friends, about whether or not they had made it out. About how they were doing. Were they crying? Were they celebrating? Did life just go on for them? And then my mind would wander to the victims and I'd have to dig my fist into my thigh and flip to another channel to try to think about something else again.

I'd spent the morning answering questions for Detective Panzella, which was totally not fun. I tried not to think about what he was doing, ever, because I was pretty sure that, no matter what it was, it didn't look good for me.

He was sure I was a shooter that day. Or at least somehow behind it all. No matter what I told him he was sure of it. No matter how much I cried, he wouldn't change his mind. And given the evidence he'd shown me over the past couple days I guess I couldn't blame him. I looked guilty as hell, even to me, and I knew I didn't do it.

He'd left snippets and tidbits of evidence with me. He'd been through my house. My room. My computer. He'd pored over my cell phone records. Recovered e-mails. Read through the notebook . . . the notebook.

From the sound of things, pretty much everybody had seen the notebook. Even the media knew all about the notebook. I'd seen pieces of it highlighted on one of those late-night TV news magazines. I'd heard it quoted on one of those morning talk shows, and I tried not to think about how ironic it was that the coiffed newspeople who found the notebook so fascinating were just the kind of people who would've ended up in it. Matter of fact, I think a couple of them actually were in it. I wondered if they knew that. Which sent me into a spiral of wondering and what-ifs and that was never a good place to be, especially with Detective Panzella sniffing around my room all the time.

I had lost count of the days, but figured I'd been there for about a week by the number of visits I'd had from the detective.

He had already been in, just after I'd gotten dressed and settled into the wheelchair. As always, he smelled like leather and he smacked his lips a lot when he talked. His suit was brown and blank like a grocery sack. And he had this sarcastic cock to his head that made me feel like I was lying, even when I knew I wasn't. He'd kept our chat short, leaving me alone with my wheelchair and cooking shows, and I was glad of it.

After the detective left, Mom came back with the clothes, a couple of magazines, and a candy bar. She seemed to be a little bit happier, too. Weird, I thought, given that she knew the detective had been in my room quizzing me. She didn't look as much like she'd been crying, either. Her red nose and swollen eyes had become almost permanent fixtures on her face and I was shocked to see her breeze in with a face full of makeup and, if not a smile, a look of complacency on her face.

She handed me the clothes and helped me get into them. Then she let me lean against her while I hopped on my good leg over to the wheelchair and she plunked me into it. She unwound the remote from where I'd had it wrapped around the bedrail and handed it to me. Then she sat on the edge of my bed and stared at me.

"Your leg is getting better," she said.

I nodded.

"You talked to the detective."

I nodded again, looking at my bare feet and wishing I'd asked her to bring socks.

"Is there anything you want to tell me about it?"

"He thinks I'm guilty. So do you."

"Now, Valerie. I never said that."

"You're never even here when he comes in to grill me, Mom. There's nobody here. I'm always alone."

"He's a very nice officer, Valerie. He's not out to get you. He's just trying to find out what happened."

I nodded again, deciding that I was suddenly too tired to fight with her. Suddenly I decided it really didn't matter what she thought. This was so big she couldn't save me even if she did think I was innocent.

We sat there for a few minutes. I flipped the channels on the TV and ended up watching Rachael Ray, who was cooking some sort of chicken or something. We were both silent, save for the shush of Mom's shoes when she shifted positions or the squeak of the vinyl seat of the wheelchair when I did. Probably Mom couldn't think of anything else to say, either, if I wasn't going to give her some big, dramatic soap opera confession or anything.

"Where's Dad?" I finally asked.

"He went home."

The next question hung heavily between us and I considered not even asking it, but decided she was waiting for it and I didn't want to disappoint her.

"Does he think I'm guilty, too?"

Mom reached over and unkinked a spot in the remote control cord, keeping her fingers busy.

"He doesn't know what to think, Valerie. He went home to think. At least that's what he says."

Now that was an answer that hung just as heavily as the question, if you asked me. *At least that's what he says.* What was that supposed to mean?

"He hates me," I said.

Mom looked up sharply. "You're his daughter. He loves you."

I rolled my eyes. "You have to say that. But I know the truth, Mom. He hates me. Do you hate me too? Does everyone in the world hate me now?"

"You're being silly now, Valerie," she said. She got up and picked up her purse. "I'm going to go down and grab myself a sandwich. Can I bring you anything?"

I shook my head, and as Mom left a thought flashed through my head like a strobe light: She hadn't said *no.*

Mom hadn't been gone long when there was a soft knock on the door. I didn't answer. It just seemed like too much energy to open my mouth. Not like I could keep anyone out these days, anyway.

Besides, it was probably Detective Panzella, and no matter what, I was determined that this time he wouldn't get a single word out of me. Even if he begged. Even if he threatened me with a life sentence. I was sick of reliving that day and just wanted to be left alone for a minute.

The knock came again and then the door swished open softly. A head peeked around it. Stacey.

I can't tell you the relief I felt at seeing her face. Her whole face. Not just alive, but not even marked. No bullet holes. No burn marks. Nothing. I almost cried seeing her standing there.

Of course, you can't exactly see emotional scars on someone's face, can you?

"Hey," she said. She wasn't smiling. "Can I come in?"

Even though I was really happy to see that she was alive, I realized once she opened her mouth and the voice that came out was the voice I'd laughed with, like, a million times over the years, I had no idea what to say to her.

This may sound stupid, but I think I was embarrassed. You know, like when you're a little kid and your mom or dad yells at you in front of your friends, and you feel really humiliated, like your friends had just seen something really private about you and it totally takes away from the "got it under control" persona you're trying to project into this world. It was like that, only times a billion or something.

I wanted to say a ton of things to her, I swear. I wanted to ask her about Mason and Duce. I wanted to ask her about the school. About whether or not Christy Bruter lived and Ginny Baker, too. I wanted to ask her if she knew that Nick was planning this. I wanted her to say it blindsided her, too. I wanted her to tell me I wasn't the only one guilty of not stopping it. Of being so incredibly stupid and blind.

But it was just so weird. Once she came in and said, "You didn't answer when I knocked so I thought you were asleep or something," it all felt so surreal. Not just the shooting. Not just the TV images of students streaming, half-bloody, out of the cafeteria doors of my high school like a nicked vein. Not just Nick being gone and Detective Panzella chanting *Law & Order* phrases at my bedside. But all of it. Every bit, going all the way back to first grade when Stacey showed me a loose front tooth that stuck straight out like a piece of gum when she poked her tongue behind it and me baring my stomach on the monkey bars on the playground. Like it all was a dream. And this — this hell — was my reality.

"Hey," I said softly.

She stood at the end of my bed, awkwardly, the way Frankie was standing on the day I woke up.

"Does it hurt?" she asked.

I shrugged. She'd asked me the same question a million times, after a million scrapes, in that other, dream world. The one where we were normal and little girls didn't care about their stomachs showing on the playground and the teeth stood out like Chiclets. "A little," I lied. "Not bad."

"I heard you have, like, a hole there," she said. "Frankie told me that, though, so who knows if you can believe it."

"It's not bad," I repeated. "Most of the time it's pretty numb. Pain pills."

She started scraping at a sticker on the bedrail with her thumbnail. I knew Stacey well enough to know that this meant she was uneasy — maybe pissed off or frustrated. Or both. She sighed.

"They said we can go to school next week," she said. "Well, some of us. A lot of kids are afraid, I think. A lot are still recovering . . ." She trailed off after the word "recovering," and her face flushed, as if she was embarrassed to have mentioned it to me. I was struck with another dream image, one of the two of us sweating under a sheet draped over a picnic table in her back yard, shoveling imaginary food into baby doll mouths. Wow, it had seemed so real, feeding those plastic babies. It had all seemed so real. "Anyway, I'm going back. So is Duce. And I think David and Mason too. My mom doesn't really want me to, but I kind of want to, you know? I think I need to. I don't know."

She turned her face up and watched the TV. I could tell that her mind was hardly on the cream puffs being pulled out of the oven by whatever food show host was cooking at the moment.

Finally she looked at me, her eyes a little watery.

"Are you going to talk to me, Valerie?" she asked. "Are you going to say anything?"

I opened my mouth. It felt full of nothing, like maybe full of clouds or something, which I think is only appropriate when you come out of a dream world like that and into an ugly, horrid reality, so horrid it has a taste, a shape.

"Did Christy Bruter die?" I finally blurted out.

Stacey looked at me for a second, her eyes sort of rolling around, all soft-like, in her head.

"No. She didn't. She's just down the hall. I just saw her." When I didn't say anything, she tossed her hair back and looked at me through squinty eyes. "Disappointed?"

And that was it. That one word. It told me that Stacey, even my oldest friend Stacey, the one who was with me when I started my first period, the one who wore my swim-suit and eyeshadow, believed I was guilty, too. Even if she wouldn't say it out loud, even if she didn't think I pulled the trigger, deep down she blamed me.

"Of course not. I don't know what to think about anything anymore," I answered. It was the most truthful I'd been in days.

"Just so you know," she said. "I couldn't believe what happened. I didn't at first. When I heard everyone saying who did the shooting I didn't believe them. You and Nick . . . you know, you were my best friend. And Nick always seemed so cool. A little Edward Scissorhands or something, but in a cool way. I never would have thought . . . I just couldn't believe it. Nick. Wow."

She started to walk toward the door, shaking her head. I sat in my wheelchair, feeling numb all over, taking in everything she had said. She couldn't believe it? Well, neither could I. Mostly I couldn't believe that my oldest and "best" friend would just assume that everything she'd heard about me was true. That she wouldn't even bother to ask me if what they were all saying was what really happened. That moldable Stacey was being molded into someone who no longer trusted me.

"Neither could I. I still don't sometimes," I said. "But I swear, Stacey, I didn't shoot anybody."

"You only told Nick to do it for you," she said. "I've gotta go. I just wanted to tell you I'm glad you're okay." She put her hand on the door handle and pulled it open. "I doubt they'd let you anywhere near her, but if you see Christy Bruter in the hallway here, maybe you should apologize to her." She stepped out, but just before the door swished closed behind her, I heard her say, "I did," and I couldn't help but wonder for, like, eight hours after that, what on earth Stacey had to apologize for.

And when it dawned on me that she was probably apologizing for being my friend, that dream world just blinked out, vanished. It never existed.

10

I thought I was going home. Mom had slipped in while I was sleeping and had laid out another outfit for me to get into, before disappearing again like smoke. I sat up, the morning light streaming through the window and across the foot of my bed, and brushed the hair out of my eyes with my fingers. The day felt different somehow, like it had possibility.

I pulled myself out of bed, grabbed the crutches the night nurse had left propped against the wall next to my bed, and used them to hop to the bathroom — something I'd been able to do by myself for a full day now. The pain medication still made me woozy, but I was off the IV now, and the wrap around my leg was still bulky, but not bad. My leg only throbbed a little, sort of like a splinter lodged in the wedge between your fingers would do.

It took me a while to maneuver myself around and get down to business in the bathroom, and when I emerged again, Mom was sitting on the edge of my bed. There was a small suitcase on the floor at her feet.

"What's that?" I asked, crutching back to the bed. I picked up my shirt and began peeling myself out of my pajamas.

"Some things I thought you might need."

I sighed, pulling the shirt over my head, and began working on my pants.

"You mean I'm stuck here for another day? But I feel fine. I can get around fine. I can go home. I want to go home, Mom."

"Here, let me get that," Mom said, leaning forward to help me shimmy into my jeans. She snapped them and zipped them for me, which felt weird and comforting all at the same time.

I hobbled to the wheelchair and plopped into it. I pulled my hair out of the back of my shirt and got settled. I wheeled to the nightstand, where a nurse had left a tray of food for me. I smelled bacon and my stomach growled.

"So have they said yet when they'll let me go home? Tomorrow? I really think I can go home tomorrow, Mom. Maybe you can talk to them about it." I opened the lid on the breakfast tray. My stomach growled again. I couldn't get the bacon into my mouth fast enough.

Just as Mom was opening her mouth to speak, the door swung open and a guy in a pair of khakis and a plaid shirt with a lab coat tossed over it came through.

"Mrs. Leftman," he said jovially. "I'm Dr. Dentley. We spoke on the phone."

I looked up, my mouth full of bacon.

"And you must be Valerie," he said, his voice measured and careful. He held his hand out like he wanted me to shake it. I swallowed the bacon and shook his hand tentatively. "Dr. Dentley," he said. "I'm the staff psychiatrist here at Garvin General. How's your leg feeling?"

I looked at Mom, but she was looking at her feet, like she was pretending we weren't in the room with her at all.

"Okay," I answered, reaching for another piece of bacon.

"Good, good," he said, the smile never leaving his face. It was a nervous smile, almost like he was half afraid, but not of me personally. It was almost like he was half afraid of life. Like it was going to jump up and bite him any moment. "Tell me about your pain level right now."

He reached behind him and whipped out my chart, which, of course, had their pain management assessment page taped to the back of the clipboard. I'd been answering this question about a hundred times a day since I got here. Is your pain a ten? A seven? Maybe it's a 4.375 today?

"Two," I answered. "Why? Am I getting out?"

He chuckled and used his forefinger to push his glasses back up on the bridge of his nose.

"Valerie, we want you to heal," he said, in this patient kindergarten-teacher voice. "And we want you to heal inside as well. That's why I'm here. I'm going to do some evaluations on you today so we can determine the best way we can help you get to a place of mental health. Do you feel like hurting yourself today?"

"What?" I looked over his shoulder again. "Mom?" But she just kept staring at her shoes.

"I asked if you're feeling like you might pose a danger to yourself or others today."

"You mean am I going to commit suicide?"

He nodded, that stupid grin hanging on like a barnacle. "Or cut yourself. Or if you're having dangerous thoughts."

"What? No. Why would I want to commit suicide?"

He shifted slightly to one side and crossed one leg over the other. "Valerie, I've spoken quite extensively with your parents, the police, and your doctors. We talked at great length about the thoughts of suicide that have apparently plagued you for a good long time. And we all fear that, given recent events, those thoughts might be increasing."

Nick had always been obsessed with death. It wasn't any big deal, you know? Some people were obsessed with video games. Some people thought about nothing but sports. Some guys were totally into military stuff. Nick liked death. From day one when he was sprawled across his bed talking about how Hamlet should have killed Claudius when he had the chance, Nick had talked about death.

But they were stories, that's all. He told stories about death. He recounted movies, books, all with tragic and meaningful death scenes. He talked about news reports and crime reports. It was just his thing. And I adopted his language; I told stories, too. It was no big deal. Really I didn't even

173

notice I'd started doing it. It felt like fiction, all of it. Shakespeare told stories of death. Poe told stories of death. Stephen flipping King told stories of death, and none of it meant a thing.

So I hadn't even noticed when the talk increased. Hadn't noticed when it got personal. Hadn't realized that Nick's stories had become tales of suicide. Of homicide. And mine had, too. Only, as far as I knew, we were still telling fiction.

When I thumbed through the e-mails Detective Panzella had given me on his first visit to my room, I was dumbfounded. How could I have not seen it? How could I have not noticed that the e-mails told an alarming story that would have made anyone sit up and notice? How could I have not seen that Nick's talk had gone from fiction to fact? How could I not see that my responses — still just fiction in my head — would make me look for all the world like I was obsessed with death, too?

I don't know, but I hadn't seen it. As much as I wished I had, I hadn't.

"You mean those e-mails? I didn't mean it. It was all *Romeo and Juliet*. It was all Nick. Not me."

He kept talking, as if I'd never said a word. "And we all believe that the best course of action for you at this juncture is to keep you safe and enter you into an inpatient residential program where you can get some help to battle those suicidal urges. Group therapy, individual therapy, some medication."

I grabbed my crutches and pulled myself to standing. "No. Mom, you know I don't need this. Tell him I don't need this."

"It's for your own good, Val," Mom said, finally looking up from her shoes. I noticed she had her fingers wrapped around the handle of the suitcase. "It'll only be for a little while. A couple weeks."

"Valerie," Dr. Dentley said. "Valerie, we can help you get what you need."

"Stop saying my name," I said, my voice rising. "What I need is to go home. I can battle whatever urges at home."

Dr. Dentley stood and leaned over to press the call button on the remote. A nurse scurried in and picked up the suitcase, then just stood at the door, waiting. Mom stood up, too, edging toward the bathroom, out of the way.

"We're just going to move up to the fourth floor, where the psychiatric wing is, Valerie," Dr. Dentley said in that measured voice. "Please sit down. We'll take you in your wheelchair. You'll be comfortable that way."

"No!" I said, and I guess from the way Mom blinked when I said it I must have been screaming, although I didn't feel it. All I could think about was tenth grade Comm Arts class when we watched *One Flew Over the Cuckoo's Nest*. All I could think about was Jack Nicholson screaming at the nurse about wanting the TV on and the creepy blank-faced Indian and the nervous little guy in glasses. And — here is the dumbest thing of all — I even had the thought that when word got around that I'd been locked up in a psych ward, everyone would totally make fun of me. Christy Bruter would have a field day with this one. And all I could think was *They're going to have to take me up there dead, because there's no way I'm going up there of my own power.*

Dr. Dentley must have had the same thought because once I started screaming, "No! I won't go! No! Get away from me!" the pleasant look on his face turned just slightly and he gave a nod to the nurse who scurried out of the room.

A few moments later two big orderlies came in and Dr. Dentley said, "Be careful of the left thigh," in this very clinical voice and then the orderlies were on me, holding me down while the nurse came at me with a needle. Instinctively I dropped back in my wheelchair. My crutches clattered against the floor. Mom bent over and picked them up.

I thrashed as best as I could with what felt like a thousand pounds on top of me and I screamed as loud as my voice would allow. So loudly, pieces of my words were silent, flinging themselves into the air so forcefully I imagined foreign-looking people in distant countries picking them up like artifacts in the dust. One of the orderlies moved to get a better hold of my arm, which gave me just enough room to kick. I kicked out with all I had, landing a good one on his shin. He let out a *shoosh* through gritted teeth, bringing his face kissing-close to mine, but it did nothing to help me. I was pinned. The nurse stole behind me and I moved the only thing I still had power over — my lungs — when she stuck the needle in my exposed hip through the open space of the wheelchair.

Within seconds, the only part of me that cooperated with fighting my fate was tears, which smeared my face and collected in my neck. Mom cried, too, and I took some satisfaction in that, though not nearly enough.

"Mom," I whimpered, as they rolled me past her. "Please don't do this. You can stop this . . ." She didn't answer. At least not in words.

They wheeled me down the hallway toward the elevator. All the way I cried, I begged, I repeated, "I didn't do it . . . I didn't do it . . ." but Dr. Dentley had disappeared and all that was left were the two orderlies and the suitcase-toting nurse, none of whom acknowledged they even heard me.

We came to an intersecting hallway with a sign that said ELEVATORS and an arrow pointing the way. Just before we turned, we passed a room, and a face that I recognized.

They say that near-death experiences change people. That they suddenly discover what tolerance and love are really about. That they have no more use for pettiness and hate.

But when the orderlies wheeled me toward that bank of elevators and we passed Christy Bruter's room, I saw her propped up slightly in her bed, staring out at me. I saw her parents standing by her bedside, and another, younger woman who was holding a little boy in her arms.

"I didn't do it . . . I didn't . . ." I was saying, crying.

Her parents stared out at me with weary eyes. And Christy looked on with just the slightest wry smile. It was the same smile I'd seen so many times on the bus. Completely unchanged.

The orderlies turned the corner and I couldn't see in Christy's room anymore. "I'm sorry," I whispered. But I don't think she heard me.

Still, I wondered if somehow Stacey did.

There would be many times in my life that I would wonder
how I survived those ten days in the hospital psychiatric
wing. How I got from my bed to the toilet. How I got from
the toilet to group sessions. How I lived through listening
to high squealy voices shouting ridiculous things through
the night. How I felt like my life had been taken down to a
disgusting level when a tech came into my room one morning and whispered that if I needed "a hit" we could "probably work something out," tugging at the front of his scrubs
while he said it.

I couldn't even succumb to my silent place again — my
comfortable space. Dr. Dentley would surely consider silence a regression and suggest to my parents that I needed
to stay longer.

Dr. Dentley made me sick to my stomach. His tartar-caked teeth and his dandruff-flaked glasses and his psychology-textbook way of talking. All the while, his eyes wandering to something more important while I answered his Super-Shrink questions.

I didn't feel like I belonged there. Most of the time I felt like everyone else was crazy — even Dr. Dentley — and I was the only sane one.

There was Emmitt, a mountain of a boy, who continually trolled the hallways asking everyone for pennies. Morris, who talked to the walls as if there were someone there talking back to him. Adelle, whose mouth was so foul they wouldn't even let her be in group with us half the time. Francie, the girl who liked to burn herself and constantly bragged about having an affair with her forty-five-year old stepfather.

And there was Brandee, the one who knew what I was there for and who regarded me with her sad, dark eyes and questions at every turn.

"What did it feel like?" she'd ask in the TV room. "You know, to kill people."

"I didn't kill people."

"My mom says you did."

"What does she know about it? She's wrong."

In the hallways, in group, there would be Brandee with her questions. "What did it feel like to get shot? Did he shoot you on purpose? Did he think you'd turn him in? Did any of your friends get shot or was it all people you hated? Do you wish you hadn't done it? What do your parents think? My parents would totally freak out. Did your parents freak out? Do they hate you now?"

It was enough to make me crazy, but I worked really hard to not let it get to me. Most of the time I would just ignore her. Shrug my shoulders noncommittally or pretend I didn't hear her. But occasionally I'd answer, thinking it would shut her up. I was wrong. Answering her would just bring on a new wave of questions and I'd regret that I'd ever said anything.

The only good thing that happened during those days in the psych wing was that Detective Panzella stopped coming in to grill me. Whether that meant Dr. Dentley was keeping him away or he'd decided I was telling the truth or he was working up a case against me, I didn't know. All I knew was it was good that he wasn't around.

I moved from place to place like I was supposed to. Changed out of my pajamas and hospital-issued robe like a good girl. Sat on the couch in the common room, watching approved TV, looking out the window at the highway below, pretending I didn't see the dried boogers smeared on the walls next to me. Pretending my heart wasn't breaking. Pretending I wasn't angry, confused, scared.

I wanted to sleep my time away there. Wanted to take painkillers, curl up in bed, and not wake up again until I was home. But I knew that would be seen as a sign of depression and would only serve to keep me there longer. I had to pretend. Pretend I was getting better. Pretend my "thoughts of suicide" had changed.

"I totally see that Nick was wrong for me now," I intoned. "I want to start over now. I think college will be good. Yeah, college."

I hid the anger that was welling up inside me. Anger at my parents for not being there for me. Anger at Nick for being dead. Anger at the people in the school who tormented Nick. Anger at myself for not seeing this coming. I learned to tamp down the anger, to force it to the back of my mind, hoping that it would just fizzle out, go away. I learned to pretend it was already gone.

I said the things that would get me out. I mouthed the words they needed to hear and somehow got myself to those group sessions and said nothing when one of the other patients would lash out at me with insults. I took my meals and tests and cooperated in every way possible. I just wanted out.

Finally, on a Friday, Dr. Dentley came into my room and sat on the edge of the bed. I didn't cringe, but curled my toes inside my socks, trying to distance myself from him.

"We're going to release you," he said, so matter-of-factly I almost missed it.

"Really?"

"Yes. We're very pleased with your progress. But you're a long way from healed, Valerie. We're releasing you to intensive outpatient care."

"Here?" I asked, trying not to sound panicky. For some reason, even though it would be outpatient, the thought of coming back to the hospital every day scared me — like if I said or did something wrong, Chester and Jock would pin me down and shove a needle in my butt again.

"No. You'll be seeing . . ." he trailed off, flipping through pages on the clipboard he was holding. He nodded in approval. "Yes. You'll be seeing Rex Hieler." He looked up at me. "You'll like Dr. Hieler. He's perfect for this case."

I left the hospital, a "case," but a free one.

A nurse wheeled me down to the front door of the hospital in a wheelchair. I was aware of every eye in the building staring at me as I went past. Probably they weren't really staring at me, but it felt like it. Like everyone in the world knew who I was and why I was there. Like everyone in the world stared at me, wondering if what they'd heard was true. Wondering if God was a cruel God for letting me live.

Mom had the car pulled up outside and was coming toward me, a pair of crutches in her hand. I took them and hobbled to the car, piling myself inside it, not saying anything to Mom or to the nurse, who was giving Mom instructions just inside the hospital door.

We drove home in silence. Mom turned the radio to an easy listening station. I opened the window a crack, then closed my eyes and smelled the air. It smelled different somehow, like something was missing from it. I wondered what I would do when I got home.

When I opened the front door of the house, the first thing I saw was Frankie sprawled on the floor watching TV.

"Hey, Val," he said, sitting up. "You're home."

"Hey. Like your hair. Maximum height on those spikes today."

He grinned, ran his hand over his head. "That's what Tina said," he said. Like nothing had ever happened. Like I didn't still smell like the hospital. Like I wasn't a suicidal freak come home to make his life miserable.

At that moment, Frankie was the best brother anyone could have asked for.

12

Dr. Hieler's office was cozy and academic — an oasis of books and soft rock music in a sea of institutionalism. His secretary, a relaxed girl with brown skin and long fingernails, was curt and professional, ushering me and Mom in from the waiting room to the inner sanctum as if we were there to buy rare diamonds. She bustled around a minifridge, bringing me a Coke and Mom a bottled water, and then waved with her arm toward an open office door. We stepped through.

Dr. Hieler unfolded himself out from behind a desk, taking off his glasses and unveiling a closed-mouthed smile that made his eyes look sad. Or maybe his eyes were always sad. I suppose if I had to listen to tales of pain and misery all day my eyes would look sad, too.

"Hi," he said, stretching his hand out to Mom. "I'm Rex."

Mom extended her arm, looking too formal and rigid to be in this office. "Hello, Dr. Hieler," she said. "Jenny Leftman. This is my daughter, Valerie." She reached behind her and touched my shoulder lightly, pushing me just slightly forward. "You were referred by Bill Dentley at Garvin General."

Dr. Hieler nodded; he knew this already, as he also already knew what was next to come out of her mouth. "Valerie goes to Garvin High School. *Went*," she amended. Past tense.

Dr. Hieler settled into an overstuffed chair and motioned with his hand for us to take a seat on the couch directly opposite. I flopped on the couch, watching Mom as she stiffly backed up and sat on the very edge of it, as if it would soil her. Suddenly everything Mom said or did was embarrassing, annoying, frustrating. I wanted to push her out of the room. I wanted to push myself out of there more.

"As I was saying," Mom said, "Valerie was there at the school the day of the shooting."

Dr. Hieler's eyes moved to me, but he didn't say anything.

"She, uh, knew the young man involved," Mom finished. It was more than I could take, this fake act of hers.

"*Knew*," I seethed. "He was my boyfriend, Mom. God!"

There was a brief silence as Mom visibly tried to gather herself up (maybe a little too visibly, I thought, and I figured this, too, was primarily for Dr. Hieler's benefit — for him to see just what a horrible child she was cursed with).

"I'm sorry," Dr. Hieler said, very quietly, and at first I thought he was talking to Mom. But when I looked up he was looking directly at me, taking me in.

There was a long period of silence, during which Mom sniveled into a tissue and I looked at my shoes, feeling Dr. Hieler's gaze on the top of my head.

Finally, Mom broke the silence, her voice sounding shrill in the close air. "Well, obviously her father and I are concerned about her. She has a lot to work through, and we just want her to get on with her life."

I shook my head. Mom still thought I had a life to get on with.

Dr. Hieler took a deep breath in and shifted forward in his seat. He finally took his eyes off of me and focused on Mom again. "Well," he said in this soft voice that felt like a lullaby, "getting on with her life is important. But right now it may be more important to put the feelings out there, deal with them, and find a way to be okay with all that's happened."

"She won't talk about it," Mom argued. "Ever since she got out of the hospital . . ."

But Dr. Hieler shushed her with an outstretched hand, his eyes once again taking me in.

"Look, I'm not going to tell you that I know what you're feeling. I wouldn't invalidate all you've been through by telling you that I have any idea of what it's like," he said to me. I said nothing. He shifted in his chair again. "Maybe if we just start off this way. How about if we kick your mom out and you and I talk for awhile? Are you comfortable with that?"

I didn't respond.

But Mom looked relieved. She stood up. Dr. Hieler stood up, too, and stepped toward the door with her.

"I work a lot with kids Valerie's age," he said in a low voice. "I tend to be really wide open and direct. Not harsh, just direct. If there's something that needs to be put on the table we put it on the table so we can work on it to see if we can find our way through it and make things better. I tend to initially listen and try to offer support." He turned and looked at me, talking to both of us — me on the couch and Mom with her hand on the doorknob. "Down the road, we may or may not think there's something that you need to change. If we do we'll talk about it. More than likely at that point, we'll talk more about your thoughts and your behaviors. Any questions?"

I said nothing.

Mom dropped her hand from the doorknob. "Have you ever dealt with anything like this before?"

Dr. Hieler glanced away. "I've dealt with violence. But I've never dealt with anything like this. I think I can help, but I don't want to lie to you and act like I think I know everything about this." He looked directly at me again and I could swear I saw real pain in his sad eyes this time. "What you've been through really sucks."

Still, I said nothing. It was easier to be silent with Dr. Hieler. Dr. Dentley would've locked me up for it; Dr. Hieler looked like he expected it.

I concentrated on my shoes as Mom left the room. "I'll be right outside," I heard her say. I heard Dr. Hieler close the door and it was suddenly so silent I could hear his clock ticking. I heard the cushions of his chair let out air as he sat down again.

"This is one of those times where there's probably not a right thing to say," he said, very softly. "I would have to imagine that this thing is awful and just keeps on being awful."

I shrugged my shoulders. I still couldn't bring myself to look up.

He cleared his throat and said, a little more loudly, "First, you went through this, you got shot, you lost somebody you loved. It's pretty well screwed up school, family, friendships, and now you're stuck in an office with a fat shrink who wants to get inside your head."

I looked up with my eyes only, keeping my head bent, so he wouldn't see me grin. But he must have because he grinned very slightly back at me. I liked him already.

"Look," he said. "Not only do I think this whole thing is terrible for you, but I'm also aware that you've probably had very little control over any of this. I'd like to do things differently here. I'd like to give you a lot of control. We'll move only as quickly as you want. If I bring up a subject that you don't want to talk about or push too hard on a topic, just tell me and I'll change the topic to something easy and safe."

I lifted my chin a little.

"The next time we get together why don't we start by just learning about you, what you've been interested in, how life was before this happened, getting to know one another a bit, and we'll move forward from there. Sound good?"

"Okay," I said. My voice was tiny, but I was surprised to hear any voice there at all.

13

When I got up the next morning, Detective Panzella was sitting in my kitchen, at the table, across from Mom, a cup of coffee in front of him. Mom was smiling, her face lighter than I'd seen it in forever. The detective was grim-looking, like always, but there was a looseness about his shoulders that suggested he might have been smiling, had he not been who he is and I not been who I am.

I limped into the kitchen, the rubber stops on the bottoms of my crutches sliding slightly under my weight on the linoleum. I fought the feeling of the world going out from under me, as it had done countless times since my surgery. I was still hopped up on a good amount of drugs, both painkillers and psychotropics, and was still a little loopy over my freedom.

"Valerie," Mom said. "The detective has good news."

I considered sitting at the table, but thought better of it and instead propped myself against the far end of the island, putting distance between Detective Panzella and myself that I had yearned for in the hospital and had been able to do nothing about at the time.

I studied him. He was in a brown suit like always, and he looked recently cleaned up, like he'd just gotten out of the shower before coming to our house. In fact, I thought I could smell soap on him and it smelled like the same kind of soap we used in our house. I could smell his aftershave, too, and it immediately sent my stomach into nauseating loops. I felt tears involuntarily spring to my eyes and, had I had the ability to use both legs, I might have sprinted out of the house screaming just to get away from him.

"Hello," he said. He turned in his seat to face me, dragging the coffee cup in a small arc on the table as he did so. Later I would scrub away the sticky trail and feel as if I were physically removing him from my life forever.

"Hi," I answered.

"Valerie," Mom said again, "Detective Panzella has come over to tell us that you're no longer a suspect in the shooting."

I said nothing. Suddenly I wasn't entirely sure I was even awake. Maybe still in the hospital, asleep, on the psych ward. I would wake in a few minutes and wheel myself to group and tell them all about this freaky dream I'd just had and Nan the schizophrenic would start yelling something about terrorists and Daisy would cry and pick at the bandages around her wrists and Andy would probably tell me to fuck off. The idiot therapist would just sit there and nod and let everyone act like that and then send us off to breakfast and meds.

"Isn't that great news?" Mom prompted.

"Okay," I said. What else could I say? *Thank God? I told you so? Why?* None of it seemed exactly right for the moment. So I stuck with, "Okay," and added, "Um, thanks." Which seemed like such a stupid thing to say.

"We've had some witnesses come forward," the detective explained. He took a sip of his coffee. "One in particular. She demanded a meeting with me and the district attorney. She was very detailed and persuasive. You won't be charged."

I felt foggy. I wanted to wake up because I was starting to feel relieved and giddy and didn't want to feel that good. It would make waking up later and finding out that I was still facing jail time feel all the worse.

"Stacey?" I croaked, shocked that she was still willing to stick up for me, even though it was obvious that she didn't trust me and that we weren't friends anymore.

The detective shook his head. "Blond. Tall. A junior. Kept repeating, 'Valerie didn't shoot anybody.'"

That didn't describe any of my friends at all.

14

"So tell me something about Valerie," Dr. Hieler said at our next visit. He settled back in his chair, slinging one leg over the arm of it.

I shrugged. As much as I hated having Mom around me all the time now, casting worried looks at me, I wished she had stayed in the office for our session.

"You mean like, why did I talk about suicide and people I hated all the time and stuff?"

He shook his head. "No, I mean tell me about you. What do you like? What can you do? What's important to you?"

I sat stone-still. It had been so long since there were things about me that were important other than the shooting. I wasn't even sure what about me other than that would be important anymore.

"Okay, I'll get us started," he said, smiling. "I hate microwave popcorn. I was almost a lawyer. And I can do a killer back handspring. How about you? Tell me about yourself, Valerie. What kind of music do you like? What's your favorite flavor of ice cream?"

"Vanilla," I said. I chewed my lip. "Um. I like that hot air balloon." I pointed to the ceiling where an antique-looking wooden hot air balloon hung. "It's really colorful."

His eyes followed mine. "Yeah, I like it, too. Partly because it's cool looking, but also partly because of the irony. It weighs a ton. In this office, anything can fly. No matter what is weighing it down. Even wooden balloons. Cool, huh?"

"Wow," I said, studying the balloon. "I never would've thought of that."

He grinned. "Me neither. My wife thought of it. I just like to take credit for it."

I smiled. There was something about Dr. Hieler that felt so safe. I wanted to tell him things. "My parents hate each other," I blurted out. "Does that count?"

"Only if you think it does," he said. "What else?"

"I have a little brother who's pretty cool. He's really nice to me most of the time. We don't fight like some brothers and sisters. I'm sort of worried about him."

"Why are you worried about him?"

"Because he has me for a sister. Because he has to go to school at Garvin next year. Because he liked Nick. Um. New subject."

195

"Vanilla ice cream, unhappy parents, cool brother. Check. What else?"

"I like to draw. I mean, you know, I like art."

"Ah!" he exclaimed, leaning back in his chair. "Now we're getting somewhere. What do you like to draw?"

"I don't know," I said. "I haven't drawn anything in a really long time. Not since I was a kid. It was stupid. I don't know why I even said it."

"That's okay. So we've got vanilla ice cream, unhappy parents, cool brother, may or may not like to draw. What else?"

I racked my brain. This was a lot harder than I thought it would be. "I can't do a back handspring," I said.

He smiled. "That's okay. I lied. I can't do one, either. But I think it would be cool to learn, don't you?"

I laughed. "Yeah, I guess. But most days I can't really even walk very well." I gestured toward my leg.

He nodded. "Don't worry. In no time you'll be running again. Maybe even doing back handsprings. You never know."

"I got cleared," I said. "Of the shooting, I mean."

"I know," he answered. "Congratulations."

"Can I ask you a question?" I asked.

"Of course."

"When you talk to Mom . . . during her sessions . . . does she blame everything on me?"

"No," he said.

"I mean, does she tell you about how much she hated Nick and how many times she tried to get me to break up with him? Does she tell you that I got what I deserved with my leg?"

Dr. Hieler shook his head. "She's never said any of those things. She's expressed concern. She's very sad. She blames herself. She thinks she should have paid better attention to you."

"She probably wants you to feel sorry for her and hate me, just like everyone else."

"She doesn't hate you, Valerie."

"I guess. Stacey hates me, though," I said.

"Stacey? A friend?" he asked, almost nonchalantly, although I had a feeling that with Dr. Hieler, pretty much no question was nonchalant.

"Yeah. We've been friends since we were kids. She came over last night."

"Great!" Dr. Hieler eyeballed me and ran a forefinger over his bottom lip contemplatively. "You don't look happy about it."

I shrugged. "Well, yeah. It was nice that she came by. It's just that . . . I don't know."

He let the sentence sit between us.

I shrugged again. "I had my brother tell her I was asleep so she would leave."

He nodded. "How come?"

"I don't know. It's just . . ." I fidgeted. "It's just that she never even bothered to ask if I was a part of the shooting. She's supposed to be on my side, you know? But she's not. Not really. And she thinks I should apologize. Not to her.

To everybody. Like, publicly or something. Like I should go to each family and ask for forgiveness for what happened."

"And what do you think of that?"

This time it was my turn to be silent. I didn't know what to think of it, other than the idea of facing all those people — the grieving ones who were screaming for justice every time I turned on the TV or opened a newspaper or saw the cover of a magazine — still made me feel sick to my stomach.

"I had Frankie send her away, didn't I?" I said softly.

"Yeah, but you didn't want her to go," he said. Our eyes locked, and then he suddenly stood up and arched his back, holding his hands over his head. "I hear it's all in the legs," he said, sort of squatting like he was going to jump up in the air.

"What's all in the legs?"

"A good back handspring."

Frankie and I were sitting at the kitchen table, just like always, him eating his cereal, me eating a banana, when I noticed the newspaper folded up on the table at his elbow. Only when I saw it did it occur to me that it was the first time I'd seen a newspaper since I came home.

"Let me see that," I said, pointing.

Frankie glanced at the paper, blanched, and shook his head. "Mom says you're not supposed to read the newspaper."

"What?"

He swallowed his cereal. "Mom says we're supposed to keep you from seeing the newspaper and, you know, TV and stuff. And we're supposed to hang up if a reporter calls.

But they don't call now as much as they did when you were in the hospital."

"Mom doesn't want me to see a newspaper?"

"She thinks it'll make you sad again if you see stuff."

"That's ridiculous."

"She must've forgotten and left this one out. I'll throw it away."

He grabbed the paper and started to get up. I lurched to standing and grabbed for it. "No you don't," I said. "Give me that paper, Frankie. I'm serious. Mom doesn't know what she's talking about. I was watching TV in the hospital when Mom wasn't around. I saw it all. Not to mention, I was there at the shooting, remember?"

He started to head for the trash again, but hesitated. I held his gaze.

"I'm fine, Frankie, really," I said softly. "I won't get sad, I promise."

Slowly he held it out to me. "Okay, but if Mom asks . . ."

"Yeah, yeah, I'll tell her you were a Boy Scout. Whatever."

He picked up his cereal bowl and took it to the sink. I sank back down at the table and read the front page article:

SCHOOL OFFICIALS SEE SOLIDARITY
IN AFTERMATH OF TRAGIC SHOOTING

ANGELA DASH

The students of Garvin High, who returned to classes last week, report a significant change in the way they see life and relate to one another, according to Principal Jack Angerson.

"If anything that came out of this tragedy could be considered remotely good," he said, "it's that the students seem to have come to an understanding of one another and of the old saying 'Live and let live.'"

According to Angerson, it's not unusual to see former enemies sit together at lunch, see old feuds end as students pair up on a more conscious level.

"Things are very much more peaceful," he says. "We don't have nearly the number of complaints coming through the counselor's office about petty things that we used to."

Behavior difficulties in the classroom are a thing of the past, as well, according to Angerson, who predicts that the school can expect to see a decline in the number of behavior problems in the years to come.

"I think students are beginning to understand that we're all friends here. That the criticism, harsh opinions, and quick dislike that are so common in children of this age just aren't worth it in the end. Unfortunately they had to find that out the hard way. But they learned and they changed. Which is why I think this generation will make the world a better place."

The students were allowed back into the building to complete the school year, although Angerson admits that curriculum has taken a back seat to what he's calling "damage control." The district has hired a team of

trained counselors to work with the students on com-
ing to terms with what happened on May 2nd.

Angerson also reports that students were not re-
quired to come back. No final exams will be admin-
istered, and teachers are working closely with the
students on an individual basis to ensure every student
has the opportunity to earn the grades they need.

"We have some teachers who are heading up study
groups in their houses at night. Some at the library.
Others are doing it online. But a lot of kids came back,"
Angerson says. "Some of them feel really strongly
about their school spirit and wanted to show support
for Garvin High. They wanted to show that they won't
be scared away. Honestly, the main reason we resumed
classes was as an answer to students' outcry."

Angerson reports that he is proud of Garvin High
students for maintaining their loyalty to their school
and feels that, in the years to come, the students of
Garvin High will emerge as strong leaders in society.
"I'm so proud of them for being the first wave of what I
believe will be the agents of change in this world some-
day," Angerson adds. "If there's ever to be world peace,
it will come through these guys."

I smuggled the article into Dr. Hieler's office later that day. No sooner had he shut the door than I dropped it on the coffee table between us.

"Does it make him a hero, Dr. Hieler?" I asked.

Dr. Hieler scanned the paper with his eyes as he eased into his chair. "Who?"

"Nick. If the people who survived are stronger and all about peace like the news says, does that make him a hero? Is he like the millennium's version of John Lennon? Peace-spreader with a gun?"

"I understand that it would be easier for you to think of him as a hero. But, Valerie, he did kill a lot of kids. Probably not a lot of people are going to think of him as a hero."

"But it seems so unfair that the school is just moving on and that finally they're accepting everyone and nobody's mean anymore and Nick is gone. I mean, I know it's his own fault that he's gone, but still. Why couldn't they have just seen it before? Why did it take this? It's just not fair."

"Life isn't fair. A fair's a place where you eat corn dogs and ride the Ferris wheel."

"I hate it when you say that."

"So do my kids."

I sulked, staring down at the article until the words blurred together. "You're probably thinking I'm an idiot for being kind of proud of him."

"No, but I don't think you're really proud. I think you're pissed. I think you wish this change of attitude at Garvin had happened sooner and then maybe none of this would've happened. And I also think you don't really believe that it's true."

And for the first time — but certainly not the last — I purged everything to Dr. Hieler. Everything. From talking about *Hamlet* on Nick's unmade bed to wishing Christy Bruter would pay big-time for what she did to my MP3 player to the guilt I was feeling. Everything I couldn't say to the cop in my hospital bed. That I couldn't say to Stacey. To Mom.

Maybe it was the way Dr. Hieler looked at me, like he was the one person in the world who could understand how everything got so out of control. Maybe it was just that I was ready. Maybe it was the newspaper article. Maybe it was my body's way of exploding — letting off the pressure before I destroyed myself.

I was a volcano of questions and remorse and anger and Dr. Hieler stood strong under the hail of all of it. He watched me intently, spoke softly, evenly. Nodded somberly.

"Do you think I would've done it?" I cried at one point. "If I had a gun, would I have shot Christy? Because when Nick said, 'Let's go get this finished,' and I thought he was going to, I don't know, embarrass her or maybe beat the crap out of her or something, I felt so good. So, like, relieved. I wanted him to take care of her."

"That's natural, don't you think? Just because you were happy that Nick was going to stick up for you doesn't mean you would've picked up a gun and shot her."

"I was pissed. God, I was really, really pissed. She broke my MP3 player and I was so pissed."

"Again, natural. I would've been pissed, too. Pissed doesn't equal guilty."

"It felt good to have him on my side, you know?"

He nodded.

"I thought he was going to break up with me, so having him stick up for me was really good. It reassured me. I thought we were going to be okay. I wasn't even thinking about the Hate List."

Again, he nodded, his eyes narrowing as I became more agitated.

His words floated softly in the air, wrapping around me. "Valerie, you didn't get her shot. Nick shot her. Not you."

I leaned back into the couch cushions and took a drink of my Coke. There was a perfunctory knock on the door and Dr. Hieler's secretary poked her head inside.

"Your three o'clock is here," she said.

Dr. Hieler's eyes never left me. "Tell him I'm running a little behind today," he said. His secretary nodded and disappeared. After she left, I was hyper-aware of the silence that stretched across the room between us. I could hear a door shut in the vestibule, someone talking in the hallway. I felt embarrassed, exposed, a little disbelieving that I'd spilled everything like that. I wanted to slink out of there, never face Dr. Hieler again, hide in my room and will the wallpaper horses to whisk me away to somewhere where I wasn't so vulnerable.

But, I realized with some amount of horror, even calm and wrought and small, I wasn't done yet. There was more. Darker, uglier things I had to know. Things that haunted me at night and wouldn't leave me, like a tickle behind my ear, an itchy spot that couldn't be identified and scratched.

"What if I wasn't serious about it then but maybe I am now?" I asked.

"Serious about what?"

"The Hate List. Maybe I thought I didn't mean for those people to die, but somewhere, I don't know, subconsciously, I really meant it. And maybe Nick saw it. Maybe he knew something about me I didn't even know. Maybe everybody saw it and that's why they all hate me so much — because I'm a poser. I set it all into motion with that stupid list and then let Nick do my dirty work. So, I don't know, maybe I should be serious about it now. Maybe that would make everyone feel better."

"I doubt more killing would make anyone feel better — least of all, you."

"They expect it of me."

"So what? Who cares what they expect? What do you expect of you? That's what matters."

"That's just it, I don't know what to expect of me! Because everything I expected about everything has all gone to shit. And I think people are disappointed that I didn't die. Christy Bruter's parents definitely think I should have killed myself afterward, just like Nick. They wish Nick had aimed better when he shot me."

"They're parents and they're hurting, too. Even so, I doubt they wish you were dead."

"But maybe I wish she was dead. Maybe a part of me always did want her dead."

"Val . . ." Dr. Hieler said, and his hesitation told all: *If you don't stop talking like this, I'll have no choice but to lock you back in the psych ward with Dr. Dentley.* I chewed my lip. A tear slipped down my cheek and, not for the first time, I ached for Nick to hold me.

"It's just that I feel like such a bad person because even now sometimes I find myself still wishing he was just in jail so I'd get to see him again," I said. Suddenly I was struck with that memory again, Nick holding me down by my wrists on his bedroom floor, telling me we could be winners. Of him leaning in to kiss me. I sat on the couch, feeling more alone than ever before. Feeling colder than I'd ever imagined possible. Feeling like, of all the horror of what happened, this was the worst of it. This was the worst because, even after everything that had been done, I still missed Nick. *Sometimes we get to win, too,* he'd told me and, hearing those words in my head again, I began to cry, miserably, achingly, Dr. Hieler moving to the couch next to me, his hand on my back. "I'm so sad without him," I sobbed, taking a tissue out of Dr. Hieler's hand. "I'm just so sad."

PART THREE

16

[FROM THE GARVIN COUNTY SUN-TRIBUNE,

MAY 3, 2008, REPORTER ANGELA DASH]
Max Hills, 16 — "I thought they were friends," one student was reported to have said about Levil's decision to shoot Hills, who was pronounced dead at the scene. "He definitely meant to shoot him," she added. "He, like, bent down to look under the table and made sure he knew who he was shooting before he did it."

Hills, described by friends as a quiet student, good at math and science, but not overly involved in many extracurricular activities, had been seen on many occasions chatting with Levil, both in school and outside of it. Many thought the two of them to be friends, which *has had a lot of students wondering why Levil targeted Hills, if, indeed, he did.*

"Maybe he thought it was someone else," Erica Fromman, a senior, said. "Or maybe he didn't care if they were friends or not," a hypothesis that has some wondering if the victims were more random than initially suspected.

Hills's mother, Alaina, however, says that she believes Max was a deliberate target. "He wouldn't let Nick borrow his truck last summer," she told reporters. "And the next day someone smashed Max's headlights in the parking lot while he was at work. Max could never prove it was Nick who did it, but we both knew it was him. They haven't been friends since then. They didn't ever talk again. Max was pretty mad about the headlights. He paid for that truck himself."

* * *

When I got home from school my second day back, I really doubted my ability to keep going back into that school. Forget transferring at the end of the semester. I'd never make it that long.

Ginny Baker never came back to class — at least not the classes that she had with me. And Tennille never looked me in the eye. And Stacey and I never sat together at lunch. But pretty much everyone else just ignored my existence, which

I thought was pretty good. But hard. Being a true outcast, without even other outcast friends, is tough.

I was really glad to get home on the second day, even though Mom kept attempting to "Mom" me, like I was still seven or something, asking me questions about homework and my teachers and — my favorite — friends. She still believed I had some of those. She actually believed the news reports. The ones that said we were all holding hands and talking about peace and love and acceptance every day. The ones that said kids are "incredibly resilient, especially when it comes to the concept of forgiveness." I often found myself wondering if that reporter, Angela Dash, was for real. Everything that woman wrote was a total joke.

As usual, when I got home, I grabbed a snack and headed for my bedroom. I kicked off my shoes, turned on the stereo, and sat cross-legged on the bed.

I opened my backpack, fully intending to get to my bio homework, but found my hand pulling out the black notebook instead. Stretching out, I opened it up. During the day I had drawn a line of P. E. students with faces dominated by enormous gaping holes for mouths, heading out to the track. A teacher — the Spanish teacher, Señor Ruiz — staring out over a staircase full of bustling students, his face blank, flat, an empty oval. And, my personal favorite, Mr. Angerson roosting on top of a miniscule version of Garvin High, his face taking on a remarkable resemblance to Chicken Little. My version of the "new and improved life at Garvin High." Seeing what was real, as Dr. Hieler suggested.

I lost track of time, fleshing out a sketch I'd made of Stacey and Duce at the lunch table, their backs brick walls, and was surprised to see that the sun was much lower in the sky when a knock at the door interrupted me.

"Later, Frankie," I yelled. I needed time to think, time to chill. I wanted to finish the sketch so I could get to my bio homework.

The knock came again.

"Busy!" I yelled.

A few seconds later, the handle turned and the door opened a crack. I silently cursed myself for forgetting to lock it.

"I said I'm —" I started, but stopped short when Jessica Campbell's head poked through the small crack in the door.

"Sorry," she said. "I can come back later. It's just that I tried to call you a few times and your mom said you wouldn't come to the phone." Ah, Mom was apparently still screening my calls.

"So she told you to come over?" I asked, disbelievingly. Mom knew who Jessica Campbell was. Everyone in the free world knew who Jessica Campbell was. Just setting her loose in my house would seem . . . risky at best.

"No, that was my idea." Jessica stepped in and shut the door behind her. She walked to the bed and stood at the end of it. "Actually, when I got here she told me you wouldn't see me. But I told her I had to try anyway, so she let me in. I don't think she likes me very much."

I chuckled. "Trust me, if she could have you for a daughter she'd probably wet her pants. It's not you she doesn't like, it's me. But that's not news." I realized as soon as I said it, that it was an awkward thing to say to someone who doesn't really know you. "What are you doing here?" I asked, changing the subject. "It's not as if you like me either."

Jessica's face got really red and for a second I thought she was going to cry. Again I was surprised at how un-Jessica-like she looked. The confidence was gone, the superiority was missing — all replaced by this weird vulnerability that didn't look right on her. She whipped her head to one side, expertly tossing her hair over one shoulder, and sat down on the bed.

"I sit with Stacey in fourth period," she said.

I shrugged. "And?"

"And we talk about you sometimes."

I felt heat rise to my face. My leg started throbbing, like it always did when I got anxious. Dr. Hieler told me that my throbbing leg was probably in my head, only he didn't use those words. He used something much nicer, I'm sure, but I only remember it that way — that it was all in my head. I rested my hand over the dent in my thigh, pressing into it through my jeans.

So this is how it was going to be — now that I was part of the mainstream again, they were going to go out of their way to make sure I knew I was officially not part of the mainstream. No longer would they wait for me to come to lunch or to my locker to make me feel like the kid everyone hates. They would to come to my house to tell me so. Was this it? Was this my punishment? "So you came to my house to tell me that you gossip with my ex-best-friend about me?"

"No," Jessica said. She crinkled her forehead, like I was crazy for even suggesting such a thing. That crinkled forehead was a look I recognized on her, one that usually preceded her saying something snotty. I braced myself for it, but instead she sighed, looked down at her hands. "No. Stacey and I talk about how we think you got messed over by Nick."

"Messed over?"

She used her middle finger to swipe her bangs over to one side and tuck them behind her ear. "Yeah. You know. You weren't guilty. But he dragged you into it. And then when they decided you weren't guilty, they never said much about it."

"They who?"

"You know. The news. The media. They only talked about how you were guilty and how the police were getting to the bottom of things, but then they never really said much when the police decided you didn't do it. It's not fair, really."

My hand eased up on my leg a little and my fingers closed around my pencil again. Something just wasn't adding up here. Jessica Campbell was sitting in my room defending me. I was almost afraid to believe it.

She glanced down at the notebook in my lap. "People keep talking about you starting another hate book. Is that it?"

I looked at the notebook too. "No!" Involuntarily, I slammed the book shut and tucked it under my leg. "It's just something I'm working on. An art project."

"Oh," she said. "Has Angerson said anything to you about it?"

"Why should he?" But we both knew the answer why he should and neither one of us said it aloud.

Jessica surveyed my room in the silence. I saw her look at the piles of clothes on the floor, the dirty dishes on the dresser, the photo of Nick that had dropped out of my jeans pocket last night when I took them off and that I hadn't bothered to pick up and hide again. Was it my imagination or did her eyes linger just a little on the photo?

"I like your room," she said. But that was lame to say so I didn't even bother to answer and I think she might have been grateful for it.

"I have homework," I said. "So . . ."

She got up. "Sure. Okay." She swished that blond hair around like a pendulum. I think that hair swish thing was on the Hate List at one point. I tried not to think about that. "Listen, the reason I came over . . . StuCo has this project going on. A memorial. For graduation, you know. Think you could work on it with us?"

I chewed my bottom lip. Work with Student Council on a project? Something was definitely up. I shrugged. "I'll think about it."

"Cool. We have a meeting Thursday in Mrs. Stone's room. Just, you know, brainstorming."

"Are you sure they want me? I mean, don't you have to be voted into Student Council?"

It was her turn to shrug. She looked toward the window when she did it, which made me think she definitely thought they didn't. "I want you there," she said, as if that's all that mattered.

I nodded, didn't say anything. She seemed to hover in the middle of my room for a few seconds, thinking. Like she couldn't decide if she should stay or go. Like she couldn't figure out how she got there in the first place.

"So everybody's saying how you were in on it. The shooting, I mean," she said in a very quiet voice. "Did you know he was planning it?"

I swallowed, looked out the window.

"I don't think so," I said. "I didn't know he really meant all that stuff. That probably sounds really lame, but it's the best I can do right now. He wasn't a bad guy."

She considered my answer, followed my gaze out the window and nodded just slightly. "Did you save me on purpose?" she asked.

"I don't think so," I said again, then changed my mind. "No, I'm pretty sure I didn't."

She nodded again. I think that was the answer she expected. She left just as quietly as she came.

Later, as I sat in Dr. Hieler's office, a can of Coke balanced on my knee, I recounted the whole strange scenario to him.

"Sitting there with Jessica Campbell on my bed was totally weird. I mean, I felt . . . naked or something with her in the room. Like everything she looked at was private. It made me nervous."

He scratched his ear, grinned. "Good."

"It was good that I was nervous?"

"It was good that you handled it."

In other words, I didn't tell her to go away.

Instead, she just left. And after she'd gone, I turned on my stereo and stretched out on my bed. I turned on my side and stared at the horses on my wallpaper. One of them seemed to shimmer just a little — the longer I looked at it, the more it looked like it wanted to take off.

17

[FROM THE GARVIN COUNTY SUN-TRIBUNE, MAY 3, 2008, REPORTER ANGELA DASH]

Katie Renfro, 15 — Sophomore Katie Renfro was not in the Commons when she became victim of the shooting. "Katie was just passing by after leaving the guidance office," Adriana Tate, the school guidance counselor, told reporters. "She didn't even know Nick Levil, I don't think," she added.

Renfro, whose injuries were not life-threatening, was hit in the bicep by a stray bullet that appeared to have ricocheted off of a locker near the Commons area.

"It didn't really hurt that bad," Renfro said. "It felt more like a sting. I didn't even know I was hit until I got outside and one of the firefighters told me there was

blood running down the back of my arm. Then I started freaking out. But mainly I think I was just freaking out because everybody else was freaking out, you know?"

Renfro's parents report that they have made the decision to pull Katie out of public high school permanently.

"It was a no-brainer for us," Vic Renfro said. "We'd always been a little bit worried about Katie going to public school. This just sealed the deal."

"You never know," added Katie's mother, Kimber Renfro, somberly, "who your child is going to school with in a public school. They let anybody in those places. Even the disturbed kids. And we don't want our daughter hanging around disturbed kids."

* * *

"She's making such a big deal out of this," I said. I was pacing — something I didn't ordinarily do in Dr. Hieler's office. Of course, ordinarily I wasn't in there under Mom's microscope, which had gotten more intense with every passing day. It was as if, rather than trusting me more as time went on, Mom actually managed to trust me less. Like she was afraid that if she stopped watching me, even for a second, I would end up involved in another shooting.

"Well, do you blame me?" Mom said. She sniffed and dabbed her nose with a balled-up Kleenex she'd pulled out of her coat pocket. "I just have a hard time believing

221

that she now wants to hang out with those people and that they want to hang out with her. And now a memorial project? Surely it can't be healthy for her to continue to focus on the incident. Surely she should be moving on now, right?"

"For the last time, Mom, I don't want to hang out with them. I'm working on a project. That's all. A school project. I thought you wanted me to get back into school projects. This *is* me 'moving on' with my life."

Mom shook her head. "Two days ago she didn't even want to be in school. And now she wants to work on a school project with the very kids that were on that list of hers," she said to Dr. Hieler. "It seems suspicious, doesn't it? Sounds like a fake to me."

This time I turned to Dr. Hieler. "She didn't talk to Jessica. I did. Jessica was serious when she asked me. It wasn't a fake."

Dr. Hieler nodded, still rubbing his lip, but didn't say anything.

Mom shook her head, like I was some fool for believing Jessica Campbell. Like I was a fool for everything I ever believed, just because I once believed Nick. It was silent in the office and Mom was staring at me.

"What?" I finally said. My voice was getting too loud. "Why are you looking at me like that? She's not going to hurt me. She didn't set me up, okay? Why is that so hard to understand? Haven't you been watching TV? Haven't you seen all the stories about how the shooting changed every-thing at the school? People aren't like that anymore. They aren't going to hurt me."

"I'm not worried about *them* hurting *you*," Mom said in a hoarse voice. She looked up at me with her red eyes. She dabbed at her nose again with her tissue.

I looked from her to Dr. Hieler. He still sat with his index finger resting on his lip. He didn't say anything. Didn't move.

"What are you worried about then?" I asked.

"Are you going to hurt them?" Mom said. "Are you join-ing up with them so you can finish the job that Nick started?"

I slumped backward into a chair. In all of her bawling and begging and forbidding and hiding newspapers and dragging me to Dr. Hieler . . . it was never to protect me from the other kids. It was to protect them from me. It was always about me hurting them. About me being the bad guy. No matter what I said, I couldn't change that in my mother's eyes.

"It's just that I wasn't paying attention before," she said, half to me and half to Dr. Hieler. "And look what hap-pened. People think I'm a horrible parent and, I don't know, I think maybe they're right. A mother should know these things. A mother shouldn't be surprised like I was. The more I let her go . . . the more I'm afraid that I'll have more deaths on my conscience."

She wiped her nose as Dr. Hieler talked to her in his soft, understanding voice. But I was too numb to listen to what he was saying.

I had changed Mom. Had changed her role as parent. No longer was her sole purpose so easy and clear-cut as it had been on the day I was born. No longer was her job to protect me from the rest of the world. Now her job was to protect the rest of the world from me.

And that was so unfair.

[FROM THE GARVIN COUNTY SUN-TRIBUNE,
MAY 3, 2008, REPORTER ANGELA DASH]

Chris Summers, 16 — Summers was said by witnesses to have died as a hero.

"He was trying to get everyone out of the way," says 16-year-old Anna Ellerton. "He was helping people out the door into the hallway. That's the kind of thing Chris would do, you know? Try to organize things."

According to Ellerton, Summers was pushed backward by frantic students trying to flee the cafeteria and as a result he fell into Levil's path.

"Nick laughed at him and asked him who was the big guy now and then he shot him," Ellerton says. "I figured he was dead so I just kept running. I don't know

if he died right then or not. All I know is he was trying
to help. All he was doing was trying to help."

* * *

I almost turned away. I looked through the long narrow window on the classroom door and saw a crowd of kids draped across chairs in a rough circle — Jessica Campbell in the middle of them, talking earnestly. Mrs. Stone, the Student Council faculty advisor, was sitting on a desk slightly off to the side. She had her legs crossed and one shoe dangling off her toe. It reminded me of a newspaper picture I'd seen during the aftermath of the shooting — a single high heel lying abandoned on the front walk outside the school, its wearer too frightened or too injured or too dead to go back and pick it up.

Was it really less than a year ago that we were sitting in the school auditorium listening to the Student Council candidate speeches? Was it really not that long ago, Nick and I filing in with our homeroom classes then immediately searching out one another from across the room, rolling our eyes as the StuCo candidates, one by one, took the stage, saying in body language what we couldn't say out loud?

"Who'd you vote for at the assembly today?" I'd asked him later that evening when we met up. He was barechested, lying next to me in a tent we'd erected in the field behind his house. We'd been coming to the tent every evening since the weather had turned, just using it as a place to

226

get away and be alone and read to each other and talk about things important to us.

He'd flipped on his flashlight and shone it across the top of the tent. A shadow spider danced in the light, struggling to climb to the summit of the tent. I wondered what it planned to do once it got there. Or was that how a spider's life was spent — forever scrabbling to reach a peak of something, the scrabbling its only goal?

"Nobody," Nick said, sullenly. "Why would I? I couldn't care less who wins anyway."

"I wrote in Homer Simpson's name," I said. We both laughed. "I hope Jessica Campbell doesn't get president."

"You know she will," he said. He turned the light off and suddenly it was way dark in the tent again. I couldn't see anything — could only tell I wasn't alone from the heat vibrating off of Nick's side next to me. I shifted in my sleeping bag and scratched my calf with the toe of my other foot, certain that now that I couldn't see the shadow spider it was surely crawling all over my body — its next conquest.

"Do you think our senior year will be different?" I asked.

"You mean if we vote in Jessica Campbell will she stop calling you Sister Death and will Chris Summers quit being an asshole?" he asked. "No."

We were both silent then, listening to the frogs outside our tent, holding a chorus around the pond off to our left.

"Not unless we make it different," he added, very quietly.

In the hallway outside the Student Council door, I started to feel a little light-headed and leaned my forehead against the cool brick of the wall. I was just going to take a few deep breaths and leave. I couldn't go through with this. No way. People were dead and if ever there was a definition of "too far gone to fix," I'd say this was it.

Someone must have seen me. The door opened.

"Hey," a voice said. "Thanks for coming."

I looked up. Jessica was hanging out the door. She gestured for me to come in. My body went on autopilot and I followed her.

Everyone was looking at me. To say that not all of the faces were kind would be inaccurate. More like none of them were. Not even Jessica's. Hers had more of a detached businesslike set to it, as if she were escorting a prisoner to the death chamber.

Meghan Norris stared at me through lowered lids, her lips set in a loose pucker, her knees bobbing up and down under the desk impatiently. I met her gaze and she rolled her eyes, then looked upward and out the window.

"Okay," Jessica said, sitting down. I sat next to her, still holding my books tight in front of me. I still wasn't sure I wasn't going to pass out. I took a deep breath, held it for ten seconds, and let it out slowly, as inaudibly as I could. "Okay," she repeated. She shuffled a few papers, all business. "I talked to Mr. Angerson and we're definitely going to have a space in the northwest corner of the courtyard, right by the doors to the Commons. We can put anything we want

228

there, as long as it passes PTA approval, which shouldn't be too hard."

"Permanent?" asked Micky Randolf.

Jessica nodded. "Yeah, we'll have a dedication ceremony during graduation, but we can leave a permanent fixture."

"Like a statue or something," Josh said.

"Yeah, or a tree," Meghan said, sounding excited — forgetting, at least for a moment, that I was fouling up her personal space.

"Statues will be expensive," Mrs. Stone pointed out. "Do we have the money for something like that?"

Jessica rifled through some papers again. "The PTA is going to pledge some money to it. And we have our account. And doughnut . . . sales . . ." There was an uncomfortable beat of silence. Doughnuts hadn't been sold since the incident. Since Abby Dempsey, Jessica's best friend, had been killed selling them on May second. Jessica cleared her throat. "Abby would've wanted us to use that money for this," she said. I felt eyes on me but didn't look up to see whose they were. I squirmed in my chair, took another deep breath, held it, let it out.

"We can have another fundraiser," Rachel Manne said. "We can sell suckers and send them out like candy-grams."

"Good idea," Jessica said. She scribbled something on a piece of paper. "And we can have an ice cream social."

"Ice cream social is a great idea. I can talk to Mr. Hudspeth about having the drama department put on a variety act for it," Mrs. Stone added.

"Oh yeah! And maybe concert choir will sing or something," someone said. Ideas were coming fast and furious now as chatter erupted about the event. I was blessedly left out, blessedly forgotten by everyone.

"That settles it," Jessica said, closing her notebook and putting her pencil down. "We'll have a variety night and ice cream social. Now we just have to decide what the memorial will actually be. Any ideas?" She crossed her arms. Everyone was silent.

"Time capsule," I said. Jessica looked at me.

"What do you mean?"

"We could have a time capsule. Put a plaque or something marking the spot and have it set to be opened in, like, fifty years or something. So people could see that there was more to this class than the . . . well . . . that there was more."

Silence stretched across the room while everyone considered this.

"We could put a bench next to it," I added. "And have the names of . . . of . . ." Suddenly I couldn't go on.

"The victims," Josh said. His voice sounded edgy. "That's what you were about to say, right? The names of the victims etched on the bench. Or on the plaque."

"Everyone or just the ones that died?" Meghan asked. The air felt very heavy around me. I kept my eyes down. Didn't want to know who they were all looking at. I had a pretty good idea it was me.

"Everyone," Josh said. "I mean, like, Ginny Baker's name should be on it, don't you think?"

"Then it's not strictly a memorial," Mrs. Stone said and everyone started talking at once again.

"But Ginny's face . . ."

". . . doesn't have to be a memorial, what about just a monument . . ."

". . . should have the names of everyone in the whole class . . ."

"That would be cool. . . ."

"Because everyone got affected by it in one way or another . . ."

". . . memorial could be about loss of life, but could also be about loss of other things, too, like . . ."

". . . not just our class, though. Freshmen died, too. . . ."

". . . can't afford to have the whole school's names put on it . . ."

"Let's just put on everyone who died," Jessica said.

"Not everyone," Josh said in a voice loud enough to stop the chatter. "Not everyone," he repeated. "Not Nick Levil. No way."

"Technically, he was a victim, too," Mrs. Stone barely whispered. "Technically, if you're going to have the names of the victims, his name should be there."

Josh shook his head. His face had gotten red. "I don't think that's right."

"I don't either," I said before I even knew my mouth had opened. "It wouldn't be fair to everyone else." I almost gasped when I realized what I had just done. Nick had been everything to me. I still didn't believe he was a monster, even after what he'd done to the school. I still didn't feel innocent about my part in it, either. But here I'd just thrown him under the bus . . . and for what? To please the Student Council? To get along with these people who, just months ago, had laughed when Chris Summers made a fool of Nick, laughed when Christy Bruter called me Sister Death? To make a show for Jessica Campbell, when I still couldn't tell if she hated me or if she'd somehow changed? Or did I really believe it? Was a part of me that I hadn't yet identified suddenly popping up, voicing my fear aloud: that Nick and I weren't the victims . . . we were the ultimate bullies?

I felt a shift inside myself so abrupt it was almost physical. I could practically see myself splitting into two people on the inside: the Valerie before the shooting and the Valerie now. And it just didn't match up.

Suddenly it felt impossible to sit there anymore, taking these kids' side over Nick's. "I've gotta go," I said. "Um, my mom is waiting for me." I grabbed my books and bolted for the door, thanking God that I'd called Mom earlier and told her to come at the normal time and wait for me, just in case I chickened out on the meeting. Thanking God that, for once, Mom's mistrust of me would pay off, that she'd be there, gnawing a fingernail and watching the school windows for sign of trouble.

I didn't even dare to think until I was safe in Mom's car in front of the school. Didn't dare to stop moving until I was sunk down into the front seat with the door locked between me and the meeting.

"Go," I said. "Just go home."

"What's wrong?" Mom asked. "What's going on? What happened in there, Valerie?"

"Meeting's over," I said, closing my eyes. "Just go."

"But why's that girl running out the door? Oh, God, Valerie, why is she running?"

I opened my eyes and peeked out the passenger window. Jessica was jogging toward the car.

"Just go!" I shouted. "Mom, please!"

Mom stepped on the gas then, maybe a little too hard because the tires actually squealed, and we whipped out of the parking lot. I watched Jessica in the side mirror getting smaller and smaller. She stood on the curb where my window had been just moments before, watching us get smaller, too.

"My God, Valerie, what happened? Did something happen? Oh, God, please tell me nothing happened. Valerie, I can't handle it if something else happened."

I ignored her. It wasn't until I felt a tickle on my chin and brushed at it only to discover that it was a tear rolling down that I realized I hadn't been ignoring her after all. I'd just been crying too hard to answer.

A few minutes later, we pulled into the driveway. When Mom paused to allow the garage door to go up, I bolted. I ducked under the garage door and into the house. I was only halfway up the stairs before I heard her barking in the kitchen:

"Dr. Hieler, please. Yes, it's urgent, goddammit!"

233

19

[FROM THE GARVIN COUNTY SUN-TRIBUNE,
MAY 3, 2008, REPORTER ANGELA DASH]
Lin Yong, 16 — "When I see what he's done, it breaks
my heart," Sheling Yong says when asked to describe
her daughter's injuries. "I'm grateful Lin's still alive, but
the bullet made permanent damage on her arm. She
was all-state violin player. Now that's gone. Her fingers
don't work right anymore. She can't play."

Yong was hit in the forearm, the impact of the bullet
shattering her wrist and causing extensive nerve dam-
age in her arm. After four surgeries, Yong still has lim-
ited use of her third finger and thumb.

"It's my right arm, too," Yong says. "So I'm having a
hard time writing. I'm trying to learn to write with my

*left hand. But my friend Abby is dead, so I don't com-
plain too much about my arm. He could definitely have
killed me, too."*

* * *

After the Student Council meeting, Mom bullied Dr. Hieler's secretary into shoving us into his schedule.

"Your mom says you left the StuCo meeting upset, Val,"
Dr. Hieler said before I'd even sat down on the couch. I
thought I detected a hint of annoyance in his voice. I wondered if he would be coming home late in order to accommodate me. I wondered if at home his wife was keeping his
plate warm in the oven, and his kids were doing their homework in front of the fire, waiting for Daddy to come home
and play cowboys and Indians with them. That's how I always envisioned Dr. Hieler's home life — sort of 1950s-TV
perfect, with a patient, loving family and never a personal
problem to be had.

I nodded. "Yeah, but it's not like it's a crisis or anything."

"You sure? Your mom says someone was running after
you. Anything happen?"

I considered his question. Should I tell him yes, something happened? Should I tell him that what happened was
that I publicly abandoned Nick, that they'd all finally gotten it through my head that Nick was bad? Should I tell him
that I felt guilty as hell about it? That I'd caved to popular
kids' pressure and I was so ashamed by it?

"Oh," I tried to sound nonchalant. "I dropped my calculator and didn't realize it. She was trying to give it back to me. I'll get it tomorrow in first period. No big deal. Mom's just paranoid."

I could tell by the way he inclined his head that he wasn't buying a word of what I was saying. "Your calculator?"

I nodded.

"And you were crying about it? The calculator?"

I nodded again, looking down at the floor. I chewed my bottom lip to keep it from trembling.

"Must be some calculator," he mused. "Must be a really good calculator." When I still said nothing, he continued in slow, soft, measured words. "I'll bet you feel really bad about dropping a calculator like that. Like maybe you feel like you should have taken better care of that calculator."

I looked up at him. His face was stony. "Something like that," I said.

He nodded, shifted in his chair. "It doesn't make you a bad person, Valerie, for forgetting a calculator every now and then. And if you end up not being able to find it and needing to get a new calculator . . . well, there are lots of good calculators out there."

I chewed my lip harder and nodded.

A few days later, Mrs. Tate was hanging out at the office copy machine when I came in to pick up my tardy slip. I tried to slip away unnoticed, but the secretary always talks so loud and when she practically screamed, "You have a doctor's note, Valerie?" Tate turned around and saw me.

She motioned at me to follow her and we walked back into her office, me with a pink tardy slip in my hand.

She closed the door behind us. Her office looked like it had been cleaned out recently. The stacks of books were still on the floor, but had been pushed into one central area. There were no used fast food burger wrappers on her desk, and her wobbly file cabinet had been replaced by a shiny new black one. She had moved all of her pictures on top of that cabinet, giving her desk a bare, uncluttered look, even though it still housed volumes of loose papers, tossed haphazardly one on top of another.

I sat in the chair opposite her desk and she edged one butt cheek up onto the corner of her desk. She used a manicured fingernail to tuck a stray piece of frizz back into her bun and smiled at me.

"How are you doing, Valerie?" she asked in this soft voice, like I was so fragile, the wrong volume would collapse me. I wished the secretary outside had used that voice and that Mrs. Tate would just talk to me normally.

"I'm good, I guess," I said. I waved the pink slip in the air. "Doctor's appointment. My leg."

She glanced down. "How is your leg?"

"It's okay, I guess."

"Good," she said. "Have you seen Dr. Hieler lately?"

"Just a few days ago. After the StuCo meeting."

"Good, good," Mrs. Tate said, nodding emphatically. "Dr. Hieler's a great doctor from what I hear, Valerie. Very good at what he does."

I nodded. When I thought about all the times I felt most validated, safest, Dr. Hieler was usually involved in one way or another.

Mrs. Tate stood and walked around her desk. She plopped into her chair, which creaked just a little under her weight.

"Listen, I wanted to talk to you about lunch," she said.

I sighed. Lunch still wasn't my favorite time of day. The Commons felt so haunted to me, and Stacey and I still passed one another at the condiment table, where she would go to my old friends, pretending she never knew me, and I would go out into the hallway, pretending that what I wanted more than anything in the world was to eat alone on the hallway floor outside the boys' restroom.

"I've seen you out in the hallway every day," Mrs. Tate said, as if she'd read my mind. "How come you're not eating in the Commons?" She leaned forward, propping her elbows on her desk. She kept her hands clasped together in front of her, like she was praying. "Jessica Campbell was in here yesterday. She said she's invited you to eat lunch at her table, but you won't do it. Is that true?"

"Yeah. She asked a while back. It wasn't anything personal or anything. I was just busy . . . working on an art project." My hand involuntarily stroked the cover of my black spiral notebook.

"You don't take art."

"This is a personal project. I take a private art class at the community center," I lied. Mrs. Tate would know it was a total lie, but I didn't care. "Look, it's nothing against Jessica. I just want to be alone. Besides, I seriously doubt Jessica's friends want me there. Ginny Baker sits at that table. She can't even look at me."

"Ginny Baker is taking a little leave of absence from school."

I had no idea. My face burned. I opened my mouth and then closed it again.

"It's not your fault, Valerie, if that's what you're thinking. Ginny has a lot of trauma to work through and she's struggled with coming back to school ever since the incident. She's worked it out with her teachers and will be fine studying from home for a while. Jessica really seems to be reaching out. You shouldn't run away from it."

"I'm not running away," I said. "I went to the StuCo meeting. It's just . . ." Mrs. Tate stared at me over her nose, her arms crossed across her chest. I sighed. "I'll think about it," I said, meaning, hell, no I'm not sitting with those guys. I stood, gathering my books tighter in my arms.

Mrs. Tate looked at me for a beat and then stood up, too. "Listen, Valerie," she said, tugging on the bottom hem of her suit jacket, which looked tight and uncomfortable. "I didn't want to have to do this, but eating outside the Commons without teacher permission is not allowed anymore. Mr. Angerson has put a ban on all solitary student activity."

"What does that mean?"

"It means that if you're seen hanging out by yourself without permission you'll be getting detentions."

For a second I didn't know what to say. *Is this a prison now?* I wanted to shout. *Are you wardens now?* But she'd probably answer *We've always been that,* so I let it go.

"Whatever," I said and started for the door.

"Valerie," she said and tugged on my elbow lightly. "Just give them a try. Jessica really wants to make it work."

"Make what work?" I asked. "Am I the class project now? Am I some sort of big joke? Why can't she just leave me alone? They were fine leaving me alone before."

Mrs. Tate shrugged, smiled. "I think she just wants to be friends."

But why? I wanted to scream. *Why does Jessica Campbell suddenly want to be my friend? Why is she suddenly nice to me?* "I don't need friends," I said. Mrs. Tate blinked at me, a crease between her eyebrows, her lips pulled in on themselves. I sighed. "I just want to get my schoolwork done and graduate," I said. "Dr. Hieler thinks that's what I should concentrate on right now. Just keeping things in line."

The last wasn't exactly true. Dr. Hieler had never given me any sort of directive to "dig deep and get it done" or any of that nonsense. Mostly Dr. Hieler was about keeping me from killing myself.

When Mrs. Tate didn't say anything else, I took that as my cue to leave. I walked out of there, my leg throbbing from being poked and prodded at the doctor's office this morning, my tardy slip in my hand, not thinking about anything other than how I was going to get out of having to go to lunch today.

20

[FROM THE GARVIN COUNTY SUN-TRIBUNE,

MAY 3, 2008, REPORTER ANGELA DASH]

Amanda Kinney, 67 — Kinney, Garvin High's head custodian of 23 years, was nicked in the knee by a stray bullet while ushering kids to safety in a nearby supply closet. "The closet was already open on account of I was putting fresh bags in the trash cans," she tells reporters from her home, her knee heavily bandaged and propped up on some pillows. "I just jammed kids up in there until I couldn't fit no more and then closed the door. I don't think he even knew we was in there. I didn't know I was shot until one of them kids told me I was bleeding. I looked down and my pants was all covered in it and there was a little tear in the knee."

Kinney, who has been known to befriend many Garvin High students, knew Levil well. "Actually he lived just a few blocks down from me so I knew him ever since he moved to Garvin. Thought he was a real nice kid. Seemed kinda mad for no reason sometimes, but nice kid. His mom's a real nice person, too. This has got to be tearing her up."

* * *

"Sorry I'm late," I said, rushing in and flopping onto the sofa. I reached out and grabbed the Coke that Dr. Hieler had set on the coffee table for me, like he always did. "Had Saturday detention and it ran over because the teacher got off on some lecture and lost track of time."

"No problem," Dr. Hieler said. "I had paperwork to catch up on anyway." But I caught him toss a little sideways glance at the clock. I wondered if he had Little League games he was missing today. Maybe his daughter's gymnastics meet. Maybe a lunch date with his wife. "Why the detention?"

I rolled my eyes. "Lunch. Didn't eat in the Commons like they want me to. So I got detentions every day and then on Friday Angerson gave me Saturday detention. Thinks he's going to break me, I guess, if I have enough detentions. But it's not going to work. I don't want to eat in there."

"Why not?"

"Who am I going to eat with? It's not like I can just walk

up to some random person and go, 'Hey, can I sit here?' and they'd be all 'Sure!' My old friends won't even let me sit with them."

"What about the other girl? The one in Student Council."

"Jessica's friends aren't my friends," I said. "They never were. That's why Nick and I had them on the Hate —" I stopped abruptly, surprised at myself for almost mentioning the Hate List so casually. I tried to shrug it off, switched gears. "Angerson's just got a thing about school solidarity so he doesn't look bad on TV. That's his problem, not mine."

"Sounds like it's not just his problem. Saturday detentions aren't ideal ways to spend your weekend, are they?" I could swear he flicked another glance at the clock.

"Whatever. I don't care."

"I think maybe you care more than you want to admit. What would happen if you gave it a try just one day?"

I had no answer for that.

Mom was gone when I got out of session. She'd left a Post-it note on the outside of Dr. Hieler's door, saying she was running an errand and would be right back, to wait for her in the parking lot. I got to the note before Dr. Hieler noticed it, ripped it down, and shoved it in my pocket. If he saw it he'd feel obligated to stay longer and I felt bad enough as it was.

Plus, I was done talking.

I left the office building and stood outside for a moment, not sure what to do with myself. I was going to have to lie low, so Dr. Hieler wouldn't see me when he walked out. I considered scooting behind the row of hedges on the side of the building, but wasn't sure if my leg would let me do much scooting. Plus there was some sort of animal under there; I could hear things rustling around and I saw the branches jerk twice.

I shoved my hands into my pockets and ambled across the parking lot, kicking pebbles with my toes as I walked. Soon I'd reached the sidewalk. I stopped and looked around. It was either the hedges or the business district across the highway. Or be spotted by Dr. Hieler and go back in for an extended session, no thanks. I pulled my hands out of my pockets and waited at the edge of the sidewalk for the cars to pass. Maybe I could find Mom's car at Shop 'N' Shop in the strip mall just on the other side of the highway. There was a clearing in cars and I jogged/limped across.

Mom's car wasn't in the lot at Shop 'N' Shop; I'd looked them all over, twice. She hadn't pulled back into Dr. Hieler's lot, either. That much I could see from the Shop 'N' Shop parking lot. And I was getting thirsty.

I hoofed it into Shop 'N' Shop and puttered around until I found the drinking fountain. I stopped at the magazine racks and flipped through a few magazines. I walked down the candy aisle, wishing I had money for a chocolate fix. But it didn't take long for me to get bored.

Back outside I stood on tiptoe and craned my neck to see Dr. Hieler's parking lot. Mom's car still wasn't there, and now neither was Dr. Hieler's. I sighed and sat on the sidewalk, my back pressed against the front window of Shop 'N' Shop until the manager came and told me I had to move on; customers didn't like to see homeless people loitering in front of the store, he said. It makes them nervous, he said. "This ain't the City Union Mission, kid," he said.

So I walked a few doors down, looking for a good place to sit.

The cell phone store was jumping, and so was the place where Mom used to take me to get my hair cut when I was little. I stared in the windows, watching a little girl cry as her mother held her head so that the beautician could have a go at her blond baby locks. I gazed into the cell phone store, too, where everyone looked angry, including the employees.

Soon I was at the end of the strip and was just about to turn around and head back to Shop 'N' Shop, when I saw a door open on the side of the building. A giant-breasted woman wearing a denim smock busy with fabric paint and costume gems stepped out and shook a cloth into the air. Glitter flew everywhere when she shook it; she looked like Cinderella's fairy godmother behind the cloud of all that glitter.

She saw me watching her and smiled at me.

"Sometimes we have a spill," she said brightly, and disappeared back inside, pulling the glittery cloth in with her.

I'll admit it, curiosity got me. I wanted to know what kind of spill would look so glorious, so shiny. Spills are usually ugly and messy, not beautiful.

As soon as the door closed behind me I could feel the whole world shut out. Inside, the place was crammed, dark, and smelled like church on Easter Sunday. There were rows and rows of ceiling-high shelves nearly toppling under the weight of plaster busts, ceramic bowls, wooden trunks. Baskets, pots, interestingly shaped cardboard boxes. I wandered down one of the aisles, feeling dwarfed.

At the end of the aisle I was dumped into a clearing and I gasped. There were easels everywhere, at least a dozen of them, and a long table covered with newspapers next to an eastward-facing window. All around were baskets and boxes of supplies — paints, cloth, ribbons, lumps of clay, pens.

The denim-smocked lady that I'd seen outside was perched on a stool in front of an easel, stroking wide purple stripes across a canvas.

"I think the morning sun is most inspiring, don't you?" she said without turning around.

I didn't answer.

"Of course, at this time of day all the people in that grocery store are getting the brilliant light. But I . . ." she raised her paintbrush and poked the air with it. "I get the most inspiring sun of the day. They can have their sunset. It's the sunrise that gets people's attention. Rebirth always does."

I didn't know what to say. I wasn't even entirely sure she was talking to me. She still had her back turned to me and was working so intently on her painting I'd wondered if maybe she was talking to herself.

I was rooted to the spot anyway, not sure where to look

first. I wanted to touch things — run my fingers along plaster vases and smell the insides of boxes and squish my hands into a lump of clay — and was afraid if I moved, even moved my lips, I'd give in to my whim and be lost in this labyrinth of un-creation forever.

She added a few dabs of purple in the corners of her canvas, then got off her stool and stood back, admiring her work.

"There!" she said. "Perfect." She placed her palette on the stool and balanced the paintbrush across it, and then, finally, turned to face me. "What do you think?" she asked. "Too much purple?" She turned and studied it some more. "Never too much purple," she muttered. "The world needs more purple. More and more, dontcha know."

"I like purple," I said.

She clapped her hands twice. "Well, then!" she said. "That settles it! Tea?" She bustled behind the cash register and I could hear china clattering around. "How do you take it?" she asked, her voice muffled.

"Um," I said, shuffling forward. "I . . . I can't. I have to get back outside. My mom."

Her head popped up — a lock of frosted brown hair had come forward over her forehead. "Oh! And I was hoping to get some company today. This place always seems so abandoned after my classes leave. Too quiet. Great for mousies, not for Bea, that's me." She sipped out of a tiny teacup with rabbits printed on the front of it — a teacup from a child's tea set. She held out her pinky while she drank.

"You teach classes here?" I asked.

"Oh yes," she said. She came around the counter with a flourish. "I teach classes. Lots and lots of classes. Pottery, painting, macramé, you name it, I teach it."

I moved to my left just slightly and pushed a finger into a bucket of wooden beads.

"Can anyone take a class?"

She frowned. "No," she answered, staring at my hand in the bead bucket. I pulled it out with a jerk and two beads fell, danced across the floor. She smiled when I blushed, as if my embarrassment were endearing to her. "Oh no, I don't teach just anyone. Some teach me."

I was just about to leave when she reached out and grabbed my hand. She flipped it palm-up and studied it, her penciled-on eyebrows shooting up into her nest of hair. "Oh!" she exclaimed. "Oh!"

I tried to pull my hand back, but didn't put much oomph behind it. As weirded-out as I was getting from her touching me, I wanted to know what her "oh's" were about.

"I should go," I said, but she ignored me.

"Well, I can spot another artist anywhere. And you are one, yes? Of course you are. You like purple!" She turned and clasped my hand harder, pulling me behind her. She took me to the canvas she'd just been working on. With her free hand she picked up the palette and brush on the stool and pointed to it. "Sit," she said.

"I really think I should . . ."

"Oh, do sit! The stool doesn't like it when its invitations go unnoticed."

I sat.

She handed me the paintbrush. "Paint," she said. "Go on."

I stared at her. "On this? On your picture?"

"Pictures are taken by photographers. This is a painting. So paint it." I stared at her a beat longer. She pushed my hand toward the canvas. "Go on."

Slowly I dipped the brush into the black paint and made a stripe across the canvas, perpendicular to the purple.

"Hmmm," she said, and then, "Ohhhh."

The best way I can describe the feeling was that it was miraculous. Or maybe soulful. Or maybe both. I don't know. All I know is that I couldn't stop at that one line or the next splotch or the tree-like dots I made along one border. And all I know is that I felt faraway when I was doing it and that I could barely hear Bea's little exclamations behind me, her humming, her talking in baby voices to the colors I dipped into ("Oh, yes, it's your turn, ochre! Does wittle cornfwower want a chance?").

Before I knew it I was ripped out of my reverie by a buzzing in the front pocket of my jeans — my cell phone startling me away from the canvas, which suddenly just looked like a canvas again.

"Oh, dratted technology," Bea muttered as I answered. "Why can't we communicate by carrier pigeons anymore?

Beautiful feathers with a lovely note attached. I could use some pigeon feathers around here. Or peacock. Oh yes, peacock! Only nobody ever communicated by peacock, I don't think . . ."

"Where are you?" Mom's voice bleated on the other end of the phone. "I've been worried sick — no Dr. Hieler, no you. For God's sake, Valerie, why can't you just stay put like I asked you to? Do you know where my mind was going?"

"I'll be right there," I mumbled into the phone. I got up from the stool as I shoved the phone back into my pocket. "Sorry," I said to Bea. "My mom . . ."

She swatted the air with one hand, picking up a broom with the other, making a beeline for a pile of sawdust under a woodworking table by the far wall. "Never be sorry about a mother," she answered. "Be sorry for a mother, yes, but about one, most certainly not. Mothers almost always love purple. I should know — I had a very purplish mother."

I scurried down the aisle I'd come in through — feeling like I was fleeing a dark and mystical forest — and had just about reached the door when Bea's voice floated across the store.

"I do hope I'll see you back next weekend, Valerie."

I smiled and plunged outside. It wasn't until I'd ducked into Mom's car, breathless and sweaty from hurry and exhilaration, that I'd remembered I'd never told Bea my name at all.

21

Lunch was some sort of petrified Mexican pizza, which was just fitting for a Monday, if you asked me. I felt like petrified pizza on most Mondays too, being forced out of my little cocoon of happiness in my bedroom and into the spotlight of Garvin High.

Other than Saturday morning, my weekend had been blissfully uneventful. Mom and Dad weren't speaking for whatever reason, and Frankie was off at some church retreat with a friend. Not that our family ever went to church, something that was brought up time and again in the media right after the shooting, but apparently there were a couple girls that went to his friend's church and Frankie was determined to get some time alone with one of them. Truth be told, if Frankie could get his hands on a girl at some point during the weekend, he'd do it without thinking twice — church retreat or not — which I thought was so wrong, but at least trying to get to third base at a church retreat kept him from having to endure Mom and Dad's cold war at home.

I could endure it just fine by staying in my room. Not like my parents expected anything different from me. They didn't even ask me to come down for dinner anymore. I'm guessing they probably didn't even have dinner. I just crept down when I figured everyone was off doing their own thing and rummaged something out of the fridge, ferreting it back up to my room like a raccoon with garbage can spoils.

Once, Saturday evening, I crept down into the kitchen after hearing the front door close only to find Dad at the table, hovering over a bowl of cereal.

"Oh," I said. "I thought you guys were both gone."

"Your mother went to some support group," he said, staring straight into his bowl. "There's nothing to eat in this goddamn house," he said. "Unless you like cereal."

I peered into the refrigerator. He was right. Other than a carton of milk and some ketchup, a small bowl of leftover green beans and a half dozen eggs, there wasn't much to be had. "Cereal's okay," I said, pulling down a box from the top of the refrigerator.

"It's goddamn stale," he said.

I stared at him. His eyes looked red-rimmed, his face unshaven. His hands looked rough and shaky and I realized it had been so long since I'd looked at Dad, I hadn't even noticed how much he'd aged lately. He looked old. Spent.

"Cereal's okay," I repeated, more softly now, grabbing a bowl out of the cupboard.

I poured my cereal into the bowl and sloshed some milk into it. Dad ate silently. As I was leaving the room, he said, "Everything in this house is goddamn stale."

I stopped, one foot on the bottom step. "Did you and Mom fight again or something?"

"What would be the point of that?" he responded.

"You . . . you want me to order a pizza or something? For dinner, I mean?"

"What would be the point of that?" he repeated. Seemed like he was right, so I just crept back up the stairs to my room and listened to the radio while I ate my cereal. He was right — it was stale.

I had slapped the petrified pizza onto my tray and was spooning some slimy canned fruit cocktail into the square next to it when I heard Mr. Angerson's voice just over my shoulder.

"Not planning to eat that in the hallway, are you?" he asked.

"Yeah, I guess I was," I said, going about my business. "I like the hallway."

"That's not what I was hoping to hear. Should I go ahead and line up a teacher for Saturday detention?"

I turned and leveled my stare at him, using every ounce

of determination that I had left. Angerson didn't even bother to try to understand. "I guess so."

Stacey, who'd been in line just ahead of me, took her tray and ducked away, scurrying toward her table. I could see her in my peripheral vision saying something to Duce and Mason and the gang. Their faces turned toward me. Duce was laughing.

"I'm not going to let you orchestrate another tragedy in this school, young lady," Mr. Angerson said to me, a little red coloring creeping up from under his tie to his chin. *So much for the medal and the letter and all that hero and forgiveness crap*, I thought. "There is a new school policy that no personal isolation is allowed in this school. Anyone who is caught regularly secluding herself from the student body will be carefully scrutinized. I hate to say but some extreme cases could be subject to expulsion. Are we clear?"

The line was moving around me and out the door now, I realized, and kids were staring as they went. Some of them had curious grins on their faces and were whispering to their friends about me.

"I never orchestrated anything," I answered. "And I'm not doing anything wrong now, either."

He pursed his lips and glared at me, the red creeping from his chin up his cheeks. "I would like you to consider your options," he said. "As a personal favor to the survivors of this school."

He let the word "survivors" drop on me like a bomb and

it worked. I felt shaken by it. Felt like he said the word extra loud and that everyone had heard it. He turned and walked away and after a minute I turned back to the fruit cocktail. I loaded more of it onto my tray with shaky hands, even though my stomach suddenly felt very full.

I paid for my food and carried my tray out into the main part of the Commons. I felt like everyone was staring at me, like a bunch of rabbits caught in the middle of the night by back porch lights. But I looked forward, only forward, and headed out into the hallway.

I could hear Angerson just inside the cafeteria talking to some boys about where French fries belonged and where they didn't, and steeled myself for another face-off when I heard footsteps coming around the corner.

"You sure you want to do this?" he asked, as I sunk to the floor, carefully balancing my tray on my lap.

I opened my mouth to answer, but was interrupted as a bustle of motion burst into the hallway. Jessica Campbell, holding her lunch tray, whisked around Angerson and slid to the floor next to me. Her tray rattled against the linoleum as she shrugged out of her backpack.

"Hi, Mr. Angerson," she said brightly. "Sorry I'm late, Valerie."

"Jessica," he said, one of those statements that sounds like a question. "What are you doing?"

She shook her milk carton, opened it. "Having lunch with Valerie," she answered. "We've got some Student Council stuff to talk about. I figured this would be the best way to talk without getting interrupted. It's so loud in there. Can't hear yourself think."

Mr. Angerson looked like he wanted to punch a hole in something. He stood around for a minute, then pretended he saw something alarming going on in the Commons and scurried off to "break it up."

Jessica giggled softly after he left.

"What are you doing?" I asked.

"Having lunch," she said, taking a bite of her pizza. She made a face. "God, it's petrified."

I smiled in spite of myself. I picked up my pizza and took a bite. We ate silently, side by side. "Thanks," I said around a mouthful of pizza. "He's totally looking for a reason to expel me."

Jessica waved her hand at me. "Angerson's such an ass," she answered, and then laughed as I opened my notebook and drew a picture of a bare butt wearing a suit and tie.

22

[From the Garvin County Sun-Tribune,

May 3, 2008, Reporter Angela Dash]

Abby Dempsey, 17 — As Student Council Vice President, Dempsey was manning a fundraising table selling doughnuts. She was shot twice in the throat. Police believe that the bullets were stray, intended for a student in line approximately three feet to Dempsey's left. Dempsey's parents had no comment for reporters, and are said by friends of the family to be "grieving deeply for the loss of their only child."

*   *   *

Mom called and left a message on my cell phone telling me she had a meeting and couldn't come pick me up. My first reaction was outrage that she would expect me to ride the bus after everything that had happened. Like I could just flop down in a seat beside Christy Bruter's posse now and everything would go fine. *How could she?* I thought to myself. *How could she throw me to the wolves like that?*

I guess it goes without saying that I wasn't going to ride the bus home, whether Mom was driving me or not. Truthfully, my house was only about five miles away and I'd walked the route more than once. But that was back when both of my legs were normal. I doubted my ability to do it now, sure that halfway there my thigh would begin throbbing and force me to sit down and wait for the nearest predator to whisk me away.

But I could probably make it a mile or so, I figured, and Dad's office was not much farther than that. True, getting a ride from Dad was definitely not top on my list. Probably not any higher up than giving me a ride was on his. But it would be better than trying to avoid the drama on a school bus any day.

There was once a time when I was embarrassed that Dad's office wasn't more imposing. Here he was, supposedly this big-shot lawyer, and he was in a tiny brick "satellite office," which, if you asked me, was just another way of saying "hole in the wall in the suburbs." But today I was glad he worked in a hole in the wall not far from school, because the October sun did nothing to warm up the air and within just a few blocks of walking I was beginning to be sorry I hadn't taken the bus after all.

I'd only been to Dad's office a couple times before; he didn't exactly put out a welcome mat for his family to show up at work. He liked to pretend it was that he didn't want us exposed to the, as he called them, "lowlifes" he represented. But I think the truth was that Dad's office was his escape from the family. If we started showing up there, what would be the point of him always being at work?

My leg felt tight and I knew I was lurching along like a horror movie monster by the time I opened the big double glass door set in the brick of Dad's office. I felt glad to have made it.

Warm air settled around me and I stood in the entryway rubbing my thigh for a minute before walking into the office itself. I could smell microwave popcorn, buoyed on top of the air and snaking around me, and I felt hunger twist inside of me. I followed the scent through the vestibule and around the corner to the waiting area.

Dad's secretary blinked at me from behind her desk. I couldn't remember her name. I'd only met her once before, at some family picnic the head office had sponsored a summer or two ago, and thought it was Britni or Brenna or something young and trendy like that. I did remember, though, that she was only twenty-four and had the most incredibly shiny straight sheath of cocoa-colored hair that hung down her back like a superhero cape and these big cow eyes that blinked slowly and housed giant trusting pupils ringed with the color I can best describe as spring green. I remembered her being cute and shy and laughing longer than anyone else every time my dad told one of his stupid corny jokes.

"Oh," she said, a blush rising to her cheeks. "Valerie." It was a statement. She didn't smile. She gulped — actually gulped like they do in the movies — and I imagined her reaching for a red security button under the desk just in case I should pull a gun or something.

"Hi," I said. "Is my dad here? I need a ride."

She pushed away from her desk in her rolling chair. "He's on a conference c —" she began, but she couldn't finish because Dad's door flung open at just that moment.

"Hey, sweetheart, could you pull the Santosh file . . . ?" he was saying, nose down in a pile of paperwork, reading. He walked around the back of Britni/Brenna's chair. She sat motionless, except for the color that crept up her face. Dad's hand landed familiarly on her shoulder as he walked by, giving it a soft squeeze, a gesture I hadn't seen him give to my mother in . . . forever. Britni/Brenna ducked her head and closed her eyes. "What's wrong, baby? You seem tense —" Dad started, finally looking up, but he stopped when his eyes landed on me.

His hand jumped from Britni/Brenna's shoulder and back up to the paperwork he was holding. The gesture was subtle, unassuming, almost so much so that I wondered if I'd seen what I thought I'd seen after all. I might have thought I was imagining things had my eyes not totally ac-

260

cidentally rested on Britni's/Brenna's face, which looked almost wet with a furious blush. Her eyes were trained only on the desk in front of her. She looked mortified.

"Valerie," Dad said. "What are you doing here?"

I tore my gaze away from Britni/Brenna. "I need a ride," I said. At least I think I said it. I'm not entirely sure because my lips were so numb. Britni/Brenna mumbled something and darted out of her chair toward the restroom. I could have guessed that she wouldn't come out again until after I'd left. "Mom um . . . Mom had a meeting."

"Oh," Dad said. Was I seeing things or was his face looking flushed too? "Oh, yeah. Sure. Okay. Give me a minute."

He stepped briskly back into his office and I could hear things shuffling around in there, drawers being shut, keys rattling. I stood rooted to my spot, beginning to wonder if I'd imagined the whole thing.

"Ready?" Dad asked. "I've got to get back, so let's move." All business. All Dad. I expected nothing less.

He opened the door, but I couldn't move.

"Is that why you and Mom hate each other?" I asked.

He looked like he considered pretending he didn't know what I was talking about. He cocked his head to the side and let the door close.

"You don't know what you think you know," he said. "Let's go home. It's really not your business."

"It's not because of me," I said. "It's not my fault that you and Mom hate each other. It's yours." And even though

261

I pretty much knew my parents weren't exactly in love before the shooting, this hit me like some great epiphany. And for whatever reason I felt worse than I had before. I guess I always thought that if it was just about me, when I left the house they would be in love and happy again. Now, with Britni/Brenna's beautiful flushed face in the picture, Mom and Dad would probably never be in love again. Suddenly all those fights they'd had over the years no longer seemed reparable. Suddenly I understood why I had clung to Nick like a life preserver — he not only understood crappy families, he understood crappy families that would never be good again. There must have been a part of me that knew all along.

"Valerie, just let it go."

"All this time I've been beating myself up about making you and Mom hate each other and you were having an affair with your secretary. Oh my God, I'm such an idiot."

"No." He sighed, put his hand to his temple. "Your mother and I don't hate each other. You really don't know anything about my relationship with your mother. This isn't your business."

"So it's okay?" I asked, gesturing toward the bathroom door. "This is okay?" He probably thought, given the context of the conversation, that I meant whatever was going on between him and Britni/Brenna. But what I really meant was about the lying. He was lying about who he was, just like I had. And it was okay. But it so didn't feel okay. And I wondered how, given everything that had happened, he couldn't see why lying about who you are isn't okay.

"Please, Valerie, let's just get you home. I've got work to do."

"Does Mom know?"

He closed his eyes. "She has an idea. But, no, I haven't told her, if that's what you mean. And I'd appreciate it if you didn't go to her and say something when you really don't know anything."

"I've gotta go," I said, pushing past him and out the door. The cold air felt so much better going out than going in.

I listened hard for him as I walked down the sidewalk back the way I'd come. I waited for him to lean out the door and yell. *Stop, Valerie! No, you've got it all wrong, Valerie! I love your mother, Valerie! But what about your ride, Valerie?*

But he never did.

23

I walked back to school. I didn't know what else to do. I left Mom a voice mail message while I walked.

"Hey, Mom. I had to get help on a homework assignment and missed the bus," I lied. "I'll just wait for you to pick me up after your meeting."

When I got to school, I went inside and dropped my stuff by the giant trophy case that assailed visitors with glittering football trophies and track trophies and giant blown-up photos of coaches long gone from the school. Long gone from their glory days. Or just plain long gone.

I sat on the floor under the case and pulled out my notebook. I wanted to draw something, to get hold of my emotion with a picture. But I wasn't sure what to draw. As jumbled up as my mind was, it was just way too hard to see reality. I couldn't make my pencil scratch out the lines of Britni/Brenna's face. Couldn't make it curve into the contours of Dad's guilty eyes — his big secret blown up. Would he marry her? Would they have children together? I couldn't make myself imagine Dad holding some creamy-faced baby, cooing down at it, telling it he loved it. Taking it to baseball games. Living some life he'd probably consider his "real life," the one he deserved rather than the one he got.

I held the point of my pencil to the paper and started to draw — immediately the curve of a woman's seeded belly took form in profile. I sketched a fetus inside it, curled into itself, sucking a tiny thumb, cradling itself around an umbilical cord. And then I drew an identical curving line on the other side. A teardrop sliding down a narrow nose. My mother's eyes. A line of fury between them. Another teardrop, clinging to an eyelash, with my name written in it.

Distantly, I heard a locker clang shut and footsteps nearing me. I shut my notebook and pretended to be staring absently out the front doors of the school. My fingers curved around my notebook, which before had always been like a fun pair of eyeglasses that would allow me to reflect the world as it really was, but now felt like a big shameful secret.

"Oh, hey." Jessica Campbell was striding toward me.

"Hey," I answered.

Jessica stopped in front of me and set down her backpack. She peered out the front doors. She sighed and sat crosslegged next to her backpack, just a couple feet from me. "Waiting on Meghan," she said, as if to justify why she might be sitting in the hallway next to me if she wasn't saving me from Angerson. "She's retaking her German test. I told her I'd give her a ride home." She cleared her throat awkwardly. "Do you need a ride? I can take you, too, if you can wait for Meghan. She shouldn't take too much longer."

I shook my head. "My mom's coming," I said. "She'll probably be here pretty soon." And then I added, "Thanks."

"No problem," she muttered, and cleared her throat again.

Another locker shut somewhere down the science hall and our heads turned toward the sound of a couple kids talking. Their voices faded and we heard the sound of a wooden door shutting, cutting their conversation off completely.

"You coming to the StuCo meeting tomorrow?" Jessica asked. "We're going to go over progress on the memorial project."

"Oh," I said. "I figured that meeting was just a one-time thing. I thought . . . well, I kind of ditched you guys last time. Plus, you know, I thought you had to be voted in to be a member of Student Council. Something tells me not too many people would vote me in."

She got a funny look on her face and then laughed a shrill, nervous little laugh. "Yeah, probably not," she said. "But I keep telling you it's okay. Everyone understands that you're going to be a part of the project. It's cool."

I arched one eyebrow and gave her an *I doubt it* look. She laughed again, this time a little more breathy and relaxed. "What? It is!" she said.

I couldn't help myself. I laughed, too. Pretty soon we were both cracking up, leaning our heads against the brick wall behind us, the tension sliding off of us.

"Listen," I said, studying the graffiti on the bottom of the trophy case above my head. "I appreciate what you're doing, but I don't want people to start leaving StuCo because of me."

"Not everyone was against it, you know. Some people thought the idea was great from the beginning."

"Yeah, like Meghan, I'll bet," I said. "She wants to be my best friend, you know. Tomorrow we're going to dress alike. Be twinkies."

We looked at each other for a beat and laughed again.

"Not exactly," Jessica said. "But she came around. I can be very persuasive." She grinned at me wickedly and wiggled her eyebrows. "Seriously. Don't worry about Meghan. She'll get cool with it. We need you to be involved. *I* need you to be involved. You're smart and you're, like, really creative. We need that. Please?"

A door opened at the far end of the hallway and Meghan stepped out. Jessica gathered her backpack and coat together. She shrugged. "You didn't shoot anybody," she said. "They don't have any reason to hate you. That's what I keep telling them." She stood up and shouldered her backpack. "See you tomorrow, then?"

"Okay," I said. She started to walk toward Meghan.

I had a sudden flash of clarity. What was it Detective Panzella had said about the girl who helped clear me? *She was blond. Tall. A junior. Kept repeating, "She didn't shoot anybody . . ."*

"Jessica?" I called. She turned around. "Um, thanks."

"No problem," she said. "Just be there, okay?"

A few minutes later Mom pulled up in front of the school and honked. I hobbled out to the car and slid in. Mom looked grim behind the wheel.

"I can't believe you missed the bus," she said. I recognized the voice — her annoyed and frustrated voice. The one she often used when coming home from work.

"Sorry," I said. "I had to get help with an assignment."

"Why didn't you just get a ride with your dad?"

The question struck me like a finger poke to the chest. I could feel my heart start to speed up. Could feel my stomach roll around, trying on the truth for size. Could hear the rational side of me screaming into my ear, *She needs to know! She deserves to know!*

"Dad was busy with a client," I lied. "I would've had to wait just as long for him."

I guess I should have felt guilty for lying to Mom about what I knew. But then again Dad didn't shoot anybody, either.

24

The following Saturday I'd begged Mom to take me over to Bea's studio after our session with Dr. Hieler.

"I don't know, Valerie," Mom said, a crease between her eyebrows. "Art classes? I've never even heard of this woman before. I didn't even know an art studio was there. Are you sure it's safe?"

I rolled my eyes. Mom had been in a mood for days. It almost seemed like the more I tried to move on with my life, the less she trusted me. "Yes, of course it's safe. She's just an artist, Mom. C'mon, can't you just let me do this one thing? You can go grocery shopping at Shop 'N' Shop while I'm there."

"I don't know."

"Please? Mom, c'mon, you're always saying you want me to do something normal. Art classes are normal."

She sighed. "Okay, but I'm coming in with you. I want to check this place out. Last time I just let you run around and do whatever you wanted, you got involved with Nick Levil, and look where that got us."

"So you remind me every day," I muttered, rolling my eyes. I pushed my thumb into the dent in my thigh to keep myself from blowing up at her. With the mood she'd been in, she'd probably change her mind about taking me to Bea's.

We walked into Bea's together and I could feel Mom hesitate at the door, once the musty and heavy air surrounded us.

"What is this place?" she said in a low voice.

"Shhh," I hissed, although I wasn't exactly sure why I wanted her to be quiet. Maybe because I was afraid that Bea would hear her and tell me I couldn't come to classes after all. That Mom's negative energy would ruin the amazing purple morning light.

I walked down the aisle toward the back, where I could hear a tinkling of music — bells tapping out rhythmically — and a soft murmuring of voices. I could see backs of artists perched on the stools in front of canvases. There was an elderly lady working with paper off to one side, folding and creasing it into intricate animals and shapes, and a little boy playing with a pair of Matchbox cars under one of the low tables. Bea was bent over a mirror, around which she was placing and pasting an elaborate design of seashells. I stopped at the end of the aisle, suddenly sure that I'd misunderstood

Bea before and that I shouldn't be here. *She was being nice. She didn't really want me here*, I thought. *I should go.*

But before I could even complete that last thought, Bea had straightened and was smiling at me, her hair teased into a glittery mound on top of her head, with ribbons and little baubles hanging from it.

"Valerie," she said, spreading her arms out wide. "My purple Valerie!" She clapped her hands twice. "You've come back. I was waiting for you."

I nodded. "I was hoping I could, er . . . take some art classes from you. Painting."

She was moving toward us, then, but was completely ignoring me. Her grin had turned to a toothy smile as she enveloped my mother. I could see Mom's body go stiff under the embrace of Bea, and then, as Bea whispered for a long time in Mom's ear, her body relaxed. When Bea pulled away again, Mom's scowl was gone, replaced by a look of curiosity. Bea was strange, no doubt about it. She was just the kind of person Mom would normally consider a kook, but Bea's eccentricity fit her so well that, even in a mood, Mom seemed to be disarmed by it.

"It's so nice to meet you," Bea said to Mom. Mom nodded, swallowed, but said nothing back. "Of course you'll paint with us, Valerie. I've got an easel right over there for you."

"How much will it cost?" Mom asked, opening her purse and digging around inside.

Bea waved her hands in the air. "Costs patience and creativity, mostly. Also time and practice. And self-acceptance. But you won't find any of those things in your purse."

Mom froze, looked up at Bea curiously, then snapped her purse shut. "I'll be at Shop 'N' Shop. You have one hour," she said to me. "Just one."

"One's my favorite number," Bea giggled. "The word *won* being the past tense of *win*, and we can all say at the end of the day that we've won once again, can't we? Some days making it to the end of the day is quite the victory."

Mom said nothing in response, just slowly and deliberately picked her way back down the aisle. I could feel the swoosh of parking lot air waft into the studio as Mom left the building.

One. Won. One hour. Just one. Won. I tossed the words around in my head.

I turned to Bea. "I'd like to paint," I said. "I need to paint."

"Then you, of course, will paint. You've been painting since this morning when you first got up." She tapped her temple with her finger. "Up here. You've been painting and painting. Using lots of purple right here. You have the painting complete. All you need to do is put it on canvas."

She led me to a stool and I sat, mesmerized by the paintings of the artists sitting, silently working, in front of me. A lady painting a snowy landscape, another weaving rusty red colors over a barn she'd painstakingly drawn with pencil. A man painting a military airplane, using a photograph taped to the upper-left-hand corner of the easel for reference. Bea bustled over to a nearby cart and came back with a palette and brush for me.

"Now," she said, "You'll want to paint your grays first, for shadowing. You'll probably get no further than that today. You'll need to give it some time to dry before you splash on your glorious colors." She opened a jar and poured some brown jelly-like stuff onto the palette next to the colors. "And don't forget to mix your paints with this. It'll help them dry faster."

I nodded, picked up the brush, and began painting. No sketching, no reference pictures. Just the picture in my mind — Dr. Hieler as I really saw him. There would be few shadows in this picture. No darkness.

"Hmmm," said Bea over my shoulder. "Oh my, yes." And then she moved to another part of the studio. I could hear her whispering gentle instruction to the other artists, giving tender support. At one point she burst into loud laughter when an artist told her he'd stuffed his cell phone in the blender that morning and turned it on the puree setting. But I couldn't look at her. I couldn't look up at all, not until the outside air brushed the back of my neck again and I heard Mom's voice, so staccato it didn't belong in the studio at all, float up the aisle at me: "Time's up, Valerie."

When I looked up, I was surprised to see that Bea was standing next to me with her hand on my shoulder. "Time's never up," she whispered, not looking at me, but at my canvas. "Just like there's always time for pain, there's always time for healing. Of course there is."

25

I had just turned the corner of the science hall when Meghan shouted out my name and jogged up behind me. I slowed, glanced worriedly in the direction of Mrs. Stone's room, where the StuCo meeting would be starting in just a few minutes, and reluctantly stopped.

"Hey, Valerie, wait up," Meghan yelled, her hair bouncing as she rushed toward me. "I want to talk to you."

Normally I would have definitely kept walking. Meghan had made it excruciatingly clear that she thought I was responsible for what happened, and I could guess that anything she'd have to say to me wouldn't be good.

But I didn't have anywhere else to turn. The hallways were empty at this time of day at this end of the building.

All the athletes were down in the field house. Everyone else had already caught their rides home.

"Hey," she breathed again when she caught up to me. "Going to the StuCo meeting?"

"Yeah," I answered uncertainly, crossing my arms over my chest defensively. "Jessica asked me to."

"Cool, I'll walk with," Meghan said. I looked at her for a second longer and then slowly began walking toward Mrs. Stone's room. After a few steps she said, "I like your idea about the time capsule. It's gonna be pretty cool."

"Thanks," I said and we walked some more. I bit my lip, considered, then said, "No offense or anything, but why are you walking with me?"

Meghan tilted her head to the side, seeming to consider this. "Truth? Jessica told me I had to be nice to you. Well, not really told me, but, you know . . . she got kind of mad at me for shutting you out and we had this fight about it. We made up and everything, but I decided she's right. I can at least try." She shrugged. "You don't act mean or anything. Mostly you're just quiet."

"I don't usually know what to say," I said. "I've always been quiet. It's just not been very noticeable before, I guess."

She glanced at me. "Yeah, you're probably right," she said.

We could see Mrs. Stone's room up ahead. A light was on inside and we could hear voices spilling out the doorway.

Mrs. Stone's voice hovering above them; a few laughs puncturing the air. We stopped.

"I wanted to ask you something," Meghan said. "Um . . . somebody told me my name was on the Hate List. And I was just wondering, you know . . . why? I mean, a lot of people are talking about how the victims deserved what they got and stuff because they like, bullied Nick, but I didn't even really know you guys. I never even talked to him."

I pressed my lips together and wished more than anything that I was already in Mrs. Stone's room, with Jessica as my buffer. Meghan was right about one thing — we didn't really know her all that well before the shooting. We'd never really talked to her or had a gripe about her personally. But we felt like we knew her well enough, given who she hung out with.

I remembered the day Meghan's name was added to the list.

Nick and I had been eating lunch when Chris Summer and his stooge friends walked past our table, practically owning the Commons, just like always.

"Hey, freak," Chris said. "Hold this for me." He pulled a wad of gum out of his mouth and dropped it in Nick's mashed potatoes. His buddies burst out laughing, hands on their chests, stumbling around like they were drunk.

"Oh man, that's disgusting . . ."

"Good one, man . . ."

"Enjoy those potatoes, freak . . ."

They ambled over to their table, taking their laughter with them. I could see the anger boil up in Nick, his eyes darkening and dulling to black holes, his jaw clenched. It was different than he'd been that day at the movies. Then he'd looked sad, defeated. Now he looked pissed. He started to push himself away from the table.

"Don't," I said, putting my hand on his shoulder. Nick had been busted for fighting twice already that month and Angerson was threatening suspension. "They aren't worth the time. Here, just eat mine." I pushed my lunch tray toward him. "I don't like potatoes anyway."

He froze, his nostrils flaring, his palms pressed flat against the table. He took a few deep breaths and lowered himself back into his seat. "No," he said softly, pushing my tray back toward me. "I'm not hungry."

We ate the rest of our lunch in silence, me flicking glances at Chris Summer's table behind us. I memorized the kids sitting there — Meghan Norris among them — all practically bowing to Chris like he was some kind of god. And when I got home that night, I opened my book and wrote each of their names down one by one.

Seemed really justified at the time. I hated them all so much for what they were doing to Nick, to me, to us. But now, standing in the hallway outside Mrs. Stone's classroom, everything felt different. Standing in the hallway outside Mrs. Stone's room, Meghan wasn't so horrible. She was just another confused person trying to get it right. Just like me.

"It wasn't about you," I told Meghan honestly. "It was Chris. You were sitting with him at lunch one time . . ." I trailed off, realizing that no matter how mad Nick and I had been that day, no matter how mean Chris had been to Nick, given everything that had happened, it just wouldn't make sense to her. It barely made sense to me anymore. "It was stupid. No, it was wrong."

Fortunately, Jessica stuck her head around the doorjamb of Mrs. Stone's room and peered out at us.

"Oh, hey," she said. "I thought I heard voices. C'mon, we're about to start."

She disappeared back into the room. Meghan and I stood out in the hallway awkwardly for a few minutes.

"Well," she said at last, "I guess it doesn't matter anymore anyway, right?" She smiled. It was forced, but not fake. I appreciated that much, at least.

"I guess not," I said.

"C'mon. If we don't get in there, Jess'll start throwing a fit."

We walked into Mrs. Stone's room and for the first time I did it without feeling like running away.

26

[*FROM THE GARVIN COUNTY SUN-TRIBUNE,*
MAY 3, 2008, REPORTER ANGELA DASH]
Nick Levil, 17 — Although witnesses and police investigation have positively identified Nick Levil, a junior, as the shooter, what remains unclear is his motivation for the crime. "He was kind of out there, but I wouldn't call him a loner or anything," junior Stacey Brinks told reporters. "He had a girlfriend and lots of other friends, too. He talked about suicide sometimes — a lot, actually — but he never said anything about killing anyone else. At least not to us he didn't. Maybe Valerie knew, but we didn't."

Police have been able, with the aid of security videos, to track the movements of Levil on the morning of

279

May 2nd, and have pieced together a clear picture of what took place in the cafeteria that day. After opening fire on a lunchroom packed with students, mostly upperclassmen, Levil shot his girlfriend, Valerie Leftman, in the leg and then turned the gun on himself. Portions of the videos, which show the grisly ending to his rampage, have been aired online and on some news channels, causing an uproar among Levil's family.

"My son may have been the shooter, but he's still a victim," Levil's mother told reporters. "Damn those media sharks who think that something like this isn't already tearing my family apart. Do they think this won't rip our hearts out to see our son put a bullet through his brain time and time again?"

Levil's stepfather added tearfully, "Our son is dead, too. Please don't forget that."

* * *

I don't know how it happened, but somehow I must have gotten used to being friends with Jessica Campbell. The end of the semester came and went and had Dr. Hieler not done this big gloating thing at one of our sessions, I might have never even noticed.

"I told you you'd make it through the semester," he'd said. "Damn, I'm good at this!"

"Don't get too full of yourself," I'd teased. "Nobody

said I'm going back after winter break. How do you know I'm not still going to transfer?"

But I did go back after winter break and the nerves that had accompanied me the first day of school were much less debilitating when I plowed through the doors in January.

People seemed to be generally getting used to the idea that I was going to be around, which seemed to be helped by the fact that Jessica and I sat together at lunch every day.

And I still had the Student Council meetings. I was beginning to participate more, even helping decorate the room for Mrs. Stone's birthday. We were going to have a special meeting — about five minutes of working on the memorial project and the rest of the time dedicated to eating cake and giving Mrs. Stone grief about being old. It was going to be a surprise, and we were working fast to get the decorating finished before Mrs. Stone came back in from bus duty.

"I'm so going to the JT concert," Jessica said. She leaned forward in her chair and it tilted under her. She wobbled for a minute, steadied herself, and hiked herself further up on her tiptoes. She tore a piece of masking tape off the roll and stuck the blue streamer in her hand on the brick of the school wall. "You going?"

"No, my mom won't let me," Meghan said. She was holding the other end of the piece of streamer. Jessica tossed her the roll of tape. Meghan reached to catch it and dropped her end of the streamer. "Dang it!"

"I've got it," I said. I hobbled over and grabbed the streamer, twisted it the way Meghan had it before, and handed it up to her.

"Thanks," she said. She stood up on her toes and secured it to the wall. While she was doing that, Jessica was busy blowing up a balloon to tape in the center of the streamer.

I plucked a balloon out of the bag on the desk behind me and started blowing it up, too. Behind me, some of the others were laying out a tablecloth and the cake. Josh had hurried down to the cafeteria to get the drinks Jessica's mom had brought in earlier that day.

"Wish *I* could go," Meghan said. "I love Justin Timberlake."

"God, he's so hot, isn't he?" Jessica added.

Meghan sighed deeply. "My mom won't let me go anywhere these days. She's so paranoid. My dad says to just let it go. But now she's talking about making me go to community college next year because she can't stand the idea of me going off to college. Like I'll be in another school shooting or something. She needs therapy."

I tied the balloon I was blowing and pulled another out of the bag.

"Well, my dad got me tickets from some guy at work," Jessica said. "He came home and was all, 'Hey, Jess, you ever heard of this singer, Dustin Timberland? Is he country or something?'" We laughed. "And I was like, 'Heck yes, I've heard of Justin Timberlake!' and he was all, 'Well I've got two tickets to go and you can have 'em but you've got to go with Roddy.' So my brother's going to come home from KU that weekend and take me, which I guess is okay. Roddy's usually pretty cool."

"No way would my parents let me go with Troy," Meghan said. "He hangs out with those losers, like Duce Barnes. I'd probably get shot with Troy along." Her face turned kind of pink and she flicked a look down at me.

I knew Troy. Sometimes Troy had hung out with Duce when Nick wasn't around. Troy had graduated from Garvin about three years ago and was sort of legendary around school as a hothead. Once he'd gotten in trouble for punching dents down an entire row of lockers. Meghan looked up to her brother and adored him. But she was nothing like him.

Nobody said anything for a minute. I tied the balloon I'd been working on and let it fall to the floor. I turned and plucked another one out of the bag and stuck it in my mouth.

"Are you going to the concert, Valerie?" Meghan asked.

I cleared my throat. I still didn't feel entirely comfortable with Meghan and I guessed the feeling was mutual. "Um," I said, testing out my voice, which sounded entirely too casual for how I felt. "I don't think so. I'm pretty much grounded for life."

"Why?" she asked. Jessica hopped down from her chair and started helping me with the balloons.

"Well. The shooting," I answered. I felt my face burning.

Meghan gave me a curious look, then said, "But it's not like that was your fault. You got shot."

"Yeah, I guess my parents don't really see it that way. They're all about my 'lack of judgment' right now."

Meghan made an *unh!* noise. "That's so unfair," she said quietly.

Jessica tied her balloon. "Have you asked them if you could go out anywhere?" she asked.

I shook my head. "I don't really have anywhere to go." I shrugged. The kids in the back were quietly bickering over the placement of the birthday candles.

"Jess, you should invite her to Alex's party," Meghan said. She jumped down off the chair and stood back to admire the streamer. "How's that look?"

Jessica put her hands on her hips and studied the wall. "I think it's perfect. What do you think, Val?"

I stood. "Looks good to me."

We all blew up balloons for a few minutes and then Jessica said, "Meghan was talking about this party we're all going to on the twenty-fifth. It's a barn party. Have you ever been to one?"

I shook my head and tied my balloon.

"It's at Alex Gold's farm. His parents are going to be in Ireland for two weeks. It should be pretty wild."

"Last time I lost my shoes," Meghan added. "And Jamie Pembroke totally got puked on. Remember that?" She and Jessica laughed. "You should come, Val," Meghan added. "It's really a blast."

"Yeah, come with," Jessica said. She reached over and nudged my arm. "Everyone's going to crash at my house."

I pretended to think it over, to be excited about the invitation, but warning bells clanged so loudly in my head I could barely think. It was one thing to come to a StuCo meeting with Jessica. To sit in the hallway with her at lunch. It was totally another to go to a party full of her friends. I could only imagine what some of them might have to say about her bringing me there. I could only imagine what Nick might have to say about me going. There was no way I could handle it.

But Jessica was looking at me so earnestly, so openly, I couldn't turn her down without at least pretending like I'd asked. "Okay," I said. "I'll try."

Jessica beamed and even Meghan smiled a little. "Great!"

"What's this?" Mrs. Stone asked from the doorway. She was still shrugging out of her coat and her nose was red from the brisk wind that had come out of nowhere this morning.

"Surprise!" we all yelled in unison, and then the room erupted in hooting and cheers.

Mrs. Stone touched her chest and looked around the room, but she seemed to spend extra time looking at me, Jessica, and Meghan, as we laughed, standing next to one another, bumping shoulders and chattering.

"What a terrific surprise," she said, wiping the corners of her eyes.

27

"Sorry, girls, but you can't sit here anymore," Mr. Angerson said. "The builders will be coming and going
through here."

Jessica and I stood holding our lunch trays in front of us.

Builders had been in and out of the building all morning,
hammering and pounding and running loud machines that
made it totally difficult to concentrate on anything. They
were installing new doors on the classrooms — ones with
no windows — and replacing the glass on either side of
them with some sort of bulletproof stuff. The doors that
they were installing locked from the inside whenever they
were shut, which meant that if you had to use the restroom
during class you had to knock to be let back in. Of course,
it also made it so that we were sitting in a little fortress of

safety, just in case someone should make it into the building with a gun or a bomb or something.

"Okay," Jessica said. We looked at one another and then both turned and faced the cafeteria.

"C'mon," she said in her old Jessica the Commander voice that I remembered so well. "You can sit with me." She tossed her hair confidently over one shoulder and hitched up her chest, walking boldly through the crowd.

My feet felt cold and heavy, but I followed her anyway. She led me to what I'd always known as the SBRB Headquarters and the thought of it made me feel panicky.

"Hey guys!" Jessica said. She set her tray on the table and wrangled a couple of empty chairs in front of it. The chatter at the table instantly died.

"Hey, Jess," Meghan said. But her voice was very quiet, her face unsmiling. The moment at the StuCo meeting blowing up balloons together could have just as easily been a hallucination. "Hey, Val."

I tried to push my mouth up into a smile, but talking was definitely out of the question.

"I thought you sat in the hallway now," Josh said. "With *her*."

"Angerson put a stop to that, of course," Jessica said. She sat, then turned to me. "Come on, Val. Sit down. Nobody will mind."

Somebody made a *tch!* sound when she said that, but I didn't catch who.

I sat down, focusing only on the food on my tray, but I

287

knew there was no way I could eat. Suddenly the gravy looked like brown jelly and the meat looked like plastic. My stomach was turning around like crazy.

"Hey, Jess, you going to the barn party?" someone asked.

"Yeah, we both are."

"Both who?"

Jessica motioned to me with her fork. "I asked Val to spend the night with me that night."

"No way," Josh said in that big Josh voice.

"Yeah," Jessica said. "What's the problem with that?" I detected a hint of snotty in that voice — a sound I recognized all too well. How many times had I heard it leveled at me? *What are you looking at, Sister Death? Nice boots, Sister Death. As if I'd be talking to your loser friends, Sister Death. You got a problem? What's your problem? Is there a problem, Sister Death?* Only this time it wasn't directed at me, but at the friends she reigned over. I felt relieved and then immediately felt guilty for being relieved. At that moment I couldn't have told you who had changed more: Jessica Campbell or me.

"Actually I haven't asked my parents yet," I mumbled to Jessica. "I was going to ask this weekend."

She waved me off, her attention focused on the other end of the table. Her eyes were slits, daring her friends to say something to oppose me being there. She held her fork steadily in front of her. The mood at the table changed, turned uncomfortable.

Everyone was peering into their own trays and talk had

quieted. Several of them were muttering just loud enough for me to know that they were talking about me, but not what they were saying.

I did hear someone say: "Is she going to bring her notebook?" and another person laughed and answered, "Is she going to bring a date?"

It was too much. Stupid of me to think I could fit in here, even after all this time. Even with Jessica on my side. *See what's real*, that's what Dr. Hieler wanted me to do. *See what's really there.* Well, I could see what was really there now and none of it was good. It was all the same as it was before. Only before I would have written down their names on the Hate List and run to Nick for comfort. Now I was a different person and I had no idea what to do, other than run away.

"I forgot," I said, standing up and picking up my tray. "I have to turn in a report for English before sixth period or I'll have to take a zero on the assignment. Duh." I tried to laugh breezily, but my mouth felt dry and I was sure that when I talked, things in my throat clicked.

I got up and carried my tray to the dishwasher's window. I dumped the entire contents of my lunch into the trash bin and scurried out of the cafeteria, vaguely hearing Dr. Hieler's voice in my head — *If you keep losing weight, Val, your mom's going to be asking about anorexia again.* I power-walked directly to the girls' restroom in the Communication Arts wing and locked myself in the handicap stall. I stayed there until the bell rang, promising myself that there was no way in hell I would go to that party.

28

I was sitting on my bed, admiring the new hot pink polish I'd painted on my toenails. I hadn't painted my nails pink in so long I doubted the polish was still good. It was all crusty around the neck of the bottle and had separated into two layers — pink on bottom with clear on top. It had even seemed pretty congealed, so I'd added a few drops of fingernail polish remover to it and that seemed to do the trick.

Normally my mainstay was black. Or navy. Sometimes a hunter green or sick corpse-yellow. But once, a long time ago, it had been pink. Everything had been pink. I think I burned myself out on pink. And then burned myself out on black. I'm not sure.

All I'm really sure about was that I had finally given in to my curiosity and dragged the old box of fingernail polishes long since gone to the Pretty Pretty Princess Valerie in the Sky out from under the bathroom sink and set about painting my toenails hot pink. It wouldn't hurt anyone for my toes to be pink for a few days, right?

I was still waiting for them to dry — puffing out little breezes of air from my mouth without giving it any real effort — when there was a knock, real soft, at my door.

I leaned over and turned my stereo down. "Yuh?"

The door opened a crack and Dad stuck his head in. He grimaced in the general direction of the stereo, so I leaned over and flicked it off.

"Can we talk?" he asked.

I nodded. He and I hadn't spoken since the Britni/Brenna incident at his office a couple weeks ago.

He came into the room and picked his way across the floor like he was coming through a minefield. He pushed a pile of T-shirts out of the way with his foot. I noticed he was wearing shoes. Running shoes. And jeans, a polo shirt. His casual, but still going out, look.

He sat on the edge of my bed. He didn't say anything at first, just stared at my toenails. I curled them under instinctively and immediately was worried that I'd messed up my painting job. I let them uncurl. Only one was marred. I used my thumb to rub most of the polish off of it and then I stared at my foot, which suddenly looked so vulnerable and imperfect with the one toe ringed in hot pink polish but bare on the inside of the nail. Like I'd started but had forgotten to finish being beautiful.

"New color?" he asked, which I thought was a really odd question coming from a dad. Were dads supposed to notice fingernail polish on their daughters? I wasn't sure, but it wasn't something my dad would notice, and the very thought of it made me feel uneasy.

"No. Very old," I replied.

"Oh." He sat some more. "Listen, Val, about Briley . . ."

Briley, I thought. *Of course. Her name is Briley.*

"Dad," I started, but he held up a hand to stop me. I swallowed. Any sentence that began, *Listen, Val, about Briley . . .* was not going to be the start of a pleasant conversation. Of that I was sure.

"Just listen," he said. "Your mother . . ."

He paused. His mouth opened and closed a few times, as if he wasn't sure where to go from there. His hands sort of flopped around in his lap. His shoulders slumped.

"Dad, I'm not going to tell Mom. You don't have to do this," I started to say, but he interrupted.

"I do," he said. "I do."

I was quiet then, my toes getting cold. I stared at them hard, expecting the hot pink to change to purple or icy blue like a mood ring. Maybe corpse-yellow wasn't so much of a thing of the past after all. I began to wonder who was the imposter, the old Valerie or the new, something I felt over and over again after the shooting, as if I could change on a moment-by-moment basis.

"I told," he said finally. "I told her everything. Your mother."

I said nothing. I wasn't sure what to say. What could I say?

"She didn't take it well, of course. She's very angry. She's asked me to leave."

"Whoa," I breathed.

"If it makes any difference to you, I love Briley. I've loved Briley for a long time. We'll probably get married."

It made a difference. But probably not in the way he'd hoped. I thought with dark satisfaction that I finally had a "stepmonster." Somehow, within the context of my life, it fit. I felt a tug of regret — having a stepmonster would've been something else Nick and I would've had in common.

We sat there in silence for a while. I wondered what Dad was thinking, why he was sticking around. Was he waiting for absolution? For me to say it was okay that he did this? For me to make some sort of magnanimous statement about accepting Briley into my life?

"How long have you and . . . um . . . *she* . . . been to-gether?" I asked.

He pulled his eyes up to look straight into mine. It might have been the only time I ever looked my dad in the eye and I was surprised at how much depth I saw there. I guess I'd always seen Dad as one-dimensional. Never a thought that didn't include work. Never an emotion that wasn't impatience or anger.

"This happened long before the shooting." He gave a half-hearted chuckle. "In some ways the shooting brought your mother and me closer. Made it more difficult to leave her. I've broken Briley's heart a million times over the past several months. I was set to move in with her over the summer. We'd hoped to have been married by now. But the shooting . . ."

He, like so many others, left the sentence hanging after those words, as if they explained anything and everything all on their own. I knew what he meant, though, without him going on. The shooting changed everything. For everyone. Even for Briley, who had nothing to do with Garvin High.

"I couldn't leave Jenny alone after that. She's gone through so much. I respect your mother and I don't want to hurt her. I just don't love her. Not the way I love Briley."

"So you're going to do it," I said. "Leave, I mean."

He nodded slowly.

"Yeah," he said. "It's only right that I do. I have to."

I wanted there to be a part of me that raged against this. *No you don't*, I wanted to scream at him. *No, you can't!* But I couldn't do it. Because the truth was, and we both knew it, he'd gone long, long ago. I'd just made him stick around when he really wanted to be somewhere else. In his own weird way he was another victim of the shooting. One of the ones who couldn't get away.

"Are you mad?" he asked, which I thought was a really strange question.

"Yes," I said. And I was. It's just that I wasn't so sure I was mad at him. But I don't think he needed to hear that part. I don't think he wanted to hear that part. I think it was important to him to hear that I cared enough to be angry.

"Will you ever forgive me?" he asked.

"Will you ever forgive me?" I shot back, leveling my gaze directly into his eyes.

He stared into them for a few moments and then got up silently and headed for the door. He didn't turn around when he reached it. Just grabbed the doorknob and held it.

"No," he said, without facing me. "Maybe it makes me a bad parent, but I don't know if I can. No matter what the police found, you were involved in that shooting, Valerie. You wrote those names on that list. You wrote *my* name on that list. You had a good life here. You may not have pulled the trigger, but you helped cause the tragedy."

He opened the door. "I'm sorry. I really am." He stepped out into the hallway. "I'll leave my new address and phone number with your mother," he said before walking slowly out of my sight.

29

As always, I decided it would be safest to skip dinner and grab something to eat after everyone went to bed. I waited until I could see the strip between the bottom of the door and the floor turn dark — lights off — and I limped out.

I padded into the kitchen and made myself a peanut butter and jelly sandwich by the light of the refrigerator. I closed the fridge and sat at the kitchen table, choosing to eat in the dark. It felt good and secluded that way. Like I had a little secret. Like I could be alone, away from all the nonsense around me. And that's what it all was, wasn't it? Nonsense. After your classmates get blown away pretty much everything else in the world — even your father bailing on your family — seems pretty trivial.

I finished my sandwich and was about to get up and

leave when I heard a noise in the living room. It sounded like a long, watery sniff and a small cough. I froze.

I heard the noise again, this time followed by the definite sound of a Kleenex being pulled out of a box.

I crept around the corner and peered into the darkness.

"Hello?" I said softly.

"Go to bed, Valerie, it's just me," Mom said from the dark fortress of the couch. Her voice sounded gravelly, her nose stuffy.

I paused. She sniffed again. Again I heard a Kleenex being pulled out of the box. Instead of heading toward the stairs I took a few steps into the living room and stood behind the recliner. I rested my hands over the top of it.

"Are you okay?" I said.

She didn't answer. I came around the recliner and started to sit in it, but thought better of it and instead took a few more steps and folded myself to my knees on the floor a few feet in front of the couch. I could now make our her shadow and see the white of her robe splitting off her knees, making her skin look super tan against it in the darkness.

"You okay?" I repeated.

There was another long silence and I began to think I should just go to bed like she'd asked. But after awhile she said, "You got something to eat, then? I told Dr. Hieler that I haven't seen you eat anything in weeks."

"I've been coming down at night. I'm not anorexic if that's what you're thinking."

"I was," she said, and I could hear tears begin anew in

her voice. She sniffed some more and the sound of silent sobbing drifted in and out of the air around me. She took a deep breath at the end of it. "You've gotten so thin and I never see you eat anything. What was I supposed to think? Dr. Hieler said he thought you were probably doing that, eating when I'm not around."

Score another for Dr. Hieler. Sometimes I forgot how much he probably stood up for me without my even knowing it. Sometimes I wondered how many times he brought my mom down off the ceiling about something ludicrous.

"So is Dad gone?" I asked after a while.

I think she nodded because the shadow shifted slightly. "He's living with her now. It's for the best."

"Are you going to miss him?"

She took a deep breath and let it out in a gust. "I already do. But not the guy who I've been living with for the past few years. I miss the guy I said 'I do' to. You probably wouldn't understand."

I chewed my lip, trying to decide if I wanted to be offended by her brushing me off like that. Trying to decide if I should argue.

"Well, I kinda do," I said. "I miss Nick, too. I miss the times we were just like bowling and stuff and we were just happy. I know you think he was all bad, but he wasn't. Nick was really sweet and really smart. I miss that."

She blew her nose. "Yeah, I guess you probably do," she said, which felt so enormously good I had no words for it. "Do you remember . . ." she said, then trailed off. I heard another Kleenex leave the box and another watery sniff. "Do you remember that summer we went to South Dakota? Remember, we went in Grandpa's old station wagon and loaded up that giant cooler with sandwiches and sodas and just took off because your father wanted you and Frankie to see Mount Rushmore?"

"Yeah," I said. "I remember you took the training potty in the car just in case we had to go on the road. And Frankie ate crab legs on a buffet somewhere in Nebraska and threw up all over the table."

Mom chuckled. "And your father wouldn't rest until we visited that godawful corn palace."

"And the rock museum. Remember I cried because I thought there was going to be like rock musicians in there and we got there and it was just all these rocks."

"And your grandmother, god rest her soul, smoked those disgusting cigarettes the entire way."

We both chuckled and trailed off into silence again. It was a horrible trip. A wonderful, horrible trip.

Then Mom said, "I never wanted you kids to have divorced parents."

I thought about it. I shrugged even though I knew she couldn't see it. "Yeah, I think I'm okay with it. Dad hated being here. He may not be the best dad in the world, but I don't think anyone should have to be miserable like that."

"You already knew," she said.

"Yeah. I saw Briley a while back at his office. I guessed."

"Briley," Mom said, as if she were testing out the name.

Did she think it sounded sexier than her own name? More appealing than Jenny?

"Have you told Frankie?" I asked.

"Your father did," she said. "Right after he talked to you. I told him I wasn't going to be the one to break you kids' hearts. I thought it was only fair that he had to tell you himself that he's shacking up with a twenty-year-old girl. I'm not doing his dirty work for him anymore. I'm tired of being the bad guy."

"Is Frankie okay?" I asked.

"No. He hasn't come out of his room, either. And now I'm afraid I'm going to have another child in trouble and I don't . . . know . . . if . . . I . . . can handle it . . . alone. . . ." Her voice drowned in a wave of tears so abrupt and soulful they drew tears out of my own eyes without my even knowing it. Had you been a passerby and heard someone crying like that you would have sworn she'd just lost everything she ever had. I wondered if she felt as if she had.

"Frankie's a good kid, Mom," I said. "He hangs out with good kids. He won't . . ." *be like me* was what was about to come out of my mouth, but that embarrassment crept up on me again and instead I said, ". . . be in any trouble."

"I hope not," she said. "I can barely keep a handle on what's going on with you most days. I'm just one person. I can't carry everyone all the time."

"You don't have to carry me anymore," I said. "I'm okay, Mom, really. Dr. Hieler says I'm making really good progress. And I'm doing those art classes with Bea. And I'm working on that Student Council project." And suddenly I felt this overwhelming need to repair something inside of my mother. Suddenly I was awash with a compassion for her that I might have sworn would never again exist. Suddenly I wanted to be the one to give her hope, to give her back South Dakota. "In fact, I was wondering if you would let me go to a sleepover at Jessica Campbell's house next weekend." My throat felt tight.

"You mean that blond girl that keeps coming over here?"

"Yeah. She's Student Council president and on the volleyball team. She's a good person, I promise. We eat lunch together every day. We're friends."

"Oh, Val," she said, her voice thick and heavy. "Are you sure you want to do this? I thought you hated those girls."

My voice raised an octave. "No, really, Mom. She's the one I jumped in front of. I saved her life. I saved her. And we're friends now."

Again there was a long silence. Mom sniffed a few times and the sound was so clouded I almost felt like I couldn't breathe. "Sometimes I forget," she said, her voice threading out to me in the darkness. "Sometimes I forget that you were also a hero that day. All I see is the girl who wrote a list of people she wanted dead."

I resisted the urge to correct her. *I didn't want those people dead*, I wanted to say. *And you would've never even known about that list had Nick not lost it. But Nick lost it, not me! Not me!*

"Sometimes I'm so busy seeing you as the enemy who dismantled my family's life I forget to see that you were the one who stopped the shooting. You were the one who saved that girl's life. I've never thanked you for that, have I?"

I shook my head, no, even though I knew she couldn't see me do it. I had a suspicion that she, like me, could feel it in the air.

"She's really your friend, then?"

"Yeah. I actually really like her." This, I discovered with some amount of shock, was the truth.

"Then you should go. You should be with your friend. You should have fun."

My stomach dropped. I wasn't sure if I even knew how to have fun with those people. Their idea of fun was so different from anything I'd ever known.

30

"So I guess you know my dad left," I said, studying Dr. Hicler's bookshelf, my back to him as he took his usual pose in his chair: leg slung over the side of the chair, right forefinger lazily tracing his bottom lip in contemplation.

"Your mom told me," he said. "What do you think about that?"

I shrugged, lifted my gaze to study the figurines on top of his bookcase. A porcelain elephant, a Precious Moments doctor and child, a polished piece of quartz. Gifts from clients. "I already knew about it. I wasn't too surprised."

"Sometimes even stuff you expect to happen can still hurt," he suggested.

"I don't know. I think I got over Dad a long time ago. I

think it hurt back then but now . . . I don't know . . . now it kind of seems like a relief."

"I can understand that."

"Thanks for doing the whole anorexia thing with Mom, by the way," I said. I abandoned the bookcase and flopped backward on the couch.

He nodded. "You have to eat, though. You know that, right?"

"Yeah, I know. I'm eating. I've even gained back a few pounds. No big deal. It's not like I'm trying to lose weight."

"I believe that. She just worries is all. Sometimes you've gotta humor the old people. Let her see you eat something every now and then. Okay?"

I nodded. "Okay. You're right."

He smiled wide, pumped his fist in the air. "Right again! I should do this for a living!"

I chuckled, rolling my eyes. "Oh! I almost forgot. I made you something."

His eyebrows raised and he leaned forward to take the canvas I had dug out of my backpack.

"You didn't have to do that," he said.

He turned the canvas around and studied it. It was the portrait I'd painted in Bea's studio last Saturday.

"This is incredible," he said. Then he repeated it, more enthusiastically. "This is really incredible! I had no idea you could do this."

I moved behind him and looked over his shoulder at my *Portrait of a Hieler*. Not the guy with the dark brown hair and sympathetic eyes that I saw every Saturday in his office, but the real him as I saw him: a pool of serenity, a burst of sunlight, a way out of the deep, dark tunnel I lived in.

I nodded. "Yeah, I think I really like painting. I've been hanging out with this lady at a studio across the street and she's been letting me paint for free. I also started a notebook. I've been drawing things as I really see them. Not like what everybody wants you to see, but what's really there. It's been helpful. Although some people think it's another Hate Book. But whatever. I just draw them, too."

He carefully propped the canvas against the lamp on the table next to him. "Can I see the book? Will you bring it next time you're in?"

I smiled shyly. "Okay. Yeah. Okay."

31

Jessica Campbell's house smelled like vanilla. It was sparkly clean, just like the minivan that her mom had driven us home in, and had colors in it that reminded me of commercials. Bright periwinkle blues, viney greens, sunshine yellow that almost hurt my eyes when I stared at it too long.

We sat at the kitchen table — Jessica, Meghan, Cheri Mansley, McKenzie Smith, and me — eating soft pretzels that her mom had handmade in anticipation of our coming home from school. She served them up on an oval platter, the Lord's Prayer hand-painted on it, along with little Pyrex dishes filled with mustard, barbeque sauce, and melted cheese.

Jessica and Cheri were talking about Doug Hobson getting pantsed in the field house after track practice earlier in the week. They were laughing and stuffing pretzels into their mouths so carelessly I felt like I was sitting in a movie theater watching them onscreen. Meghan and McKenzie were studying a magazine article about hairstyles. I sat at the far end of the table silently nibbling on a pretzel.

Jessica's mom stood by the sink and beamed at her daughter, laughing along with them every time the girls dissolved into another funny story, but without intruding on their conversation. I tried not to notice how her smile wavered every so often when she'd flick a glance at me.

We finished eating, then moved upstairs to Jessica's bedroom where she turned on some song that I didn't know. The four of them got up and danced, talking over the music and making squealing noises I didn't think my vocal cords were even capable of making. I sat on the bed and watched them, smiling without trying or even really realizing it. I imagined that, if I had my notebook with me, I would be able to draw everyone exactly as they looked at that moment. For a change I felt like I was in reality.

After a while Jessica's mom knocked on the door and opened it just a crack with that smile pasted over her perfect teeth. She announced that dinner was ready and we headed down to find homemade pizza on the counter. Three kinds. The crusts perfectly flaky and brown. The meat perfectly baked. The veggies perfectly soft. A measured and even crust stuffed painstakingly with garlic butter and cheese. They almost looked too perfect to eat.

I couldn't help but wonder what would have happened

to Jessica's mom if I hadn't jumped in between Nick and Jessica. If she'd lost her baby girl. Would she still make perfect pizzas and set bowls of lemons on the kitchen table for decoration and burn vanilla candles? She didn't seem like someone who tolerated bullying. Did she know that Jessica used to call me Sister Death? Was she disappointed in Jessica for treating me that way? Disappointed in herself for raising a daughter who would do that? And what would she have done if she were my mom? Would it have broken her more to know that her daughter was dead or that her daughter might have been the shooter?

After dinner we piled into Jessica's car and left, her mom waving at us out the front door like we were preschoolers heading off on our first field trip. The drive to Alex's house was long and over gravel roads. After a while I didn't recognize where we were — we'd driven down country roads I didn't even know existed in Garvin.

Alex's house was a rambling brick farmhouse all but hidden behind a grove of crabapple trees. No lights were on in the house, which made it look ominous in the night, even though the driveway was clogged with cars.

Just past the driveway, a large gate to a pasture had been pulled open and Jessica pulled onto the grass. Up ahead it looked like a parking lot, as if all of Garvin had shown for the party, and Jessica eased her car in with the others. As soon as we tumbled out of it we could hear thumping music off to our left. Ahead we could see the barn, the door thrown wide open, a square of black light and spinning crescents of colored light spilling out onto the cropped grass.

Over it all we could hear laughter and little squeals and above even that we could hear the sounds you would expect to hear on a farm — a faraway dog barking, intermittent mooing, frogs chattering near a pond.

Jessica, Meghan, McKenzie, and Cheri practically raced toward the barn, talking excitedly and bumping to the beat of the music. I followed slowly behind, chewing on my bottom lip, my heart pounding, my legs feeling leaden.

Inside, the barn was packed, and I couldn't find Jessica or the others in the sea of people. I pushed through as well as I could and eventually found myself standing at a giant metal tub filled with ice and drinks. Mostly there was beer inside, but after searching for a few minutes I found a soda and pulled it out. I hadn't drunk a drop of alcohol since Nick died and I wasn't sure I could handle it.

"Don't you want one of these?" someone called to me from behind. I turned to see Josh holding up a beer. "This is a party, man."

He stepped forward and took the soda out of my hand and tossed it back into the ice, then rummaged around in the tub and pulled out a bottle of beer. He twisted off the top.

"Here." He flashed me a smile that showed all of his teeth.

I took the beer with shaking hands. I thought about Nick. About the times we partied together. The times we sneered over how we imagined people like Jessica and Josh partying. About how disappointed Nick would be to see me drinking with Josh. About how it didn't matter any-more, what Nick thought, because Nick was gone. And somehow that thought seemed to make the difference. I took a long gulp.

"You come with Jess?" Josh shouted over the music.

I nodded and took another swig.

We both listened to the music for a while and watched the crowd. Josh finished his beer and tossed the bottle into a pile of empties behind some hay bales. He reached into the tub and grabbed another, wavering slightly as he did so.

I took another gulp and was almost surprised to find more than half of the bottle gone. My arms and legs started feeling warm. My head felt lighter, too, and I was begin-ning to think that this party might be a great idea. I took another drink and bounced my head slightly to the rhythm of the music.

"Want to dance?" Josh asked.

I looked behind me at first, sure he wasn't talking to me. He could barely look at me in those student council meet-ings. He hadn't exactly pulled a seat out for me at the lunch table, either. The change seemed so . . . sudden.

He laughed. "I'm talking to you," he said.

I laughed, too. And not a little laugh, which sort of sur-prised me. I tipped the bottle back up to my mouth and discovered that it was already empty. I tossed the empty bottle behind the hay bale with a clink and pulled another one out of the ice. Josh grabbed it out of my hand and twisted open the top, then handed it back.

"I don't really dance anymore," I said, taking a big swig. "My leg . . ."

But when I looked down, my leg looked like anyone else's leg. And, come to think of it, it didn't throb at the moment, either. I took another long swallow.

"C'mon," he said, tossing an arm over my shoulders and leaning in to me. "Nobody will even notice."

I drank again and licked my lips. He smelled good. Like soap. Some of that masculine soap like Nick used. I loved that smell on Nick. And suddenly a longing opened up in me so big it hurt. Suddenly I was so lonely I felt as if I were in a cage. I closed my eyes and leaned my head back into Josh's arm. Things swam in front of my closed eyelids. I smiled, then opened my eyes and downed the rest of my beer. I tossed it into the pile and grabbed his hand.

"What are we waiting for then?" I shouted. "Let's dance!"

I was amazed at how easy the moves came to me. Came back to me, I should say. I could remember a time when dancing was one of my favorite things to do, and with the alcohol in my system, it was difficult to stay in reality. I remembered a thousand times dancing in Nick's arms, him breathing into my neck, saying, *"You're gorgeous, you know that? These school dances are really lame, but at least I get to be with the most gorgeous girl in the room."*

The song changed to something slow and I allowed Josh to hug me tight around the middle. I leaned into him, my eyes closed. The leather sleeves of his letter jacket creaked against my cheek and I soaked up the sound, along with the smell of him, and the rough feel of his football letter pressing against my ear. With my eyes closed, I could imagine that I was smelling Nick's leather jacket, feeling one of its zippers pressing up against my ear. Hearing him telling me he loved me. Telling me he'd always love me.

For a minute my fantasy was so real I was surprised when I looked up into his eyes and saw Josh there instead.

"I think I should get some air or something," I said. "My head's spinning. I think I drank that too fast."

"Sure," he said. "Okay."

We plowed our way back through the crowd and made our way outside the barn. A few kids were scattered here and there, making out, smoking, playing grab-ass in the wedge of lights and music that slipped through the open door. We rounded the corner to the side of the barn where nobody was. Josh sat down on the grass and I dropped down next to him, wiping my hands across my forehead, which was beginning to sweat.

"Thanks," I said. "I haven't had a lot of exercise in the past few months. I'm kind of out of practice."

"No problem," Josh said. "I was ready for a break anyway." And he smiled at me. A genuine smile. And it was cool, this party. Nothing like Nick and I had guessed these parties would be.

Suddenly there was a rustling in the nearby weeds and a trio of guys burst out of the overgrown pasture, heading toward us. I recognized one as Meghan's brother, Troy. The other two I knew as older guys who hung around with Troy, but I didn't know their names.

"Well, what do you have here, Joshy?" Troy said, standing over us, his arms folded across his chest. "Gettin' busy with the murderer's girlfriend? Risky! Hey, I hear blowing people away gets her hot."

Josh's smile blinked out like a lightbulb, replaced by a hard edge I recognized all too well. "With her? No way, man. I'm just keeping an eye on her. For Alex. Making sure she doesn't cause any trouble."

I was almost surprised at how much I felt like someone had punched me in the chest when I heard him say that. It almost felt like a physical blow. Here I was again, thinking Josh was actually into me, too stupid to see what was real. The old blind Val back in action. My head was buzzing and I felt tears spring to my eyes. *Idiot,* I thought. *Val, you're a real idiot.*

"Thanks, but I don't need a babysitter," I said. I tried my best to sound tough, unaffected, but a quaver rode on top of the words and I found myself pressing my lips together instead. "You can go now," I said when I was able to pry them apart again. "I was just leaving."

Troy crouched down and squeezed my knees with his hands, staring directly into my face, too close for comfort. "Yeah, Joshy. You can go. I'll hang with Sister Death."

"Cool," Josh said. He scrambled to his feet and was gone. As he rounded the corner of the barn, he looked over his shoulder at me one last time. I could almost swear I detected a look of regret in his face when he did that, but how could I possibly trust anything I saw anymore? I was, like, the world's worst at reading what anybody was thinking. I might as well have GULLIBLE stamped across my forehead.

"If she gets out of line," Troy said, leaning in so close my hair moved in puffs when he talked. "I'll just talk to her in her own language." He cocked his forefinger and thumb into a gun shape and pressed it to my temple. I shrugged away from him angrily.

"Get away from me, Troy," I snarled, trying to stand up. But his grip on my leg tightened, his pinky digging into my thigh dangerously close to my scar. "Ow, you're hurting me. Let go."

"What's the matter?" Troy said. "Not so tough without your boyfriend?" His mouth was so close now I felt little pieces of spittle hit my ear. "Alex told me you were coming tonight. Seems your new buddies aren't too thrilled to have you hanging around their parties."

"Alex isn't my buddy. I'm here with Jessica," I said. "It doesn't matter. I'm leaving anyway. Let go."

His fingers gouged into my leg harder. "My sister was in that cafeteria," he said. "She saw her friends die, thanks to you and that puke boyfriend of yours. She still has nightmares about it. He got what he deserved, but you got a free pass. That ain't right. You should've died that day, Sister

Death. Everyone wishes you would have. Look around. Where is Jessica, if she wants you here so bad? Even the friends you came here with don't want to be with you."

"Let go of me," I said again, pulling on his fingers. But he only pinched tighter.

"Your boyfriend isn't the only one who can get his hands on a gun, you know," he said. Slowly he eased himself up to standing again. He reached into the waistband of his jeans and pulled out something small and dark. He pointed it at me, and when the moonlight hit it, I gasped and pressed myself against the barn wall.

"So was this the kind of gun your psycho boyfriend used?" he asked, turning the gun in his hand contemplatively. He aimed it at my leg. "Do you recognize it? It's not so tough to get ahold of one. My dad hides this one in the rafters downstairs. If I wanted, I could make people go away, just like Nick did."

I tried to look away, to force myself to be strong, to get up and run at least. But I couldn't look at anything but the gun gleaming in Troy's hand and I felt boneless, my muscles useless. My ears started ringing just like they had on the day of the shooting, and I felt like I couldn't take a breath. Images of the Commons tried to force themselves in on me. "Stop," I half-grunted. Tears sprang to my eyes and I wiped them away with shaking hands.

"Stay away from my sister and her friends," he said.

"This is lame, man," his friend said. "C'mon, Troy, I'm losing my buzz. That thing isn't even loaded."

Troy stared at me, his face pulling into a smile. He wiggled the gun at me and laughed like it was all some big funny joke. "You're right," he said to his friend. "Let's get out of here." He shoved the gun back in his waistband and they took off around to the front of the barn.

I sat on the ground making a raw, ragged sound in my throat that was not quite a cry and not quite a gasp, but something in between. I felt like my eyes were bugging out of their sockets and all I could think about was getting away. I struggled to my feet and ran with all my might through the pasture and toward the road, ignoring the pain in my leg that throbbed every time my foot hit the ground.

I kept running until my lungs felt molten and then I walked, first down gravel roads and then onto paved ones, following the railroad tracks to the highway. Once, I stopped and sat on a low wall by a pond to catch my breath and let my leg rest. I crawled to the edge of the pond and lay on my belly, splashing my face with the cold water. And then I sat there, my jeans soaking up the damp ground under me, staring up at the sky, which looked so clear and full of promise.

Finally I made it to the highway and shortly to a gas station. I pulled my cell phone out of my pocket and dialed Dad's cell phone number. The one I'd added to my contacts list, thinking, *I'll never call it. I'll never call him.*

I waited through two rings.

"Dad?" I said. "Can you come get me?"

32

Dad came to get me at the gas station in his pajamas, his face angular and intense, his hands gripping the steering wheel tightly. He didn't look directly at me as I slid into the front seat next to him, just sat there staring straight ahead, his jaw clenched.

"You been drinking?" he asked as he pulled out of the gas station parking lot onto the street.

I nodded.

"Dammit, Valerie," he said. "This is why you called me? Because you're drunk?"

"No," I said, leaning my head back against the seat. "I'm not drunk."

"I can smell it on you."

"I just had a couple beers. Please don't tell Mom. Please. It'll kill her."

He gave me a look that clearly said, *And what about me?*, but thought better of it. Maybe he realized it wasn't only me that was killing Mom. He had something to do with the death of her dreams, too.

"I can't believe your mother is letting you go to parties," he muttered under his breath.

"Maybe she's trying to trust me," I said.

"She shouldn't," he answered, glancing at me as he pulled onto the highway.

We drove on in silence, Dad shaking his head every few seconds disgustedly. I stared at him, wondering how it was that we got to this place. How the same man who held his infant daughter and kissed her tiny face could one day be so determined to shut her out of his life, out of his heart. How, even when she reached out to him in distress — *Please, Dad, come get me, come save me* — all he could do was accuse her. How that same daughter could look at him and feel nothing but contempt and blame and anger and resentment, because that's all that had radiated off of him for so many years and it had become contagious.

Maybe it was the alcohol or maybe it was the rawness I felt after Troy's threat, or maybe it was both, but for some reason I couldn't shut out the outrage I felt coursing through me. He was my dad. He was supposed to protect me, to at least be concerned when I called him from a gas station out in the middle of nowhere in the middle of the night, asking him to pick me up.

"Why not?" I blurted out before I could stop myself.

He glanced at me again. "Why not what?"

"Why shouldn't Mom trust me, Dad? Why are you so determined to make me out to be the bad guy all the time?" I stared at the side of his face, willing him to make eye contact. He didn't. "I've been doing really good lately and you don't even care."

"Yet you still managed to get into trouble tonight," he said.

"You have no idea what happened tonight," I said, my voice ratcheting up a notch. "All you know is that, because I was involved, I'm somehow guilty of something. You could at least pretend to care, you know. You could at least try to understand."

Dad gave a sardonic little laugh. "I'll tell you what I understand," he said, his voice getting a courtroom causticity to it. "I understand that when you're left to your own devices you get into trouble, that's what I understand. I understand that I was trying to have a happy, restful evening with Briley and once again you screwed it up."

I sat back against the seat and snorted laughter. "Sorry to bother your perfect little life with perfect little Briley," I said. "Sorry you had to be bothered by your real family. But in case you —"

But Dad cut me off, his voice booming in the car. "I

understand that your mother lets you run wild. If I'd been there, you wouldn't have been going to any damn party tonight."

My eyes widened. "But you weren't there, Dad. That's the whole point. You're never there. Even when you're around, you're not there. Briley's not your family. I'm your family. *I* am. Briley's just a . . . stupid affair."

Dad yanked the steering wheel and the Lexus swerved to the shoulder of the road. The car behind us screeched to a stop and honked. Then slowly it started to pull around us, the driver glaring at Dad. But Dad didn't notice. He slammed the car into park and got out. He took several long strides to my side of the car and jerked my door open, reached in and grabbed my shoulder with incredible force, and yanked me out. I yelped and stumbled in the gravel.

He pulled me close to his face, his fingers still digging into my shoulder.

"Listen here, young lady," he said through clenched teeth. "It's time you understood something. You've had a good goddamn life, you spoiled goddamn brat, and I'm sick — " he shook when he said the word "sick" and spittle flew out from between his teeth and cheeks and landed on my chin. "Sick of you ruining everyone else's life. You either pull your shit together and start acting right or I'll have your ass out on the street before you can say 'unappreciative brat,' do you hear me?"

My eyes were wide and I was breathing in short gasps.

My shoulder ached where he clasped it and I could feel my legs shaking. My anger had vanished; I was too scared to be mad. I nodded numbly.

He relaxed a little, but didn't let go, and still spoke in angry staccato little reports through his teeth. "Good. Now I'm about to take you to my home with Briley who, like it or not, is my family, too, and you better not fuck with her while you're there. And if you feel like you just can't handle acting normal for one goddamn night then I'll take you home right now, but you'll have five minutes to gather your shit and move the fuck out. Out of this family. Period. And don't test me."

A silver car came up beside us and slowed, the passenger window rolling down. A woman's face appeared in the open space, curious and worried. "Is everything okay here?" she called out. Neither of us moved at first, our eyes locked, our bodies still in the shadow of the car.

Finally, Dad, breathing hard through flared nostrils, let go of my shoulders and looked up. "Fine. We're fine," he said, walking around the front of the car.

"Miss?" she called out. "You okay? You need us to call someone?"

Slowly, as if through water, I turned and looked at her. She had a cell phone in her hand and waved it at me slightly, her eyes flicking to Dad, as he opened the driver's door and got back inside the car. Part of me wanted to run to her, duck into the back seat of her car and beg her to take me away from here. Take me anywhere else.

But instead I shook my head. "I'm fine," I said. "Thanks." I reached up dazedly and smoothed the sleeve of my shirt, which was bunched and wrinkled where Dad's fingers had wound in it.

"You're sure?" she asked. Her car started rolling slowly forward.

I nodded. "Yeah," I said. "I'm okay."

"Okay," she said uncertainly. "Have a good night." She kept her eyes on me as her window rolled up again and the car began to move away, disappearing into the night.

I leaned up against Dad's car, shaking. My heart was pounding and I felt nauseated. I gulped in a few deep breaths and tried to calm myself before ducking back in and shutting my door. We drove the rest of the way home in silence.

When we got to Dad's apartment, Briley, wrapped tidily in a thick pink robe, was waiting at the door. She eyed me as we came through the door and then gave Dad a startled glance.

"What's going on?" she asked.

Dad tossed his keys on a side table and kept walking. I followed him in sheepishly and looked around. The place looked like Dad, although I recognized nothing in it as being Dad's stuff. That stuff was all at my house. Yet this stuff could just as easily have been his stuff, too. There was a flat-screen TV in the corner of the living room, a lot of leather furniture — black — and two giant bookcases crammed with books. On the coffee table were two wine glasses with a quarter of an inch of red wine splashed in the bottom of each one. I imagined the two of them, hanging out in their pajamas and robes, watching Letterman, holding hands, having a drink before bed, when the phone rang. Had Briley rolled her eyes when he left? Had she tried to get him not to go?

I heard a refrigerator door open and close around the corner. I stood rooted in the hallway, under Briley's gaze.

"Come on," she said. She touched my shoulder lightly, not unlike the touch Dad had given her in the office the other day. The touch that had outed them. "I'll get you some pajamas."

I followed her into a cool and boxy bedroom. She motioned for me to sit on the bed and I sat while she rummaged through a bureau for a pair of pajamas.

"Here," she said, handing them to me. She stood back and studied me, her hands resting on her hips. "He's your father," she said. "He deserves to know what went on."

I blinked and looked down into my lap.

"Will it be easier to tell me, then?" she asked. She didn't say it in some overly nice voice and she didn't try to get all gentle or reach out to me, which I appreciated. Had she reached over to tuck my hair behind my ear or rub the small of my back or something I might have lost it. She just sat next to me on the bed and rested her palms neatly on the mattress beside her and said, "Tell me and I'll tell him. Either way he's got to know. You can't stay here if you're not going to tell him. I'll call your mother myself."

I told her everything. She never said a word while I talked, and she didn't try to hug me when I finished. Just stood up and smoothed the robe down the sides of her legs with her palms and said, "You can change in the bathroom right there on your left," and walked out of the room.

Next thing I knew I was sitting cross-legged on the leather couch, drinking the glass of milk she'd given me, and listening to them fight in the kitchen.

"She can't let him get away with it," Briley's voice hissed from the kitchen. "You know that."

"She's afraid. Surely you can understand that." Dad's voice, not bothering to hiss. "Besides, she's not going to listen to a damn thing I say tonight anyway. That much is perfectly clear."

A part of me wanted to feel smug about causing their fight. About causing a rift between the happy couple. Like I'd had the last laugh, despite Dad's threat. But I couldn't. All I could feel was tired and numb. And stupid. Incredibly stupid.

"She has a hard enough time in school as it is. He didn't hurt her. He doesn't even go to that school anymore. He graduated," Dad was saying.

"That's not the point, Ted. He threatened her. He scared the hell out of her. And he had a gun."

"But it wasn't loaded. We don't even know if it was a real gun. Besides . . . this isn't up to us. Let her mother deal with it, if she decides to tell her mother. Jenny let her go out; she can handle the problem."

"She needs a parent right now, Ted."

"But you're not her parent!" Dad roared.

My mouth dropped open when he said that and I actually found myself feeling sorry for Briley. She must have reacted because suddenly his voice got lower — controlled angry.

"I'm sorry . . . I'm sorry. I know you want us to be a family, but right now it's still too soon. You're not her parent yet. I am."

"Then act like one," came the garbled response, and then footsteps, the sound of slippers slapping the wooden floor of the hallway, and a door shutting softly in the bedroom.

I heard Dad sigh in the kitchen. Then more footsteps. Dad coming into the living room.

"I'll take you home in the morning," he said in a measured voice. "What about the girl who you were supposed to be spending the night with tonight? Don't you think she's going to call your mother when she realizes you're missing?"

"I called her cell and told her I was feeling sick and had you pick me up. She won't be looking for me."

He nodded.

"Listen," he said, sighing, rubbing his forehead. "As a lawyer, I'm telling you, you really should just tell the police that the guy threatened you. See what they say. That way at least they have it on record."

"I'll think about it," I said.

"Think hard," he said, and then paused. "And you have to tell your mother."

"I know," I said, but in the back of my mind I promised myself I wouldn't do it. This party was her South Dakota.

And besides, he was right. It's not like I'm some big gun expert or something. It could have been a fake. How would I know the difference?

He turned as if to leave the room. "Better get to bed soon," he said, gesturing at the pillow and blanket next to me on the couch. "I'm taking you home first thing in the morning. I have things to do tomorrow."

He switched off the floor lamp and the living room was bathed in darkness. I stretched back on the couch and stared at the ceiling until my eyes ached, afraid to close them for fear of what images of the night might replay in my head. My brain had so many frightening ones to choose from now. One thing was for sure: I was sick and tired of feeling scared. But from where I lay, every path I could take from here was scary as hell.

And something else was clear as well. Dad would never come around. It wasn't worth my time to keep trying. He'd already made his decision about me.

In the morning, Dad loaded me into the Lexus and drove me home. Neither of us spoke until he pulled up against the curb outside the house. It was still so early the sky was gray and the house looked asleep.

"Tell Frankie I'll pick you guys up on Saturday morning," he said. "We'll go out to eat or something."

I nodded. "I'll tell him, but I think I'll stay home."

He considered this, searching my face with his eyes. After a while he gave a curt little nod. "I guess I'm not surprised by that."

33

After Dad dropped me off, I traipsed upstairs to my bedroom and fell asleep facedown on my bed. Mom came in
after a while to tell me it was time for therapy and I waved
her away, promising I'd call Dr. Hieler that evening instead.
I lied, telling her I'd stayed up too late with Jessica and
needed to sleep in a little.

But after Mom left I'd rolled onto my back and found
myself staring at the ceiling once again, unable to go back
to sleep. After a while I'd gotten up and asked her to take
me to Bea's.

"Oh my," Bea said, taking in the look on my face
when I walked into the art studio an hour later. "Oh goodness." But she didn't say any more. Just went back to her

jewelry-making, shaking her head piteously every so often and clucking her tongue.

I didn't say anything to Bea, either. I just wanted to be left alone. Wanted to paint, to get away from it all.

I pulled a blank canvas off the shelf and brought it to my easel. I stared at it for so long I was sure Mom would be back to pick me up and I'd have nothing to show for my sitting here, other than a blank canvas that held a thousand images for me only.

Finally I picked up a paintbrush and poised it over the palette, unsure what color to choose.

"Did you know," Bea murmured, plucking a shiny green bead out of a box with her fingernails and threading it onto a bracelet, "that some people mistakenly think that all paintbrushes do is paint? How closed-minded some people can be."

I stared at my brush. My hands suddenly went to work without me, as they'd done so many times before, turning the brush so that the bristles were curled into my palm. I made a tight fist around them. I felt the bristles crush and roll in my fist.

I brought the tip of the paintbrush handle to the canvas and put pressure behind it. A little, and then a lot. And then I felt a pop and heard a small tear as the brush poked through the canvas, gouging a hole in the center. I pulled the brush out and looked at it, then did it again, about an inch away from the first gouge.

To say I was creating anything in particular would be a lie. I had no thought running through my mind as I worked. I only knew that my hands were moving and that with each punch through the canvas I felt an unidentifiable relief pour from me. It wasn't a feeling I was seeking, but something that was being drawn from me.

Soon I had ten slashes in my canvas. I painted them red. I surrounded them with a lot of black, dotted with watery droplets that looked like tear stains.

I sat back and looked at it. It was ugly, dark, uncontrolled. Like a monster's face. Or maybe what I saw there was my own face. I couldn't quite tell. Was the face the image of something evil or the image of myself?

"Both," Bea muttered, as if I'd spoken my question aloud. "Of course it's both. But it shouldn't be. Goodness, no."

Still, I knew then what I had to do. In a way, Troy was right. I didn't belong. Not with Jessica, not with Meghan, definitely not with Josh. I didn't belong at those parties. I didn't belong in Student Council. I didn't belong with Stacey and Duce. With my parents who'd suffered so much. With Frankie who made friends so easily.

Who was I kidding? I never even really belonged with Nick. Because I totally betrayed him, made him think I believed what he believed, made him think I would be on his side no matter what, even if he killed people.

Bea was wrong. I was both the monster and the sad girl. I couldn't separate the two.

And as I dropped the paintbrush, which clattered to the floor, flicking dots of paint all over the bottoms of my jeans, and slunk out of there, I pretended not to hear the encouragement Bea was shouting to my back.

34

"You can't drop out now," Jessica said. An annoyed little line drew itself across her forehead. "We only have a couple months left to get this together. We need your help. You committed."

"Well, now I'm un-committing," I answered. "I'm out."

I shut my locker and walked toward the bank of glass doors.

"What is your problem?" Jessica hissed, rushing behind me. For a moment I could almost see the old Jessica shining through — could almost hear her voice echoing *What are you looking at, Sister Death*? Somehow it made what I had to do easier.

"This school is my problem!" I said through clenched teeth. "Your asshole friends are my problem. I just want to be left alone. I just want to finish and get out of here. Why can't you understand that? Why are you always pushing me to be someone I'm not?" I didn't slow down.

"God, when are you going to get past that 'I'm not one of you' thing, Valerie? How many times do I have to tell you that you are? I thought we were friends."

I stopped and whipped around to face her. That was almost a mistake. I felt so guilty — I could see hurt in her face — but knew I had to get away from her. To get away from Student Council. To get away from Meghan. Away from Alex Gold who wanted me gone so bad he had Josh babysit me and Troy threaten me at his party. Away from all the confusion and hurt.

I couldn't tell Jessica the truth about what had happened with Troy at the party. She'd already strong-armed Meghan into accepting me. She would probably go breaking down Troy's door and put him under citizen's arrest. I could imagine her making me her cause, forcing everyone in Garvin to accept me again, whether they wanted to or not. I was sick of being Garvin's charity project, always under scrutiny, always in the spotlight. I just couldn't do it anymore.

"Well, you were wrong. We're not friends. I was only doing this because I felt guilty about the notebook. They don't want me there, Jessica. And I don't want to be there anymore. Nick couldn't stand your little crowd and neither can I."

Her face reddened. "In case you haven't noticed, Valerie,

Nick is dead. So it doesn't matter what he thinks anymore. And for the record, I don't think it ever did except for a few minutes in May. But I thought you were different. I thought you were better. You saved my life, remember?"

I squinted my eyes and peered right into hers, pretending I had confidence to match hers. "Don't you get it? I didn't mean to save you," I said. "I just wanted him to stop shooting. You could have been anyone."

Her face showed no emotion, although her breath started coming in harder rasps. I could see her chest rise and fall with it.

"I don't believe you," she said. "I don't believe a word."

"Well, believe it. Because it's true. You can finish your little StuCo project without me."

I whirled around and continued walking.

Just as I was about to reach the double doors, Jessica's voice rang out at my back. "You seriously think this has been easy for me?" she called. I stopped, turned. She was still standing where I'd left her. Her face looked funny, almost writhing with emotion. "Do you?" She dropped her backpack on the floor and started walking toward me, steadily, one hand on her chest. "Well, it's not. I still have nightmares. I still hear the gunshots. I still . . . see Nick's face every time I look at . . . you." She had begun crying, her chin wrinkling like a little kid's, but her voice was steady and strong. "I didn't like you . . . before. I can't change that. I've had to fight my friends to include you. I've had to fight my parents. But at least I'm trying."

"Nobody told you to try," I said. "Nobody said you had to make me your friend."

She shook her head wildly. "You're wrong," she said. "May second told me. I lived, and that made everything different."

"You're crazy," I said, but my voice was wobbly and uncertain.

"And you're selfish," she said. "If you walk away from me now, you're just plain selfish."

She got within just a few paces of me and all I could think about was getting out of there, whether that made me selfish or not. I plunged through the doors and into the open air. I fell into Mom's car and sank back into the seat. My chest felt heavy and cold. My chin spasmed and my throat felt full.

"Let's go home," I said as Mom drove away.

35

"Still not talking?" Dr. Hieler asked, settling into his chair. He handed me a Coke. I said nothing. I hadn't said a word since he came out into the waiting room to get me. Hadn't said a word when he asked if I wanted a Coke, nor acknowledged him when he told me he was going to step out to get us both something to drink and would be right back. I just sat, sulkily, on his couch, slouched back into the cushions with my arms crossed and a scowl darkening my face.

We sat in silence for a while.

"Did you bring me that notebook? I still want to see your drawings," he said.

I shook my head.

"Chess?"

I moved from my seat on the couch and sat across the chess board from him.

"You know," he said, slowly, making his move on the chess board. "I'm beginning to think something's upsetting you." He tipped his eyes toward me and grinned. "I read a book about human behavior once. That's what makes me so adept at recognizing when someone's upset."

I didn't return his smile. Just looked back down at the board and made my move.

We played for a while in silence, me promising myself all the while that I wouldn't say anything. That I'd just go back to that friendly place of quiet and solitude that had cradled me in the hospital. Just curl up into myself until I disappeared. Never speak to anyone again. The problem was, it was so hard to be silent with Dr. Hieler. He cared too much. He was too safe.

"Want to talk about it?" he asked, and before I could do anything to stop it, a tear rolled down my cheek.

"Jessica and I aren't friends anymore," I said. I rolled my eyes and swiped at my cheek angrily. "And I don't even know why I'm crying about it. It's not like we ever really were friends anyway. It's so stupid."

"How'd this come about?" he asked, abandoning the chess game and sitting back. "She finally decide you were too much of a loser to be her friend?"

"No," I said. "Jessica would never say that."

"So who did? Meghan?"

"No," I said.

"Ginny?"

"I haven't even seen Ginny since the first day of school."

"Hm," he said, nodding his head. He looked at the chess board thoughtfully. "So you're the only one talking then, huh?"

"She still wants to be friends," I added. "But I can't."

"Because something happened," he said.

I glanced at him sharply. He had crossed his arms and was running his forefinger over his bottom lip like he always does when he's ferreting out information on me.

I sighed. "It has nothing to do with why I blew Jessica off."

"Just a coincidence," he said.

I didn't answer. Just shook my head and let the tears roll. "I just want it to go away. I just want all the drama to stop. Nobody would believe me anyway," I whispered. "Nobody would care."

Dr. Hieler shifted, leaned forward in his chair, and leveled his eyes so they looked deeply into mine. "I would. On both counts."

I believed him. If anyone would care about what happened at the party, about what happened with Troy, it was Dr. Hieler. And holding it all in, what felt comforting just a week ago, suddenly felt heavy and almost physically painful. Next thing I knew, I found myself, unbelievably, talking. Like even the silence wasn't friendly to me anymore.

I told Dr. Hieler everything. He sat back in his chair

and listened, his eyes growing more and more vivid, his body growing more tense as I talked. Together we called the police to report Troy's threat. They'd check into things, they said. There probably wasn't much of anything they could do. Especially if you're not even positive it was a real gun, they said. But they didn't laugh at me for telling. They didn't say I deserved it. They didn't accuse me of lying.

When my session was over, Dr. Hieler walked me out to the waiting room, where Mom sat alone reading a magazine.

"Now you need to tell your mom what happened," he said. Mom looked up, startled. Her mouth made a small *o* shape as she looked from him to me. "And you're going to work your ass off to get better," he warned. "You don't get to just check out now. I won't let you. You've worked way too hard. You have more hard work ahead of you."

But I didn't feel like working hard, and when I got home all I could think about was flopping back on my bed and sleeping.

I told Mom everything in the car, including Dad's threat on the side of the highway when he picked me up. She looked impassive, disinterested while I talked, and said nothing when I finished. But as soon as we got home she called Dad. I climbed the stairs to my bedroom, listening to Mom's voice ratchet up notch by notch as she talked, blaming him for knowing and not telling. For picking me up without calling her. For not being at home where he belonged in the first place.

After a while I heard the front door open, followed by Mom's murmurs again. I opened my door and peeked downstairs. Dad was standing in the entryway, his hands on his hips, his face lined with annoyance.

I noticed he was in street clothes, which I found odd because it was a work day and Dad never left work before dark. But then I noticed some splotches of paint on his shirt and realized that he must have been at home today, painting Briley's apartment. Making it theirs. I quietly closed my door and paced to the window. Briley was sitting in the car at the curb waiting for him.

I heard my mother's anxious voice mumble again. Heard him thunder back at her, "What was I supposed to do?" A pause and then his voice again, "Send her back to the damn psych ward, that's what I think. I don't give a shit what that shrink says about progress!" And then I heard the front door slam. I paced to the window again and watched him get into the car with Briley and drive away.

Not long after Dad left, I sensed movement around the door and opened one eye. Frankie stood leaning tentatively up against the doorframe. He looked somehow older, with his hair buzzed short and glistening with gel and his button-down shirt buttoned loosely over an Abercrombie T-shirt and his factory-faded jeans. His face looked unnaturally smooth and innocent and he had these permanent little pink patches over his cheeks that made him look constantly embarrassed. Maybe he *was* always embarrassed. Look at the life he had to deal with.

Ever since Dad moved out, Frankie had pretty much gone to live with his best friend, Mike. I'd overheard Mom telling Mike's mom that she needed some time to get things straight with her oldest and sure appreciated Mike's family for taking Frankie in. I figured it was this time spent with Mike that accounted for Frankie's transformation. Mike's mom was one of those perfect moms who wouldn't ever have a kid with spiked hair, much less one who shot up a school. Frankie was a good kid. Even I could recognize that.

"Hey," he said. "You 'kay?"

I nodded, sat up. "Yeah, I'm okay. Just tired I guess."

"Are they really gonna send you back to the hospital?"

I rolled my eyes. "Dad's just blowing off steam. He wants me out of his hair."

"Do you need to go back? I mean, are you crazy or something?"

I almost laughed. In fact, I did chuckle just a little, which made my head ache. I shook my head no. I wasn't crazy. At least I didn't think I was. "They're just upset right now," I said. "They'll get over it."

"Well, if you go . . ." he started and then stopped. He picked at my bedspread with chewed fingernails. "If you go, I'll write to you," he said.

I wanted to hug him. Console him. Tell him it wouldn't be necessary because there was no way I was going to go to some stupid psych ward. That I'd just stay away from Dad and he'd eventually calm down. I wanted to tell him our family would be repaired — would be better, even.

But I didn't say any of those things. I didn't say anything at all, because somehow saying nothing seemed more humane than giving him all these reassurances. After all, how was I supposed to know anything at all?

He brightened suddenly. "Dad's getting me a four-wheeler!" he said excitedly. "He told me on the phone last night. And he's going to take me out and show me how to ride it. Isn't that awesome?"

"That's awesome," I said with as much conviction as I could muster. It was cool to see Frankie smile and get excited again, even if I didn't believe for a minute that Dad was going to buy him anything. That would be so . . . dad-like . . . and we both knew that our dad was totally not dad-like.

"You can ride it, too," he said. "If, you know, you come over to Dad's sometime."

"Thanks. That'd be fun."

He sat around some more, looking uncomfortable the way boys do when they're sitting somewhere under extreme duress. If I were a good sister I would have told him to go ahead and do something more fun. But I didn't mind sitting there with him. He radiated something that made me feel good inside. Hopeful.

But pretty soon he got up. "Well. I gotta get to Mike's. We're going to church tonight." He ducked his head, as if church were embarrassing. He walked toward the door. "Well . . . see ya," he said awkwardly. And he was gone.

I sank back into my pillows and watched the horses on my wallpaper go nowhere. I closed my eyes and tried to imagine myself on one of them again, the way I used to do when I was little. But I couldn't see it. All I could see was the horses bucking me off time and again, dumping me on my butt on the hard ground. They had faces, too — Dad's, Mr. Angerson's, Troy's, Nick's. Mine.

After a while, I rolled to my back and stared up at the ceiling, realizing at once that there was something I had to do. I couldn't change the past. But if I were ever to feel whole again I would have to say goodbye to it. *Tomorrow,* I told myself. *Tomorrow is the day.*

36

Even though I'd never been to Nick's grave, I knew exactly where it was. For one thing it was on the news about every ten seconds for the first two months after the shooting. For another I'd heard enough people talking about it to get a pretty good idea.

I hadn't told anyone I was coming here today. Who would I tell? Mom? She'd cry, forbid me, probably follow me, screaming at me out the open driver's side window. Dad? Well, we weren't exactly on speaking terms. Dr. Hieler? I would have, but I didn't exactly know I was going to do this the last time I saw him. I probably should have; Dr. Hieler probably would have driven me, and right now my leg wouldn't hurt so much from walking all this way. My friends? Well, I had kind of kicked all of them out of my life, one way or another.

I walked down a few rows of neatly kept graves with polished new headstones and unweathered bouquets and found it between his grandfather Elmer and his aunt Mazie, both of whom I'd heard of, but neither of whom I'd ever met.

I stood and stared for a minute. The wind, which had only begun to shake off the winter, played around my ankles and made me shiver. It all felt right — my desperation, my chest aching from exertion, the chill, the wind, the gray. This was how graves were supposed to be, right? It's how they always were in the movies anyway. Cold, murky. Did the sun ever shine when you visited the eternal resting place of someone you loved? I doubted it.

Nick's grave gleamed just like those around it, the light of the overcast sky playing great gray shadows across the words. Still I could read them:

NICHOLAS ANTHONY LEVIL

1990–2008

Beloved Son

The words "Beloved Son" took me by surprise. It was small, italicized, almost hiding in the grass. As if in apology. I thought about his mom.

Of course I'd seen her on TV, but it never seemed like the real woman. I knew her as "Ma," just as Nick had called her, and she was always so laid-back and nice to me. Always sort of in the background, intent to let Nick and me do our own thing — never suffocating, never issuing edicts about proper behavior. Just cool. I liked her. I often thought of her as my mother-in-law and enjoyed the fantasy.

Of course Ma would have wanted Nick remembered as a "Beloved Son." Of course she'd do it in the most laid-back way possible — whispering it to him in tiny letters on his headstone. Just a whisper. *You were beloved, son. You were my beloved. Even after all of this, I still remember the beloved you. I can't forget.*

There was a bouquet of plastic blue roses sticking up from a built-in metal vase at the top of the headstone. I bent and touched one of the brittle petals, wondering if Nick would've been the type to want flowers on his grave, and then I was taken aback that I had never bothered to know that about him. Three years together and I'd never bothered to ask him if he liked flowers, if his favorites were roses, if he found the unnatural color of blue on plastic roses to be absurd. And suddenly that felt like a great tragedy in itself, my not knowing.

I lowered myself to my knees, my leg screaming under me. I reached out with my forefinger and traced Nick's name. *Nicholas*, I smirked, remembering how I teased him about his name.

"Nicholas," I had sung, dodging around the corner between the kitchen and dining room, holding the framed photo I'd just snatched off the fireplace mantel in my hands. "Oh, Nicholas! Come here, Nicholas!"

"You're going to regret it," he said from somewhere in the living room. There was a smile in his voice and, even though I was teasing him over a given name that he truly hated being called, I knew he wanted to catch me not to punish me but to be playful. "When I get my hands on you . . ."

He jumped around the corner with an "Aha!" I squealed and ran, laughing through the kitchen and up the stairs toward the bathroom.

"Nicholas Nicholas Nicholas!" I yelled through my laughter. I could hear him laughing and grunting behind me, just on my tail. "Nicholas Anthony!"

"That's it!" he cried, lunging for me and catching me around the waist just short of the bathroom. "You're gonna pay!" He'd knocked me to the floor and flopped on top of me, tickling me until I cried.

Seemed so long ago now.

I traced the name on his headstone again with my finger. And then again. Somehow it made me feel like the old Nick — the one tickling me on the hallway floor outside the bathroom on the second floor of his house — was more alive than he'd ever been.

"I don't hate you," I whispered, and then I repeated it, louder. "I don't." A bluejay answered me in a tree off to my left. I searched the leaves and branches with my eyes, but never found it.

"It's about time," said a voice behind me.

I jumped and whirled around, falling off my knees and onto my butt. Duce was sitting on a concrete bench behind me, leaning forward, hands dangling between his knees.

"How long have you been sitting here?" I asked, trying to slow my heart by resting my palm on my chest.

"Every day since he died. What about you?"

"I didn't mean that."

"I know."

We stared at each other for a minute. Duce's stare felt like a challenge. Like the way a dog will stare down another dog when it's ready to fight.

"So what are you doing here now?" he asked.

I locked eyes with him, this time doing the challenging myself. "You can't chase me away from here," I said. "And I don't know why you blame me so much anyway. You were his best friend. You could've stopped the shooting, too."

"You were the one with the list," he countered.

"You were the one who spent the night at his house two days before the shooting," I snapped, and then added softly, "We could do this all day. It's stupid. It's not going to bring anyone back."

A car rolled up and an old man gingerly piled out of the back seat, then picked his way to a grave nearby, holding flowers at his hip. We watched him as he knelt slowly, his head bent over, his chin nearly touching his chest.

"The cops, they questioned me too," Duce said, still looking at the old man. "They thought maybe I was in on it because I hung around with him so much."

"Seriously? I never heard that."

"Yeah, I know," he said, his face sour. "You were all about poor you, poor Valerie. You were shot. You were

347

grieving. You were a suspect. You never even considered any of the rest of us. You never even asked, man, how the rest of us were doing. You totally just ditched us."

I looked at him, stricken. He was right. I hadn't asked Stacey during our one visit how anyone else was doing. I hadn't called anyone. E-mailed. Nothing. I hadn't even considered it. "Oh my God," I whispered, and suddenly I could hear Jessica's voice in my ear: *You're just selfish, Valerie*. "I'm sorry. I didn't think . . ."

"That Detective Panzella practically lived at my house, man. Took my computer and everything," Duce said. "But the real kicker is . . . I really had no idea. Nick never said anything to me about shooting anybody. He never even warned me or anything."

"He didn't warn me either," I said, but my voice was almost a whisper. "I'm so sorry, Duce."

Duce nodded, fumbled in his pocket for a cigarette, took his time lighting it. "I felt really stupid for a while, not knowing. I figured maybe we weren't as good of friends as I thought. And guilty, too. Like I should've known and then I could have done something. Helped him. But now . . . I don't know. Maybe he didn't tell us to spare us."

I let out a sarcastic grunt. "Well, if he did plan to spare us, it so didn't work."

Duce chuckled softly. "No kidding."

The old man was struggling to his feet again, pulling his jacket tight around him as he headed back toward his car. I watched him. "You remember the time we went to Serendipity together? The water park?" I asked.

Duce chuckled. "Yeah, you were a drag that day. All whiny about being cold and hungry and nag nag nag. You wouldn't let him have any fun."

"Yeah," I said. I looked back at the grave. *Nicholas Anthony*. "And at the end of the day when you guys took off and Stacey and I had to look all over for you and we finally found you eating Oreos with those two blond girls from Mount Pleasant . . ."

Duce's grin widened. "Those girls were hot."

I nodded. "Yeah, they were. And do you remember what I said to Nick when I found you there?"

I looked up at Duce. He shook his head no. Smiling. Hands dangling.

"I told him I hated him. I said it, in those words. 'I hate you, Nick.'" I reached down and picked up a dried leaf and began flaking it to bits with my fingers. "Do you think he knows I didn't mean it? You don't think he died thinking I hated him, do you? I mean, it was forever ago and, you know, we made up that day. But sometimes I worry that he still thought about me saying that and that maybe, on the day of the . . . the shooting . . . when I tried to stop him he remembered me saying I hated him back at Serendipity and that's why he killed himself. Because he thought I hated him."

"Maybe you do hate him."

I thought about this and then shook my head. "I loved him so much." I let out an exasperated laugh, shaking my head. "My tragic flaw." That's what Nick would have called it, had I been one of the suffering characters in one of his beloved Shakespeare tragedies.

I heard a scraping of clothing against concrete. Duce had moved to one side of the bench and was patting the concrete next to him. I got up and sat next to him. He reached down and picked up my hand. He was wearing gloves and the warmth of his hand enveloped mine, radiating through my whole body.

"Do you think he did it for me?" I asked softly.

Duce thought about it, spat on the ground at his feet. "I think he had no idea why he did it, man." It was a possibility I'd never considered before. Maybe I couldn't have known what Nick was about to do, because Nick himself didn't even know.

He let go of my hand, which quickly grew chilly again without the warmth of his glove around it, and slid his arm around me. It made me feel weird, but not entirely in a bad way. In some ways Duce was the closest to Nick I'd ever be again. In some ways it felt like Nick's hand behind me, Nick's warmth beside me. I leaned my head back into the hollow of his shoulder.

"Can I ask you something?" he said.

I nodded.

"If you loved him so much, why weren't you here before now?"

I chewed my lip. I thought it over. "Because I didn't really feel like he was here. He was still so much everywhere else I looked, I didn't think it was possible for any part of him to be here."

"He was my best friend," Duce said. "You know?"

"He was mine, too."

"I know," he said. There was an edge to his voice but it was very soft. "I guess. Whatever."

We sat there in silence for a while, both of us staring at Nick's grave. The wind picked up and the sky darkened and the leaves swirled around my ankles in tighter and tighter circles, making them itch. When I began to shiver, Duce pulled his arm away from me and stood up.

"I've gotta go."

I nodded. "See ya."

I sat there for a few more minutes after Duce left. I stared at Nick's grave until my eyes watered and my toes felt numb from the cold. At last I stood up and brushed a leaf off of the headstone with my toe.

"Bye, Romeo," I said softly.

I walked away, shivering, and didn't look back, even though I knew I'd never again go visit his grave. He was Ma's *Beloved Son*. The words carved in the granite said nothing about me at all.

37

A police cruiser was sitting in the driveway when I got home, Dad's car parked behind it and a battered red Jeep behind it. A feeling of dread washed over me. I trudged up the driveway and let myself in the house.

"Oh, thank God!" Mom cried, rushing from the living room to the front door. She wrapped herself around my neck. "Thank God!"

"Mom . . . ?" I said. "What's . . . ?"

A uniformed officer followed her into the entryway. He looked none too pleased to be there. He was followed by Dad, who looked even less happy than the officer. I peered into the living room and saw Dr. Hieler, sitting on the couch, the lines in his face making it look harsh and tired.

"What's going on?" I asked, pulling away from Mom. "Dr. Hieler . . . ? Did something happen?"

"We were about to issue an Amber Alert," Dad said, his voice ragged with anger. "Jesus, what next?"

"Amber alert? Why?"

But then the officer was ambling toward me. "You probably don't want to be picked up as a runaway," he said to me. "Just so you know."

"Runaway? I'm not. I wasn't. Mom . . ."

He headed for the front door and Mom followed him, thanking him and apologizing. The radio on his shoulder was squawking and I missed most of what they said.

Dr. Hieler got up and shrugged into his jacket. He came toward me, his face looking confused and sad and angry and relieved all at the same time. Once again I thought about his family at home. What domestic serenity had I kept him from tonight? Was his wife at home, secretly wishing I had run away for good?

"The grave?" he asked very quietly. Neither Mom nor Dad heard him. I nodded; he nodded. "See you Saturday," he said. "We'll talk then." And then he, too, was speaking softly to Mom in the doorway — apologies on both sides of the conversation now — and shaking Dad's hand as he left. I watched the officer race away in his cruiser and Dr. Hieler climb into his Jeep and pull away without fanfare.

"I've got to get back," Dad said to Mom. "Let me know if you need anything. And my opinion still stands. She needs more help than she's getting, Jenny. You've got to stop letting her make all of us miserable." He cut his eyes to me. I looked away.

"I've heard you, Ted," Mom said with a sigh. "I've heard you."

Dad put one hand on Mom's shoulder and gave it a quick pat, then disappeared through the front door.

Mom and I stood in the empty entryway regarding one another.

"This was quite a show," she said bitterly. "Once again. We had reporters in our yard. Once again. Dr. Hieler had to chase them away. I was giving you the benefit of the doubt, Valerie, and once again look what's happened. Maybe your father's right. You can't have an inch or you'll take a mile."

"I'm sorry," I said. "I didn't know. I swear, I wasn't running away. I just took a walk."

"You've been gone for hours, Valerie. You didn't tell anyone where you were going. I thought you'd been kidnapped. Or worse. I thought that Troy kid had done something to you like he threatened."

"I'm sorry," I said. "I really didn't realize."

"Bull," said a voice from the landing above us. We both looked up. Frankie was standing there in a pair of boxers and a T-shirt, his hair sticking straight out to one side.

"Frankie," Mom warned, but he cut her off.

"Dad's right — all she does is cause trouble."

"I said I was sorry," I repeated. It seemed like the only

thing I could do. "I wasn't trying to cause anything. I went to the cemetery and started talking to Duce and lost track of time, I guess. I should've called."

Mom looked at me, startled. "Duce Barnes?"

I looked down.

"Oh, Valerie, he's one of them," she breathed. "He's one of those Nick-types. Didn't you learn? Everything you've got going on and all you can do is hang around with boys and get into trouble?"

"No, it's not like that," I said.

"I had soccer tryouts today," Frankie yelled from the top of the stairs. "But I couldn't go because both Mom and Dad were here, freaking out because you were missing. God, Valerie, I try to be on your side, but all you think about is yourself. You think you and Nick were everybody's victims," he said. "But even now that Nick's gone, you still do stuff to make people miserable. It's impossible. Just like Dad says. You're impossible. I'm sick of my life always having to revolve around yours." He stomped back into his room and slammed the door shut.

"Very nice," Mom said, gesturing to the space where Frankie had just been standing. "Why is it that you can't let us have just one good day? Here I was trusting you and —"

"And I did nothing wrong," I interrupted, practically shouting. "I took a walk, Mom. I didn't ruin your day. You ruined it by not trusting me." Mom's mouth hung open, her eyes wide. "When are you guys going to get it? I didn't shoot anybody! I didn't do it! Stop treating me like a criminal. I'm sick and tired of taking all the blame around here." I heard Frankie's door squeak open a crack, but didn't look up. Instead, I briefly closed my eyes and took a deep breath, trying to calm myself. The last thing I wanted was to cause more drama for Frankie. "I took a walk to say goodbye," I said evenly, opening my eyes and looking at Mom. "You should be really happy. Nick's officially out of my life forever. Maybe you can trust me now."

Mom closed her mouth, dropped her hands to her sides. "Well," she said after a long while. "At least you're safe." She turned and walked up the stairs, leaving me in the entryway alone. Above me, I heard Frankie's door click shut again. *Yeah*, I thought. *Safe.*

38

Frankie went to live with Dad during the week and only came home on the weekends. Mom swore it wasn't because of me, but I had a really hard time believing it after the scene he'd made, especially since he left without saying goodbye. I felt really guilty about it. I'd never meant to hurt Frankie. I'd never meant for his life to revolve around mine. But I seemed to have a way of doing that — hurting people without meaning to.

By the time spring wrapped around us full force, I had noticed that he'd cut his hair to match the rest of the soccer players and was wearing a pair of glasses that completed a clean-cut look for him that I'd never have imagined.

He didn't speak to me much, except to give reports on how Dad and Briley were doing when Mom wasn't around.

"Dad's got a new car," he would say, or, "Briley is so nice, Val, you should give her a chance. She listens to punk, can you believe it? Can you see Mom listening to punk?"

I pretended not to care one way or another what was going on with Dad and Briley, but once while Frankie was in the shower, I dug around in his backpack for his cell phone and scrolled through the photos he had stored on it until I found pictures of them. I then sat on the floor and stared at them until my eyes felt sandy.

The divorce was almost final. I noticed, though, that Mel, Mom's attorney, was still coming over pretty much nightly and sometimes he'd bring hot sandwiches from Sal's with him or a bottle of wine. And I noticed, too, that Mom wore makeup on the days he came over and would sit raptly at the kitchen table with him and laugh every few minutes and touch his forearm lightly with the pads of her fingers when she did it.

I could hardly stand the thought of it, but every so often I'd wonder what kind of stepdad Mel would make. I brought it up with Mom once and she blushed and simply answered, "I'm still married to your father, Valerie." But she'd walked away sort of dreamily after that, fiddling with her necklace and smiling softly, like Cinderella did the morning after the ball.

Even though Duce and I had technically made a truce that day at Nick's grave, it didn't change anything for us at school. We didn't talk. We didn't meet at the bleachers in the mornings. And we didn't eat lunch together. Instead, I managed to finagle Mrs. Tate into letting me eat lunch in her office with her, by promising to look through college catalogs while I was there.

It was the time of year when school seemed interminably long and boring. Somehow, hearing the birds chirping right outside our open classroom windows made the hours of the day multiply and pile one on top of another. Schoolwork seemed stupid, too, this close to graduation. Like we were just filling time. Hadn't we learned everything we needed to know already? Couldn't we just go out and play like we did when we were kids? Don't seniors deserve recess?

May second came and went without a lot of fanfare. We held a moment of silence in the morning, followed by a reading of the victims' names over the intercom with morning announcements. There were a few prayer vigils at some local churches that night. But mostly people just went on about their lives. Already. After only a year.

Everyone was talking about graduation. About party plans afterward. About dreadful family parties before. About what they were wearing, how they were keeping their hats from falling off, what joke would be played on Mr. Angerson.

It was tradition in our school for each graduating senior to hand the administrator something small and concealable as he shook your hand on stage during graduation. One year it had been peanuts. One year pennies. One year it was plastic bouncy balls. Angerson would be forced to put whatever was handed to him in his pockets, and by the end of commencement his pockets would be bulging under the strain of seven hundred bouncy balls or pennies or peanuts. Rumor had it this year it was going to be condoms, but the cheerleaders were heading a strong campaign against it. They wanted jingle bells, so he couldn't move without making noise. I, personally, liked the jingle bell idea. Or maybe nothing. Maybe what poor Angerson needed from our class was simply a break. A great big handful of nothing.

And when the graduation talk ebbed, conversation turned to college talk. Who was going to MU? Who was going overseas? Who wasn't going at all? And did you hear the rumor that J.P. was going to join the Peace Corps? What's the Peace Corps? Will he get malaria and die? Will local rebels kidnap him and behead him in a hut hidden by banana trees? The talk never ended.

Every day at lunch, Mrs. Tate would grill me about my future plans.

"Valerie, it's still not too late to grab a scholarship to one of the community colleges," she'd say, looking pained.

I'd shake my head. "No."

"What are you going to do?" she'd asked me one day as we ate lunch together.

I'd considered this, believe me. What would I do once graduation was over? Where would I go? How would I live? Would I stay at home and wait for Mom and Mel to possibly get married? Would I move in with Dad and Briley and Frankie and try to repair the relationship that I was pretty

360

sure Dad didn't want anyway? Would I move out and get a job? Get a roommate? Fall in love?

"Recover," I'd said. And I'd meant it. I needed some time to simply recover. I'd consider my future later, when Garvin High had slipped off me like a heavy coat in a hot room and I'd begun to forget the faces of my classmates. Of Troy. Of Nick. When I'd begun to forget the smell of gunpowder and blood. If I ever could.

Everything seemed to be going along all right until one rainy Friday, the smell of wet grass clippings permeating the hallways. The storm clouds were thick outside and made inside the school feel like evening. The final bell had just rung and the hallways were a flurry of activity. As usual I wasn't part of it, just moving around in my bubble, waiting to mark another X on the calendar — another day closer to graduation.

I stood at my locker, trading out my math book for my science text.

"So who's the chick who tried to axe herself?" I heard a girl ask a few lockers away. I perked my ears and looked over at them.

"What do you mean?" her friend asked.

The girl's eyes got big. "You didn't hear? Some senior tried to kill herself a couple days ago. Took pills, I think. Or maybe slit her wrists, I don't remember. Name was Ginny something."

I gasped. "Ginny Baker?" I asked aloud.

The girls looked at me, their faces confused.

"What?" one of them asked me.

I took a few steps toward them. "The girl who tried to kill herself. You said her name was Ginny something. Was it Ginny Baker?"

She snapped her fingers. "Yeah, that's her. You know her?"

"Yeah," I said. I rushed back to my locker and crammed my books inside. I slammed my locker and headed for the office. I rushed past the secretaries and into Mrs. Tate's office, where Mrs. Tate looked up from a book, startled.

"I just heard about Ginny," I said, trying to catch my breath. "Can you drop me off at the hospital?"

39

I had to bite my palms when I stepped out of the elevator on the fourth floor into the vestibule of the psychiatric ward at Garvin General. I had a sick feeling in my stomach like if I messed up even the tiniest bit, someone would step around the corner with restraints and take me back into my old room, make me stay there and go to those insane group sessions. Make me listen to Dr. Dentley's idiotic "Let me repeat what I've heard, Miss Leftman. Let me validate you."

I stepped up to the nurse's station. A bristle-haired nurse looked up at me. I was surprised to find that I didn't recognize her at all, which either meant I was too drugged up and stupid to take in her face when I was here, or she was new. She didn't act as if she recognized me either, so I was betting on the latter.

"Yes?" she asked with that weary and suspicious face all mental health nurses have, like I was going to help a patient escape and seriously mess up her day.

"I'm here to see Ginny Baker," I said.

"Are you family?" the nurse asked. She rifled through some papers on her desk as if I didn't exist at all.

"I'm her half-sister," I lied, surprising even myself with how smoothly it came out.

The nurse glanced up from her paperwork at me. She looked like she didn't believe it for one second that I was Ginny's half-sister, but what could she do — demand a DNA test? She sighed, motioned over her right shoulder with her head, and said, "Four-twenty-one, on the left there."

She went back to her paperwork and I shuffled past the desk and into the hallway, praying I wouldn't run into anyone who most certainly knew that I wasn't a Baker stepchild, especially Dr. Dentley. I took a deep breath and ducked into Room 421 before I could think about it too long.

Ginny was propped up in bed, her arms hooked up to IVs and monitors. She was staring blankly up at the TV. A big Styrofoam cup with a striped bendable straw was sitting on the bed table in front of her. Her mother sat next to the bed, also looking up at the TV, which was playing some sort of dramatic daytime talk show. Neither of them was talking. Neither of them looked like they'd washed their hair today.

Mrs. Baker was the first to glance at me when I entered the room. A string of tension wound itself around her torso when she placed my face, and her mouth opened just the tiniest bit.

"I'm sorry to interrupt," I said. At least I think I said it. My voice felt like a squeak.

Ginny looked at me then, and once again I was struck by how disfigured her face was. Once again I felt sorry. No matter how many times I looked at her spoiled cheekbones and flayed lips now it was always shocking.

"What are you doing here?" she mumbled.

"I'm sorry to interrupt," I repeated. "I wanted to talk to you."

Ginny's mom had gotten out of her chair, but she stood behind it, almost like she was hiding behind it. I half expected her to pick it up and use it to fend me off, sort of like a lion tamer.

Ginny's eyes roved to her mom and back to me, but neither of them spoke. I took a few more steps into the room.

"I was in Room four-sixteen," I said. I didn't know why this was important for me to tell her, but for some reason it felt right when it came out of my mouth. "It's better on this side, because they keep the insomniacs over in the four-fifties."

Just then I heard a voice that I recognized and the squeak of cheap shoes coming down the hallway. I braced myself to be kicked out, which sucked because even though I wasn't sure what I wanted to say to Ginny, I knew I hadn't yet said it.

"Well, how's Ginny today?" the voice said behind me, coming into the room. Dr. Dentley.

He walked to Ginny's bedside and lifted her wrist to take her pulse, the whole time yammering on about what a good group they had this morning and did she feel restless and how did she sleep last night before noticing that both Bakers were still staring at me. He turned, surprise dawning on his face.

"Valerie," he said, "what are you doing here?"

"Hi Dr. Dentley," I said. "I'm just visiting."

He turned from Ginny and put his hand on my back between my shoulder blades, shoving me lightly toward the door. "I don't think, given the circumstances, that you should be here. Miss Baker needs this time to —"

"It's okay," Ginny said. Dr. Dentley stopped pushing me. Ginny nodded when we looked at her. "I don't mind if she's here."

Both Dr. Dentley and Ginny's mom looked at Ginny as if she might have truly lost her mind. I wondered if Dr. Dentley was making plans in his head to send her off to the schizophrenic wing.

"Really," Ginny said.

"Well," Dr. Dentley blustered. "Regardless, I need to do some evaluating . . ."

"I'll wait in the hallway," I said.

Ginny nodded wearily, looking as if the last thing she wanted to do was spend a little alone time with Dr. Dentley.

I scuffed out of the room, feeling much freer now that I'd

been recognized and invited to stay. I lowered myself to the floor and sat in the hallway, listening to the low rumble of Dentley's voice coming through the door of Ginny's room.

Soon I heard footsteps and Ginny's mom came out into the hallway. She paused when she saw me sitting there, but only for the briefest moment. Had I not been paying attention I might have missed the hesitation entirely. She cleared her throat, looked at the floor, and began walking again. She looked so tired. Like she hadn't slept in years. Like maybe she'd never in her life had a good night's sleep. Like if they put her in Room 456, next to Ronald, who liked to sit up into the long hours of the night picking scabs off his elbows and singing old Motown songs, she'd be right at home.

She'd almost passed me but thought better of it. Her face was a straight line when she looked at me.

"I couldn't see it coming," she said.

I stared at her. I wasn't sure if I was supposed to respond.

Mrs. Baker looked straight ahead again. Her voice was toneless, as if even it had been worn out and could no longer do its job properly.

"I suppose I should thank you for stopping the shooting," she said, and then she walked briskly down the hallway away from me. She glanced at the nurse's station and then hit the double doors with a bang and was gone. She supposed she should . . . yet she didn't. Not exactly.

Still. It was almost good enough.

Soon Dr. Dentley was leaving, too, whistling. I stood up.

"Dr. Hieler says you're doing well," he said. "I hope you're still taking your meds."

I didn't respond. Not that he was waiting for my response, anyway. He simply walked down the hall, tossing a light "She'll need to rest today, so don't stay long," over his shoulder.

I took a couple deep breaths and stepped into Ginny's room again. She was wiping her eyes with a Kleenex.

I sidled over to a chair, the farthest from her bed, and sat down.

"He's such an idiot," she said. "I want out of here. He won't let me go. Says I'm a threat to myself and it's law that I have to stay. Stupid."

"Yeah," I said. "They make suicides stay for three days or something like that. But most of them end up staying longer because their parents are so freaked out. Is your mom freaked out?"

Ginny gave a sardonic little laugh and blew her nose. "She is so beyond freaked," she said. "You have no idea."

We sat for a moment and watched TV, which had turned over to one of those entertainment magazine shows. A photo of a dark-haired teen celebrity splashed across the screen. She looked neither glamorous nor happy. She looked like any other kid. I thought she even looked a little like me.

"When Nick first moved here, we were friends," Ginny said out of the blue, breaking the silence. "He was in my homeroom freshman year."

"Yeah?" Nick had never said anything about being friends with Ginny Baker. "I didn't know that."

She nodded. "We talked, like, every day. I liked him. He was really smart. And nice, too. That's what gets me. He was really nice."

"I know," I said. Suddenly it felt like Ginny and I had worlds in common now. I wasn't the only one who saw it. There was someone else. Someone else saw the good in Nick. Even through her marred face she still saw it.

She leaned her head back against her pillow and closed her eyes. Tears were slipping out from under her lids, but she made no attempt to brush them away. We were both quiet for a while and finally I leaned over and plucked a tissue out of a box on the chair next to me. I leaned forward and gently placed it on her face, beneath her closed eyes.

She flinched slightly, but didn't open her eyes and didn't try to make me stop. Slowly, my strokes on her cheeks grew bolder and I followed the curved scars along her cheeks with my fingers under the wet tissue. When her face was dry I leaned back in my chair again.

Her voice sounded croaky when she talked again. "When I started going out with Chris Summers at the end of that year, Chris saw me talking to Nick and completely freaked out about it. Totally jealous. I think that's what started it. I think if I hadn't ever been friends with Nick, Chris would have ignored him. He was so mean to Nick all the time."

"Ginny, I . . ." I started, but she shook her head.

"I had to stop talking to Nick. I had to because Chris

would just never let up about it. *What do you want to be friends with a freak like that for?*" she said in a low voice meant to mimic Chris Summers.

"But Chris was the one who . . ." I said, but she cut me off again.

"It's just that I keep thinking . . . maybe if I hadn't been Nick's friend back then . . . or maybe if I'd stayed his friend and told Chris to shove it . . . maybe the shooting . . ." she trailed off, her face crumpling in on itself again. "And now they're both dead."

The images on the entertainment show turned to some rapper I'd never heard of. He was wearing one of those giant gold dollar signs around his neck and was flashing some sort of hand signal to the camera. Ginny opened her eyes at last, blew her nose, and gazed at him.

"It wasn't your fault, Ginny," I said. "You didn't cause this. And I . . . um, I'm really sorry about Chris. I know you really liked him." In other words, I thought, Ginny could see the good in Chris, too. Which made her somehow better than me, because I never did. Did that make Chris and Nick more alike than different — both bound by a side of themselves that wasn't the only, or even the best, side of them?

Ginny tore her watery eyes away from the TV. She looked directly into mine. "I've wanted to die ever since Nick did this to me," she said. She pointed to her face. "You have no idea how many surgeries I've had and still look at me. I didn't want to die before, you know, when he was shooting.

370

I was, like, praying that he wouldn't kill me. But in some ways I wish he would've gone ahead and killed me. I hear people talking when I'm out in public all the time and when they think I can't hear them they always go, 'That's such a shame. She was a pretty girl.' Was. Like a thing of the past, you know? And it's not like being pretty is the most important thing in the world. But . . ." she trailed off again, but she didn't need to finish the sentence. I knew what she was thinking: Being pretty isn't everything, but sometimes being ugly is.

I didn't know what to say. She had been so outright about it — so bold. I looked at my jeans. There was a tiny rip in the thigh. I poked my finger into it.

"You know," she said. "I don't remember everything that happened that day. But I know you weren't part of it. I told the police that. Went with Jessica to the police station and everything. My parents were really pissed. I think they wanted to be able to blame it on someone who was still alive. They kept telling me I didn't know everything I thought I knew. That I could be forgetting things, you know? But I knew you didn't shoot anybody. I saw you running after him trying to get him to stop. I saw you kneeling down trying to help Christy Bruter, too."

I fished around in the hole in my jeans with my finger. Ginny leaned back against her pillow and closed her eyes again, like she was worn out. And, I suspected, there was probably a big part of her that was.

"Thank you," I said. Very softly. More to the hole in my

jeans than to her. "And I'm sorry. I mean, I'm really, really sorry for what happened to you. Not that it matters, but I still think you're pretty."

"Thanks," she said. She laid her head back on the pillow and closed her eyes again. Her breathing came soft and steady as she began drifting off to sleep.

My gaze landed on a newspaper, which was lying in the chair where Ginny's mom had been sitting. A headline screamed out at me:

SHOOTING VICTIM ATTEMPTS SUICIDE:
PRINCIPAL REAFFIRMS HEALING EFFORTS
OF GARVIN HIGH STILL FIRM

The piece was written by Angela Dash, of course. Suddenly I was struck with an idea. I reached over and picked up the paper, folded it into a small square and tucked it into my backpack.

"I should go and let you sleep," I said. "I think I have something to do. I'll come back later," I added, almost sheepishly.

"Yeah, that'd be good," Ginny said, never opening her eyes as I headed out the door.

40

"I think you should do it," Dr. Hieler said, dumping half a cup of coffee down the drain in the tiny office kitchen.

When I'd left the hospital, I'd walked straight to his office down the street, not sure where else to go, and totally sure that I needed to talk. He was in between clients, but had a few minutes while he prepared. I followed him around the office, watching him pick up leftover soda cans from old clients and stack paperwork together on his desk.

"Write something. Doesn't have to be any sort of apology or anything. Just something that represents the class to you."

"What, like a poem or something?"

"A poem's a good idea. Just something." He puttered back into his office and I followed on his heels.

"And just make the suggestion that I read this poem or whatever at the graduation ceremony?"

"Yep." He used his hand to scoop a small pile of potato chips off his desk into the trash can below.

"Me."

"You."

"But aren't you forgetting that I'm Sister Death, the Girl Who Hated Everyone? The one everyone loves to hate?"

He stopped and leaned forward on his desk. "That's exactly the reason you should do it. You're not that girl, Val. You never were." He glanced at his watch. "I've got someone waiting . . ."

"Yeah, okay," I said. "Thanks for the advice."

"Not advice," he said, heading out the door with me at his heels. "Homework."

41

"Can you wait here for me?" I asked Mom. "I'll only be a minute."

"Here? At the newspaper office?" she asked. "What would you be doing here?" She peered out the windshield at the brick building, the words SUN-TRIBUNE cast across the front of it.

"It's for a school project," I said. "The memorial project. I have to pick up some research from a lady who works here."

Probably every warning bell Mom had was clanging in her head right now. Here she was, coming home late from work already and she had to pick me up at Dr. Hieler's office, totally unplanned, and drive me directly to the *Sun-Tribune* office, with no more explanation than *I'll tell you every-thing later, I swear.*

She seemed highly skeptical that I was doing exactly what I said I was doing, but she was probably so relieved that no police cruisers were following us home and I wasn't in handcuffs that she didn't push it.

"Mom, everything's okay," I said, my hand resting on the door handle. "Trust me on this."

She gave me a long look, then reached out and brushed my hair off my shoulder. "I do," she said. "I do trust you."

I smiled. "I won't be long."

"Just do what you need to do," she said, settling back behind the wheel. "I'll be here."

I got out of the car and pushed my way through the double front doors of the *Sun-Tribune* office. A security guard sitting up front pointed to a sign-in sheet without a word. Once I'd signed in, he turned it and read my name.

"And your business here . . . ?" he said.

"I need to talk to Angela Dash."

"She expecting you?" he asked.

"No," I admitted. "But she's written about me a lot, so I think she'll want to talk to me."

He looked doubtful, but reached over and picked up the phone, mumbled something into it.

A few minutes later, a dumpy brunette in a too-tight denim skirt and out-of-style boots came plodding toward me. She opened the door to let me in the inner offices.

"I'm Valerie Leftman," I said.

"I know who you are," she answered. Her voice was full, a little masculine. She whisked down the hall and I stumbled behind her to keep up. She disappeared into a dingy little office with almost no light, save for the gray lighting of the computer screen. I followed her in.

She sat at her desk. "Boy, have I tried and tried to talk to you," she said, her attention on her computer screen, her fingers clicking madly on the mouse. "You've got some protective parents."

"I didn't know they were screening my calls until a lot later," I said. "But I probably wouldn't have talked to you anyway. I didn't really talk to anyone back then. Not even my protective parents."

She glanced briefly, uninterestedly, from her computer screen. "What brings you here now? Finally ready to talk? Because, if so, I've gotta tell you I don't think we'll need you after all. This is a pretty overdone story already. Except for the suicide attempt and the moment of silence, there's really nothing new here. We're ready to move on. The shooting's old news."

While Angela Dash didn't look like the person I thought she was going to be, she definitely acted like her, which only emboldened me. I unzipped my purse and pulled out the article I'd filched from Ginny's hospital room. I tossed it on her desk.

"I want you to stop writing this stuff," I said. "Please."

Her mouse finger stopped clicking. She pulled off her glasses and used the hem of her shirt to clean them. She put them back on and blinked. "Excuse me?"

I pointed at the paper. "The stuff you write isn't true. It's not like what you're saying in your articles. You're making everyone think that we've all moved on and it's one big love fest in that school, but it's not."

She rolled her eyes. "I never said love fest . . ."

"You made Ginny Baker look like some suicidal freak who can't get over what happened when everyone else has," I said. "And it's a lie. You didn't even talk to Ginny Baker. You never have. The only person you've talked to is Mr. Angerson and you're spinning the lies he wants you to spin. He doesn't want to lose his job, so he has to make it sound like everything's normal at Garvin High again."

She leaned forward on her elbows and gave me this cocky little grin. "Spinning lies, huh? And where are you getting your information?" she asked.

"From living it," I said. "I'm in that school every day. I'm there to see what people are still doing to each other. I'm there to see that Ginny Baker is not the only girl still suffering. I'm there to see that what Mr. Angerson sees and what Mr. Angerson wants to see are two totally different things. You've never been there. Not one day. You've never been to my house. You've never been to a football game or a track meet or a dance. You've never been to the hospital to check on Ginny."

She stood. "You don't know where I've been," she said.

"Stop writing," I said. "Stop writing about us. About Garvin. Leave us alone."

"I'll take your advice under consideration," she said in this fake pleasant drawl of a voice. "But you'll forgive me if I listen to my editor first and you second."

I noticed for the first time how squat she looked behind her desk — this person who I'd always considered a giant with tons of power.

"I have a story to get back to," she said. "If you want to see 'the truth' in writing, maybe you should consider writing a book. I ghostwrite on the side, if you're interested."

And suddenly I knew that the story Angerson wanted the world to be told about Garvin High was the story that would be told. That Angela Dash was lazy and a bad journalist and would say whatever he wanted her to say. That the truth about Garvin would never be heard. And there was nothing I could do about it.

Except maybe there was.

I walked briskly back outside, where Mom was still waiting for me at the curb.

"Get what you need?" she asked, scanning me with her eyes. "You got the research?"

"Actually, yeah," I said. "I think I got exactly what I needed."

42

I wasn't sure if it was too late to get back on the StuCo project or not, but I wanted to give it a try anyway. There were only a couple weeks of school left and I wanted to share with Jessica my plans for the memorial.

I walked hesitantly into the room, bracing myself to face the entire Student Council, but the only one in the room was Jessica, bent over a pile of papers.

"Hey," I said from the doorway. She looked up. "Where is everyone? I thought there was a meeting."

"Oh, hey," she said. "Canceled. Stone has the flu. I'm just studying for my Calc final." She rubbed her elbows and squinted at me. "You wanting to come to a meeting? I thought you quit."

"I have an idea for presenting the memorial," I said. I

380

moved across the room and sat in the desk next to her. I pulled out the piece of paper I'd been working on all night long — an outline of my plan — and handed it to her. She took it and started reading.

"Yeah," she said, a smile growing slowly across her face. "Yeah. This is good. This is great, Val." She glanced up at me sideways. "Need a ride?"

I grinned at her. "Okay."

Our first stop was Mr. Kline's house. It was a small, cozy brown house with untended flower gardens in the front and a skinny orange cat sitting on the porch steps.

Jessica pulled into the driveway and shut off the motor.

"You ready for this?" she asked. I nodded. Truth was, I'd probably never be ready for this, but it was something I had to do.

See things for what they really are, I reminded myself. *See what's really there.*

We got out of the car and climbed the steps to the front door. The cat meowed at us plaintively and scurried under a bush. I rang the bell.

I could hear a small dog yapping ferociously just inside the door and some shushing noises that were doing nothing to quell the noise. Finally the door was pulled open and a mousy woman with mussed hair and giant glasses peered out at us. She was flanked by a squinty-eyed kid sucking on a popsicle.

She pushed open the storm door a crack.

"Can I help you?" she asked.

"Hi," I said nervously. "Um, Mrs. Kline? I'm Val —"

381

"I know who you are," she said flatly. "What do you want?"

Her voice was like shards of ice and I felt my bravado melting off of me. Jessica glanced at me and must've seen me looking scared because she piped up.

"We're sorry to bother you," she said. "But we were wondering if we could talk to you for a few minutes. It's for a project that will involve your husband."

"A memorial," I added without thinking. My face immediately burned afterward. I felt embarrassed for mentioning her husband's death in front of her. As if mentioning it would somehow make it more real to this sturdy little woman having to mother her children alone.

She looked at us silently for a long time. She seemed to be considering things very carefully. Maybe worried that I was carrying a gun and might blow her away and make her children orphans.

"Okay," she said, pushing the door open a little further. At the same time she backed to the side, giving Jessica and me enough room to squeeze into the cluttered living room behind her. "But I've only got a few minutes."

"Thanks," Jessica breathed and we went in.

Forty minutes later we were at Abby Dempsey's house — an emotional journey for Jessica, who was Abby's friend and who hadn't seen Abby's parents since the funeral — and an hour after that we were talking to Max Hill's older sister, Hannah, on lawn chairs in their garage.

As evening pressed in on us we sat in Ginny Baker's hospital room, watching her cry into a mountain of crumpled used tissues. Ginny was having a bad day. She wanted to go home. But the night before she'd broken a compact mirror and used a shard to try to slit her wrists. She'd be there for a while, and she wasn't happy about it. We talked to her mom in the hospital waiting room.

By eight o'clock, we were starving and we had one stop left to make. Jessica pulled into a gas station and we filled up on Slim Jims and bags of chips. I called my mom and told her I'd be home a little late and almost cried with happiness when she told me it was no problem, to just check in and be careful. Something she'd have said before the shooting. We sat in the gas station parking lot, stalling.

"Maybe this isn't such a good idea," I said, feeling nauseated after all that grease.

"Are you kidding me?" Jessica said, popping a Cheez Doodle into her mouth. "It's a great idea! And we're almost done! Don't doubt yourself now."

"I'm just thinking maybe it will be more hurtful than helpful. I'm just thinking — "

"You're just thinking you're scared of going to Christy Bruter's house. I don't blame you, Val, but we're going."

"But she's the reason it all happened. My MP3 player . . ."

"She is not the reason it all happened. Nick was the reason it all happened. Or fate. Or whatever. It doesn't matter. We're going."

"I'm not sure."

She crumpled up her empty Cheez Doodle bag into a

ball and tossed it into the back seat. She turned the key in the ignition and the car fired into life. "I'm sure. We're going," she said. She pulled out of the parking lot. I had no choice. We were going.

"It only hurts sometimes," Christy said, sitting between her mom and dad on the couch. She would only look at Jessica when she talked. I didn't blame her. I had a hard time looking at her, too. "And I wouldn't really even say 'hurts' anymore. Just feels weird. Like my body's weird.

"The worst part, honestly, is not getting to play softball anymore. I had already been offered a scholarship. Plus, my dad used to coach me and now . . ."

Her dad interrupted, clamping down on her knee with his palm. "Now he's glad he got to coach for all those years," he said. "Now he's glad to have a daughter who's alive to go to college."

Christy's mom made a small noise that sounded like "Amen" and dabbed at the corner of her eye with her fingertip. Mrs. Bruter hadn't said much since Jessica and I got there. She sat by Christy's side, alternately patting Christy's knee and nodding her head in agreement to things Christy said, a trembling and not very convincing smile holding up her mouth the whole time. She nodded again when Christy's dad mentioned that he had only prayed for a daughter who would be happy and have a long life, not one who could play softball.

"Do you . . ." I blurted, but faltered, unsure of what I wanted to ask her. *Do you blame me?* I wanted to ask. *Do you hate me even more now? Do you wish Nick had killed me? Do you have nightmares with me in them?* My mouth opened and closed. I swallowed.

Mr. Bruter must have sensed my discomfort because he leaned forward with his elbows on his knees and looked me straight in the eye. His hands dangled between his legs.

"We've learned a lot about forgiveness since this happened," he said. "We have no interest in seeing anyone else suffer over this tragedy. Not anyone."

Christy stared at her hands in her lap. Jessica shifted toward me slightly.

"There are heroes who died for their school," Mr. Bruter said softly. "And there are heroes who almost died for their school. And there are heroes who stopped the shooting. Who called nine-one-one when Christy went down. Who held her stomach to stop the bleeding. Heroes who . . . who lost people they loved. We appreciate all of the heroes of Garvin High."

Jessica reached over and touched the back of my arm. I felt surrounded. I — God, how did this happen? — felt proud.

When I got home, totally exhausted, Mom and Mel were sitting on the couch watching TV.

"It's getting late," Mom said, wrapped in her cocoon of Mel. Her feet were pulled up to the side. She looked comfy in a way I'd never seen before, not even when Dad was her cocoon. "I was getting worried about you."

"Sorry," I said. "This project has to be done before graduation."

"Did you get it finished?" Mel asked and I found, to my surprise, that I didn't mind him asking. All in all, Mel was a pretty good guy. And he made Mom smile more, which, in my opinion, made him a pretty great guy.

"Well, I got the research finished," I said. "I got all the interviews done, anyway."

He nodded in approval.

"I saved dinner," Mom said. "It's in the oven."

"No thanks," I said. "Jess and I ate something already." I walked over and stood behind the couch. "I think I'm just going to go to bed." I gave Mom a kiss on the cheek — a gesture I hadn't given her in years. She looked surprised. "'Night, Mom," I said, walking toward the stairs. "'Night, Mel."

"'Night," Mel called back loudly, drowning out Mom's voice.

43

I burst into my last session with Dr. Hieler practically buzzing.

"I think I'm starting to figure out who I am," I said, smiling wide as I dropped back onto the couch and popped open my Coke.

"Who you are?" Dr. Hieler asked, grinning widely. He flopped into his chair and draped one leg over the arm of the chair like always.

"Yeah, I mean, I know this sounds stupid, but I think talking to all those people reminded me of who I really am."

"And who are you? Who did you remember yourself to be?"

"Well," I said. I stood and paced the room. "For starters, I liked school. I really did. I liked being with my friends and hanging out and going to basketball games and stuff. I was smart and driven, you know? I wanted to go to college."

Dr. Hieler nodded, pressing his forefinger to his lips. "Good," he said. "I would agree with all those things."

I stopped pacing and sat back on the couch, a knot of excited energy. "And the Hate List was real. I really was angry. It wasn't a show for Nick. I mean, I wasn't as angry as he was, you know. I didn't even realize how angry he was. But I was angry, too. The bullying, the teasing, the name-calling . . . my parents, my life . . . seemed so messed up and pointless and I really was pissed about it. Maybe back then a part of me was suicidal and I just didn't know it."

"Possible," he said. "You had good reason to be angry."

I jumped up again. "Don't you see? I wasn't faking it. Not entirely." I turned and looked out the window. Mist was settling down on the cars in the parking lot. "At least I wasn't a poser," I said, staring at the water beading on the hoods of the cars. "At least I wasn't that."

"Yeah," he said, "But can you do a killer back handspring?"

"No, still can't do that."

"Really? I can."

"You cannot. You're such a liar."

"But I'm good at it," he'd said. "And I'm proud of you, Val. I'm not lying about that." And we'd moved over to the chess board, like always. He beat me, like always.

44

"I know you don't want me to get excited," said Mrs. Tate. A doughnut sat, half-eaten, on the desk in front of her. Her coffee cup steamed. It smelled good in Tate's office first thing in the morning. It smelled like waking up was supposed to smell — rich and bright and comforting. "But I can't help it, you know. This is exciting news."

"It's not news," I said sleepily from the chair across from her desk. "I'm just saying I want those catalogs now. For later."

She nodded enthusiastically. "Of course! Of course, for later! Absolutely. Who would blame you? Later's a good thing. How much later?"

I shrugged. "I don't know. However long it takes. I need some time to think things over. But you're right, college was always part of my plans before and I shouldn't just let go of who I am." Now that I knew who I wasn't, I was determined to remember who I was. Who I would become.

Mrs. Tate opened a file cabinet and pulled out several thick catalogs. "I can't tell you, Valerie, how proud I am to hear that," she said, beaming. "Here you go. Lots to choose from. You know you can call me if you ever have any questions or need help deciding."

She handed the books to me and I leaned over to take them. They felt heavy in my palms. I liked the feeling of it. For once the future seemed heavier than the past.

PART FOUR

*"Alas, how shall this bloody
deed be answer'd?"*

— SHAKESPEARE

I can't say the TV cameras didn't make me a little bit nervous. There were so many of them. We'd expected some — were banking on it, really — but this many? I felt my throat go dry and scratchy when I tried to talk.

It was hot for May and the gown was sticking to my legs when the wind blew. Graduation was, as it had always been, held outside, on the vast lawn on the school's east side. Someday, administration had always warned, graduation would be moved to a big auditorium to accommodate school expansion and unpredictable Midwest weather. But not today. Today we were following tradition. At least we could do that, this troubled class of 2009. Tradition felt good to us.

I could see my family — Frankie sitting between Mom and Dad, off to the side, near the back. Briley sat on the other side of Dad.

Mom had a grim set to her face and kept shooting hostile glances at the cameramen. I was suddenly struck with gratefulness that she'd somehow managed to keep the cameras mostly away from me throughout all of this. The only reporter I'd even spoken to was Angela Dash, when I'd made the trip to her office. It made me realize, with something akin to shock, that despite all of the accusatory things said and the mistrust placed over the past year, Mom didn't just work to protect the rest of the world from me; she also protected me from the world. Beneath the struggle there would always be that basic love, that safe place to come home to.

Dad looked fairly miserable, caught between Mom and Briley, but whenever our eyes would catch, a glint of relief would flash across his face. And that relief was real, I could tell. In his eyes I saw hopefulness and knew, with some amount of certainty, that despite what we might have said to one another we would both eventually forgive each other. Even if we could never forget. All it would take was time.

Every so often, Briley would lean in and whisper something in his ear and he would smile. And I was glad that he was getting a reason to smile. A part of me wished Mel had come with Mom. That way she could have a reason to smile, too.

Frankie looked bored, but I suspected this was a planted

look. Next year would be Frankie's turn to test the corridors of Garvin High. His turn to scurry under the watchful eye of Mr. Angerson. His turn to sit in Mrs. Tate's office, shocked and comforted by the unruliness. I had a feeling Frankie would do all right. Despite everything, he'd be okay.

Dr. Hieler was there, too. Sitting in the row behind Mom and Dad. He had his arm curled around his wife. She looked nothing like I'd expected her to look. Neither beautiful nor glamorous. She didn't have a Madonna-like set of unending patience and grace to her face, either. She checked her watch often and squinted against the sun and once barked something into her cell phone. I liked my version of her better. I really wanted to believe families like the one I'd imagined for Dr. Hieler existed. Especially for him.

Behind Dr. Hieler was a splash of purple. Bea, her hair ratted up high and adorned with so many purple baubles she jingled when she moved, sat there. She wore a gauzy purple suit and clutched in front of her a purple handbag the size of a small suitcase. She grinned up at me, her face serene and beautiful, like a painting.

Angerson stood and shushed the ceremony to a start. He gave a short speech about perseverance, but he seemed not to know exactly what to say about this class. All of the old standbys just didn't work here. What could he say about a future to those parents who couldn't let go of the past, who could do nothing but watch their hopes for their children's futures fade away, their children gone for more than a year now and never coming back? What could he say to the rest of us, so marred by what happened within those hallowed halls of education we knew and once loved? There would be no sweet memories — those would be forever eclipsed. There would be no reunions — those would be traumatic.

Soon he turned things over to Jessica, who rose confidently and climbed the steps to the podium. She spoke in an even, soothing voice about college and academia — bland stuff that would elicit no tears. And then she hesitated, her head bent toward the sheaf of papers in her hand.

She paused so long people began coughing and shuffling, a wave of awkwardness. It almost looked as if she were praying, and, I don't know, maybe she was. Angerson looked flustered and a couple of times wavered slightly toward her, as if he were going to prod her along or usher her off stage. When she finally looked up again, her face had changed. Softened, somehow, from the resolute Student Council president to the girl who patted my arm as Christy Bruter's dad talked about forgiveness.

"Our class," Jessica began, "will forever be defined by a date on the calendar. May second, 2008. Not a member of this class will pass that date without remembering someone he or she loved, who is now gone. Remembering the sights and sounds of that morning. Remembering pain and loss and grief and confusion. Remembering forgiveness. Just remembering. We, the class of 2009 Student Council, are gifting Garvin High a memorial to remember . . ." her voice cracked on the word and she paused, her head bent again, to compose herself. When she looked up again, her nose was very red and her voice quavered. ". . . Remembering the victims of that day. Those we will never forget."

Meghan stood from her chair and walked to a mound in the grass near the stage. It was covered by a sheet. She grabbed the edge of the sheet and pulled it off. A concrete bench, almost blinding in its white-grayness, sat above a hole in the ground about the size of a television set. Next to the hole was a pile of fresh dirt and a metal box, the time capsule, its lid open. From my chair I could see that the box was mostly full of various items — pompom strands, fuzzy dice, photographs.

Jessica nodded at me and I stood. My legs felt like rubber as I climbed the steps to the podium. Jessica moved to the side as I came toward her, but lunged toward me and wrapped me in her arms as I stepped closer. I let her cling to me, feeling the heat of her absorbing into my gown, making it stick to me even more. But I didn't care.

I remembered her walking toward me in the hall the day I tried to quit the Student Council project. Her eyes had been wet, desperate, her hand on her heart, her voice full and thick. *I lived and that made everything different*, she'd said. At the time I'd told her she was crazy, but now, clinging to her on the stage of our graduation, our project complete, I knew what she meant, and knew that she was right. That day did change everything. We'd become friends not because we'd wanted to, but because somehow we'd had to. And call me crazy, but it almost felt like we'd become friends because we were *supposed* to.

Distantly, I could feel, rather than see, camera flashes popping. I could hear the murmur of reporters in the background. When Jessica and I parted I stepped up to the podium and cleared my throat.

I saw all my old friends: Stacey, Duce, David, and Mason. I saw Josh and Meghan and even Troy, sitting in the back with Meghan's parents. I saw everyone, a shifting sea of discomfort and sadness, each person carrying his own pain, each telling her own stories, no story more or less tragic or triumphant than any other. In a way, Nick had been right: We all got to be winners sometimes. But what he didn't understand was that we all had to be losers, too. Because you can't have one without the other.

Mrs. Tate gnawed at a fingernail as she watched me. Mom sat with her eyes closed. She looked like she wasn't breathing. It occurred to me, only briefly, that maybe I should go with my first instinct after all and use this time to apologize. Formally. To the world. Maybe, more than what I was about to give them, an apology was what I owed them.

But I felt Jessica's hand slip into mine, her shoulder rub up against mine, and at the same time I saw Angela Dash dip her head down to a notebook and begin writing. I glanced at my speech.

"At Garvin High we were dealt a hard dose of reality this year. People hate. That's our reality. People hate and are hated and carry grudges and want punishments." I glanced at Mr. Angerson, who seemed to be perched on the edge of his chair, ready to jump up and stop me should I go too far. I felt myself shudder, falter a little. Jessica's hand tightened around mine just slightly. I went on. "The news tells us that hate is no longer our reality."

Angela Dash shifted back against her chair. Her arms were crossed, her reporter's notebook and pen forgotten. She glared at me with pursed, ugly lips. I blinked, swallowed, willed myself to go on.

"I don't know if it's possible to take hate away from people. Not even people like us, who've seen firsthand what hate can do. We're all hurting. We're all going to be hurting for a long time. And we, probably more than anyone else out there, will be searching for a new reality every day. A better one." I looked back, past my parents, toward Dr. Hieler. His arms were crossed over his chest, his forefinger rubbing his bottom lip. He nodded at me ever so slightly, almost not a nod at all.

I shuffled a half step to the side. Jessica leaned in to the microphone, still grasping my hand.

"We do know that it's possible to change reality," she said. "It's hard, and most people won't bother to try, but it's possible. You can change a reality of hate by opening up to a friend. By saving an enemy." Jessica looked at me. She smiled. I smiled back, sadly. I wondered if we would go on to be friends after this. If we would even see one another again after today.

"But in order to change reality you have to be willing to listen and to learn. And to hear. To actually hear.

"As president of the senior class of 2009, I am asking all of you to remember the victims of the May second shooting and hear the reality of who those people were."

I cleared my throat.

"Many of the people who died, did so because the shooter . . ." I trailed off. I couldn't even look up at Dr. Hieler, who I knew would be wiping his eyes and nodding encouragement to me. ". . . my boyfriend, Nick Levil, and I thought they were bad people. We only saw what we wanted to see and we . . ." I swiped at one eye. Jessica let go of my hand and began instead rubbing my back. "Um . . . we didn't . . . Nick and I didn't . . . we didn't know . . . the reality of who these people were."

Jessica leaned forward again.

"Abby Dempsey," she said, "was an avid horseback rider. She had her own horse named Nietzsche, and she rode Nietzsche every Saturday morning. She was scheduled to perform next summer in the Knofton Junior Rodeo. She was so excited about it. She was also my best friend," she added huskily. "We've put a lock of Nietzsche's mane into the time capsule on Abby's behalf."

She stepped back and I stepped forward again. My fingers were shaking around the note cards I was holding and I still couldn't look up. But it was getting easier as I remembered the faces of all the parents Jessica and I had talked to.

All the parents I had finally personally apologized to. All the parents who accepted my apology — some who forgave me. Some who didn't. Some who said I never owed them one. We'd cried together and they'd been thrilled to share stories of their children with us. Most of them were out in the audience right now, I suspected.

"Christy Bruter," I said, "has been accepted to Notre Dame University and plans to study psychology. She wants to work with trauma victims and is already co-writing a book about her near-death experience. Christy has placed a softball in the time capsule."

Jessica leaned forward again. "Jeff Hicks had just come from the hospital seeing his new baby brother for the first time the morning of May second. He was running late to school, but was thrilled when he left the hospital, excited to have another boy in the family. He even suggested a name for the baby — Damon, after a favorite football player. In honor of Jeff, his parents named the baby Damon Jeffrey. We placed Damon Jeffrey's hospital wristband in the time capsule on Jeff's behalf."

"Ginny Baker," I said. I took a deep breath. There was so much I wanted to say about Ginny. Ginny, who'd suffered so much. Who'd keep suffering. Who couldn't be here because she was busy trying to find ways to finish the job Nick started. To punish herself for the bullying she felt she'd set in motion. "Ginny was winner of the Lads and Lassies contest when she was two years old. Her mom says she was always putting on talent shows and taught herself how to twirl the baton when she was only six. Ginny has elected . . ." I paused, trying not to cry, "not to put anything in the time capsule." I lowered my head.

We went on like that — taking turns offering trinkets and stories about Lin Yong and Amanda Kinney and Max Hills and the others. Mr. Kline's widow sobbed out loud when we placed a quarter in the time capsule on his behalf, symbolizing his habit of tossing quarters at students who answered questions correctly in his class. One of his daughters kept her face buried in the folds of her mother's dress, immobile.

We got to the last one and I walked back down the steps to my seat. I tried not to make eye contact with anyone — the sound of noses blowing was too deafening.

Jessica stood at the podium alone then, her feet planted firmly, her nose red but her eyes fierce. Her blond hair wisped in the wind like cobwebs.

"There are two others," she said into the microphone. I frowned, counted on my fingers. I'd thought we'd gotten them all. Jessica took a deep breath.

"Nick Levil," she said, "loved Shakespeare." I held my breath. When had Jessica talked to Nick's family? Why had she? Did she do it without me on purpose? I squinted at the bench. Sure enough, Nick's name was there, last on the list of victims. I made a small noise in the back of my throat and covered my mouth with my hand. This time I couldn't keep the tears from falling, especially when she dropped

Nick's old battered copy of *Hamlet*, the one he'd read passages of to me so many times, into the time capsule.

I barely heard her say, "Valerie Leftman is a hero. More courageous than anyone I've ever known — a bullet the least of the scary things I've seen her face this year. Valerie single-handedly saved my life and stopped the shooting of May second, 2008, from being worse than it already was. And I'm so blessed to be able to call her my friend. Valerie has placed a book of drawings in the time capsule." She produced my black spiral notebook and dropped it in on top of Nick's *Hamlet*. My reality and Nick's escape . . . one on top of the other.

At first nobody clapped as Jessica thanked the crowd and took her seat. But then, building up like water coming to a boil, smattering applause broke into steady clapping. A few people — those who had themselves under control — stood in front of their chairs.

I turned my head and looked: Mom and Dad were both clapping and wiping their eyes. Dr. Hieler was standing in front of his chair, not bothering to wipe his.

Mr. Angerson stepped back up to the podium and got us back to the business of graduating, of getting on with our lives.

I thought about the suitcase that lay opened on my bed. My things, nearly packed. The picture of me and Nick sitting on that rock at Blue Lake nestled under the underwear and extra bras. The copy of *The Gift of Fear* that Dr. Hieler had bought me, with an admonition to "stay safe." The stack of calling cards Dad had wordlessly pressed into my hand last Saturday when he came to pick up Frankie. The college catalogs I'd gotten from Mrs. Tate.

I thought about the train that I would catch in the morning — destination unknown — and how Mom would probably cry at the station and beg me once again not to go, at least not without a plan. And how Dad would probably look relieved as I watched him grow small through the window as the train pulled away. And how I wouldn't blame him for it if he did.

I imagined the things I might miss while away. Would Mom and Mel get married without me there? Would I miss seeing Frankie get his first job, maybe lifeguarding at the neighborhood pool? Would I miss the announcement that Briley was pregnant? Would I miss it all and, hearing about these things, would I feel that they deserved at least that much, my absence during those happy things?

"You sure about this?" Dr. Hieler had asked me at our last session. "You have enough money?"

I nodded. "And your number," but I think we both knew I'd never call it, not even if I woke in the shadows of a musty-smelling hostel, my leg aching and Nick's voice echoing in my ears. Not even if my brain finally allowed me to remember the hazy image of Nick putting a bullet in his brain in front of my bleary eyes. Not even to say Merry Christmas or Happy Birthday or I'm fine or Help me.

He'd hugged me and rested his chin on top of my head.

"You'll be fine," he'd whispered, although I wasn't sure if he was whispering to himself or to me.

And I'd gone home and packed, leaving the suitcase open on my bed, next to the horses in the wallpaper, which were — as they'd always been, of course — completely motionless.

Acknowledgments

First and foremost, deep thanks to Cori Deyoe for taking a chance on me, for being my mentor and friend, for giving me the courage to put fingers to keyboard time and again, and for always being my loudest and best cheerleader.

A huge thank-you to T. S. Ferguson for believing in my story, for teaching me so much about the craft of storytelling, for patiently answering an insane amount of questions, and for making me dig deeper than I ever knew I could. Also thanks to everyone at Little, Brown who read and helped shape this book, particularly Jennifer Hunt, Alvina Ling, and Melanie Sanders. Also, special thanks to Dave Caplan for the amazing cover design.

Thanks to my writing friends, Cheryl O'Donovan, Laurie Fabrizio, Nancy Pistorius, and my girls at Café Scribe—Dani,

Judy, Serena, and Suzy—for being there for shoulder-lending when the "I can'ts" set in.

Thank you to my mom, Bonnie McMullen, for not only telling me, but showing me daily that anything in life is possible. And thank you to my dad, Thomas Gorman, for always telling everyone whatever story I'm working on is the best one out there. Thanks, as well, go to my stepparents, Bill McMullen and Sherree Gorman. Also to my extended "mom" and "dad," Dennis and Gloria Hey, and "sister" Sonya Jackson, who told me decades ago that this day would come.

To my husband, Scott, there aren't words big enough to say thank you for your enduring belief, support, and love. And to my children, Paige, Weston, and Rand, thank you for your patience and inspiration. I feel so hopeful about any future that includes you three at the helm.

And finally, deep love and thanks to whoever's pulling the strings "up there." Jack, I 'spect it's you. I owe you a big smooch!